*"We'* [obscured] *We both try* [obscured] *."*

Profe[obscured] s words were true. But pe[obscured] remaine would be shocked to discover just how far apart they were.

Cade moved closer to Shae, his head tilted intimately toward hers, and his voice went low and persuasive. "C'mon, Doc. What's the harm?"

With new eyes she reassessed him, not as a doctor but as a female. He had a smoker's voice, slightly raspy, with more than a hint of the South in it. Coupled with those penetrating jade eyes and rangy build, she didn't doubt that he found it far too easy to persuade women to do just about anything he asked.

He reached for one of her hands, held it in his as his thumb skated over her knuckles. At the touch, she let her eyelids lower, her lips part.

"Tell me something," Shae murmured throatily.

Although he hadn't moved, somehow he seemed closer. "Hmm?"

"Does this little act of yours usually work?"

Dear Reader,

This is definitely a month to celebrate, because Kathleen Korbel is back! This award-winning, bestselling author continues the saga of the Kendall family with *Some Men's Dreams,* a journey of the heart that will have you smiling through tears as you join Gen Kendall in meeting Dr. Jack O'Neill and his very special daughter, Elizabeth. Run—don't walk—to the store to get your copy of this genuine keeper.

Don't miss out on the rest of our books this month, either. Kylie Brant continues THE TREMAINE TRADITION with *Truth or Lies,* a dicey tale of love on both sides of the law. Then pick up RaeAnne Thayne's *Freefall* for a haunting, mysterious, page-turner of a romance. Round out the month with new books by favorites Beverly Bird, who's *Risking It All,* and Frances Housden, who'll introduce you to a *Heartbreak Hero,* and brand-new author Madalyn Reese, who gives you *No Place To Hide* from her talented debut.

And, as always, come back again next month, when Silhouette Intimate Moments offers you six more of the best and most exciting romances around.

Enjoy!

Leslie J. Wainger
Executive Editor

Please address questions and book requests to:
Silhouette Reader Service
U.S.: 3010 Walden Ave., P.O. Box 1325, Buffalo, NY 14269
Canadian: P.O. Box 609, Fort Erie, Ont. L2A 5X3

# Truth or Lies

## KYLIE BRANT

# INTIMATE MOMENTS™

Published by Silhouette Books

**America's Publisher of Contemporary Romance**

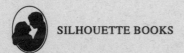 SILHOUETTE BOOKS

ISBN 0-373-27308-8

TRUTH OR LIES

Copyright © 2003 by Kim Bahnsen

Visit Silhouette at www.eHarlequin.com

**Printed in U.S.A.**

**Books by Kylie Brant**

## KYLIE BRANT

lives in Iowa with her husband and children. Besides being a writer, this mother of five works full-time teaching learning-disabled students. Much of her free time is spent in her role as professional spectator at her kids' sporting events.

An avid reader, Kylie enjoys stories of love, mystery and suspense—and she insists on happy endings! She claims she was inspired to write by all the wonderful authors she's read over the years. Now most weekends and all summer she can be found at the computer, spinning her own tales of romance and happily-ever-afters.

She invites readers to check out her online read in the reading room at eHarlequin.com. Readers can write to Kylie at P.O. Box 231, Charles City, IA 50616, or e-mail her at kyliebrant@hotmail.com. Her Web site address is www.kyliebrant.com.

# Prologue

The dim spill of light from the nearby street lamp barely disturbed the oppressive shadows deep in New Orleans's City Park. Even the glow of the night's half moon couldn't penetrate the thick canopy of trees. Darkness held untold fears for some, but for others it provided a much-needed cover. Some business was best conducted far from the light of day.

"He's late." Detective Cade Tremaine checked his watch. "I thought you said he was dependable."

"Freddie's reliable as long as he hasn't been shooting up or snorting." Brian Hollister, Cade's partner, shrugged. "If he's using again, I can't vouch for him."

Scanning the area, Cade said, "We'll give him a couple minutes." He wasn't thrilled with the idea of losing any more sleep. But the snitch represented a chance for a lead in a case that had been damn short of clues lately. And catching the dealer responsible for at least three deaths from overdoses was well worth the inconvenience.

He heard footsteps moments before a figure stepped out of the shadows. "Is that him?"

"Yeah." Hollister straightened, waited for the man to get closer. "You must have us confused with one of your junkie bitches, Freddie. We don't much like being kept waiting." The words were accompanied by a slap alongside the man's head.

Freddie flinched away. "Stuff came up, Hollister. You know how it goes."

Cade shoved the snitch under the street lamp, noted the pinpoint pupils, the glassy stare. "He's high," he said with disgust. Releasing the man's filthy shirt, he turned to his partner. "Let's go. We're wasting our time."

"No, hold on," the snitch said hastily. "You wanted information and I have some for ya." He gave a look around as if they were in danger of being overheard and lowered his voice. "That guy you're investigating? The one who's putting pure stuff on the streets? I can get you in contact with someone who knows him."

"Then start talking, Freddie, 'cause we're ready to walk," Hollister said impatiently.

"Okay, okay." The man turned to the side, dug in his pocket. "I got his name written right here on this napkin. Not the dealer, but the guy I told ya about. I can tell ya where he hangs out, too."

He'd finally managed to get Cade's attention. Not that he was ready to believe a hopped-up junkie, but a name would give them a contact they didn't have right now. Hollister stepped forward to snatch the creased napkin from Freddie, and while he unfolded it, Cade moved closer.

In the next moment, however, Freddie was backpedaling furiously, the words tumbling from his mouth. "Got you what you wanted, didn't I? So pay up, guys, pay up."

At first Cade thought the words were directed at them. Then he saw the glint of metal. "Gun!" Reacting instinctively, he reached for his own weapon. He'd barely cleared it from his holster when the first bullet hit him in the chest, the impact sending him stumbling backward. He squeezed off a couple of shots before the next two slugs hit him, knocked him to the ground.

After the first searing jolt there was no pain, only a cold numbness that seemed to spread from one internal organ to the next, shutting down physical functions. Distantly Cade was aware of more shots being fired, shouting, but he couldn't move. Couldn't feel. He could only lie on the sidewalk, cheek pressed to its gritty surface. It took every ounce of his rapidly draining energy to drag his eyes open. He saw the stream of blood eddying out from him to join an ever-widening pool. Saw his partner's body crumpled in a heap next to his.

Cade didn't see his life flash before his eyes. Didn't see a powerful white light that drew him deeper into its center. Death was a yawning black hole that sucked the life from his body bit by bit until there was finally only darkness.

Then there was nothing at all.

# Chapter 1

*Two months later*

"**G**unshot wound to the abdomen. Blood pressure is one-ten and dropping. His name is Jon LeFrenz." The paramedics helped transfer the moaning patient from the ambulance cot to an emergency-room cart. They ran alongside as the Charity Hospital E.R. employees rolled it through East Hall to triage.

"Room four is open," Dr. Shae O'Riley said to her colleagues. Then she addressed the closest paramedic. "How're his sounds?"

"Lungs are clear. But we had trouble stopping the bleeding. That's the third pressure dressing. We already gave him a unit of O negative. He's lucid and responsive."

Nodding, she said, "Okay, thanks." She left the ambulance crew behind as the cart was rolled into the tiny trauma cubicle. The area was jammed with people and equipment. Drawing the curtain to separate the area into two separate compartments left barely enough room to move. "Okay, Jenna, type him and get a couple of units of blood ready." The lab tech nodded, reached for the patient's hand.

Shae looked up, saw the lines the ambulance crew had put in to replace fluids. Both IV bags were nearly empty. "Let's get another couple of bags in him. How's his blood pressure doing?"

The emergency room RN looked at the screen. "One hundred over sixty."

Not dangerously low yet, but dropping. "Roll him to his side." Shae leaned in and lifted the dressing used to staunch the bleeding on the abdomen. The bullet had torn through the flesh, leaving a relatively small entry. She looked up at Boyd DuBois, the emergency-room resident. "Is there an exit?"

He lifted the dressing on the man's back and nodded. Shae moved around the cart and looked at the angry gaping hole, which was oozing sullenly. "Wessels and Lyndstrom still on duty in surgery?"

DuBois checked his watch. "I think so."

Shae looked at the triage nurse next to her. "Could you give them another call, get someone down here for a consult?"

"I called as soon as we heard he was coming in."

"But no one's here yet, are they?"

The woman shrugged and headed to the phone on the wall. The consultation would be merely a formality. Virtually all gunshot wounds to the abdomen had to be explored.

Shae turned her attention back to stabilizing the patient. The paramedics had cut his blood-soaked T-shirt up the center, baring his chest. He was awake, his face sheened with sweat. No more than twenty, she guessed, although it was difficult to tell for sure with pain and shock twisting his surprisingly innocent features. Leaning down, she shone a flashlight into each eye, noting normal pupil reaction.

The patient turned his head from the light, raised his hand to knock the flashlight away. "Get that outta here." The oxygen rebreather mask the paramedics had placed on him made his words difficult to make out, but his meaning was clear enough.

"You're in Charity Hospital, Mr. LeFrenz, and we're going to help you." She put a stethoscope to his chest to check his sounds. "You will probably require surgery. Do you have any family you want us to call?"

"No," he muttered, turning his head back toward her. His eyelids fluttered open and he stared fixedly at her. Then he reached up and dragged down the mask. "Must be alive. Ain't no angels where I'm going."

Shae pushed it back into place. "We're stabilizing you now, and a surgeon will come to assess your condition." As she spoke, she pressed lightly on the skin surrounding the wound, watching his face carefully for signs of increased pain. When he flinched and moaned loudly, she said to Boyd, "Slight swelling to the upper quadrant." She probed the area a bit longer. The belly was hard, rigid, indicating possible internal bleeding. "Let's do a DPL and see what's going on in there."

She stepped aside to allow the RN to prepare an area on the skin where they could insert the catheter. Moving back up to the patient's head, she spoke evenly, pitching her voice above the man's loud moaning. "Mr. LeFrenz, we're going to do a test that will let us know the extent of the bleeding in your abdominal cavity. The discomfort will be minimal, but one of us will let you know what we're doing every step of the way.''

"No! Just patch me up and let me go!'' He'd pulled his mask down again to scream the words. Then he spewed a stream of obscenities as he rolled from side to side, grimacing in pain. Boyd made a grab at him, but not before one of his flailing arms had knocked Shae back a step.

With no more than a look she directed two of the staff to restrain the man. Preparing the plastic catheter, she performed the direct peritoneal lavage and withdrew the catheter, handing it to the RN. "Get that to the stat lab and have them do a cell count.'' The woman nodded and exited. It was only then that Shae noticed the man leaning against the far wall.

Her first thought was that he was a family member. She immediately realized her mistake as second and third impressions followed on the heels of the first. She didn't need the gold shield hanging around the man's neck to identify his occupation. There was cop in his eyes, in the cold steady way he was regarding her.

"Detective Cade Tremaine,'' he said by way of an introduction. "I need to talk to him. Is he lucid?''

"Pressure's dropping, Doctor. Ninety-eight over sixty.''

Shae acknowledged the resident's words with a quick nod, but never looked away from the detective. "He's as lucid as anyone would be with a bullet in his belly. Did you put it there?'' She wasn't even certain where the note of censure had come from, but she heard it in her voice.

If it had any effect on him, it didn't show in his expression. "Yes.'' He brushed by her, took up a stance next to the patient. "Hello, Jonny.'' The patient abruptly stopped struggling. Tremaine turned to look at Shae. "Does he need that mask on?''

It was on the tip of her tongue to assure him that the man did. To tell him in no uncertain terms to get out of her trauma room and wait as long as it took for his little talk. But that urge sprang from the personal side of her, not the professional. So instead, she stepped in next to him, took out her stethoscope and listened to the patient's breathing. It was shallow, but still even. Without a word, she reached up and pulled the man's mask down.

"Sorry it took so long." Jenna appeared around the edge of the curtain, holding two units of blood. "The lab was pretty backed up."

Shae looked up at the monitor again. The pressure was still dropping. "Use a power infuser to transfuse him." The device would warm the blood and deliver it far more rapidly than an ordinary infuser.

"You gonna keep protecting him, Jonny? What the hell for? You don't see him here asking after your health, do you?"

The conversation between the detective and her patient diverted Shae's attention as she flushed the wound of particles of fabric and dirt. There was no doubt in her mind which of the pair was the more dangerous. Tremaine's six-foot-plus frame seemed overly spare, his unshaven angled face just shy of gaunt, as if he'd recently been through his own trauma. But the aura of quiet menace that radiated from him effectively quelled any sympathy his appearance might have elicited.

"I got nothing to say to you. Angel Eyes, get him away from me." LeFrenz grasped her fingers.

Shae gave Boyd a sharp glance and the resident restrained the man again. The monitor beeped and her gaze flicked to the screen, noting that the pressure was hovering at ninety-six.

Tremaine shoved his face closer to the patient's. "All

you need to do is give me a name. No one has to know where it came from. That kid's death is on your hands, LeFrenz.''

"Not my hands," LeFrenz wheezed. His face twisted in pain and he cried out at Shae's ministrations. "His choice…to take it…all at once."

"But you're the one who sold it to him." The detective's voice was unforgiving. "If you cooperate, I can arrange for your protection, but otherwise you're going down for this kid's death. I'll bury you."

"Doctor, I've got the labs."

It took a moment longer than it should have for the lab tech's voice to register, for Shae to turn away from the human drama unfolding before her. As she was looking over the results, Dr. Lyndstrom hurried into the room.

She looked up at the surgeon, then pointedly at her watch. "Busy up there?"

"We're starting to stack them up, so don't give me any grief. It'd be best if your guy could wait an hour or two."

"I don't think so." Deliberately Shae shifted her attention from the detective's hard persistent voice, LeFrenz's moans interspersing his belligerent replies. Handing the results to the surgeon, she gave him a rundown of the case, ending with, "His count is high. There's rebound tenderness in the upper quadrant and his BP is dropping, despite two transfusions. His liver may be bleeding."

The surgeon's muttered curse was drowned out by the RN's voice. "Blood pressure's ninety."

Shae leaped back to the patient's bedside, elbowing the detective out of the way. DuBois and Lyndstrom joined her, and the cubicle became a flurry of emergency maneuvers to save the patient from flat lining.

"Let's get him upstairs." Lyndstrom and Shae helped

Boyd shove the cart out of the room, the RN running alongside with the IV stands and infuser.

"Wait a minute. Where are you taking him?" The detective jogged after them to the elevator.

"Surgery." Shae switched her attention to the intern, Sara Gonzalez. "Stay with him for the duration, okay?" The woman nodded.

"LeFrenz." Frustration laced the detective's voice. "Dammit, LeFrenz, do the right thing."

The elevator doors opened and the surgeon and intern stepped in, pushing the cart. The patient had gone silent, pale, his limbs shaking with shock. Shae threw up an arm to prevent the detective from following the patient even as the doors began to close. And when the man rounded on her angrily, she met his gaze with a steady one of her own.

"He's unconscious. You aren't going to get anything more from him right now." She watched the man tuck away his frustration and fury with a control that looked as dangerous as it was deliberate. And when he turned the intensity of his focus on her, it was all she could do not to take a step back.

She had enough experience dealing with cops to last her a lifetime, but she'd never met one like this. The gold shield he displayed didn't in any way mask his lethal air. "Is he going to make it?"

"Since I don't have my crystal ball handy, I really couldn't say." Shae turned to walk away, but she didn't get more than a step before a hard grip on her elbow spun her back around.

"In your professional opinion, Dr.—" his gaze dropped to her name tag before recapturing hers again "—O'Riley, what are his chances?"

Boyd DuBois passed them, turning to quiz Shae with

raised brows. Aware that her reaction to the detective hadn't gone unnoticed, she forced a neutral tone. "I'm sorry." And she was. There was little she despised more than allowing her private life to splash over into the professional. "It's been pretty wild today with the crash on Interstate 10." Most of the victims of the pileup had been transported here, straining both emergency-room personnel and surgery.

"I heard about that." His gaze never left hers. His eyes were an unusual shade of dark jade, and every bit as unyielding. She imagined his penetrating stare was used to great advantage during interrogations.

The observation wasn't a comfortable one. Shae began walking toward the front desk, and Tremaine fell into step beside her. "I really can't predict what LeFrenz's outcome will be. He lost a lot of blood and it's a good bet there's still bleeding going on inside. His chances for surviving surgery depend on the path of the bullet and the extent of the internal damage."

"How long before he's out of surgery?"

Again she shrugged. Reaching the front desk, she sneaked a glance at her watch. Seven o'clock. Technically she was due to go off shift, but there were still reports to be dictated and paperwork to sign off on. "It could be four hours or more. It's hard to tell."

He gave a short nod, started to turn away. "I'll be back then."

"You'll be wasting your time." Shae didn't know what made her say it. She was more than ready to part ways with the enigmatic detective. But she couldn't shake the impression that he'd recently been ill. He possessed a runner's body, taut and lean, but his bordered on gaunt. "No use losing sleep. From surgery, LeFrenz will go directly to a PACU—post-anesthetic-recovery unit. In all likelihood you won't be able to speak to him until tomorrow morning.''

"Don't worry.'' It was clear from his tone that he'd misinterpreted the cause of her concern. "I'll leave my rubber hose at home.''

"It's not him I'm worried about.'' She made no effort to soften the bluntness of her words. "You look like one of the walking wounded. We can't really spare an extra bed if you collapse during your all-night vigil.''

Oddly her tart remark brought an almost smile to his lips, a softened expression that was as arresting as it was fleeting. "Despite your underwhelming concern, I'll be back in a few hours. Maybe I'll see you then, *Angel Eyes*.'' He sauntered away, leaving her to burn over his use of LeFrenz's name for her.

Turning back to the desk, she snatched down the most recent patient's chart, aware that DuBois was eyeing her.

"You know, that guy looks familiar.''

"Yeah, well, he's a cop. They all look alike.''

Her attempt at humor fell flat. Boyd continued to stare in the direction of the double doors Tremaine had disappeared through. "No, I mean I think we worked on him not long ago.'' The E.R. resident stared into space, as if searching his memory. "A month ago? No, more like two. Maybe it was when you were out on personal leave.''

She flipped over a page on the chart, continued to make notations as if uninterested. In actuality every nerve was on alert. It was far more comfortable to attend to the reason for Tremaine's visit here two months ago than on the reason for her leave at the same time. "What'd he present with?''

DuBois had already given up trying to remember. He took down another chart and began to read through it. "I don't recall. I wasn't primary. Aren't you supposed to be going off duty?''

"Pretty soon," she answered vaguely. But it was another two hours before she'd finished with the charting and dictation. And even then she couldn't force herself to head for the parking lot. Instead, she sat down in front of a computer, typing in a name.

*Cade Tremaine.*

The file unfolded slowly on the screen, and Shae leaned closer, scrolling down as she scanned it quickly before she stopped, paused to read more carefully. Minutes later she logged off, more shaken than she cared to admit.

She didn't know many men who took three bullets to the chest in the line of duty, only to be back on the job two short months later. He'd been dangerously close to death by the time he'd arrived at the hospital, and his recovery must have depended on equal parts luck, science and sheer force of will. Even from the limited time she'd spent with the detective, his tenacity was apparent. She could only assume he'd browbeaten his physician into granting him a release without giving many details of the danger of the job he was returning to. From what she'd witnessed today, it didn't appear as though he'd allowed his condition to slow him down much.

It shouldn't matter. As she made her way to the parking lot, she tried, and failed, to convince herself of that. In all likelihood she'd never see the detective again, and a flicker of relief accompanied the thought. What kind of person, after all, exhibited that kind of dedication to his job? A very determined man. Or a very driven one.

Either way, he seemed like an excellent man to avoid.

At dusk St. Jude's had emptied of the usual tourist tours. In New Orleans cemeteries were notoriously unsafe

at night. Row after row of white monuments provided end-
less hiding places for thieves and muggers waiting to
pounce on the unwary. Only foolish or dangerous souls
would take a chance and be caught there alone. The
woman standing before the narrow gleaming tomb didn't
fit either description.

Cade reached her, placed his hands on her shoulders.
"Carla." She didn't turn; she must have heard his approach. She covered one of his hands with both of hers.

"We just got the marker up."

"I saw that. It looks good." Silently they both stared
at the shiny gold plaque.

*Brian Hollister, beloved husband of Carla, father of
Benjamin and Richard. Died too young in the line of duty.*

"He was a good cop, wasn't he, Cade?"

"The best." There was no doubt in his voice, none in
his mind. He'd partnered with Brian since he'd made detective four years ago, was godfather to both his children.
He'd spent as much time at the Hollister home as he did
at his own apartment. And not a day had passed in the
past two months that he didn't feel guilty for being alive
while his friend lay lifeless in the family vault.

"I can't tell you what it means to hear you say that."
Carla turned to face him, and he saw the toll the recent
weeks had taken on her. Always delicate, the Creole
beauty looked as though a good wind would tumble her
over. There was no sign of her familiar teasing smile, but
the haunted look in her dark eyes struck a chord. He saw
the same in his own each time he looked in the mirror.

"Have they gotten to you yet, Cade?"

He frowned, not understanding her meaning. "Has who
gotten to me?"

"Internal Affairs." The venomous tone sounded foreign to her usually soft voice. "They've been to the house

at least three times, most recently yesterday. At first they danced around things, saying how sorry they were about Brian. Then they started asking questions. Had he said where he was going that night, what he was going to be doing? Yesterday they asked if they could go through his things.''

Her words seemed to come from a distance. *Internal Affairs?* Cade tried, and failed, to imagine a positive reason for them to be looking into the shooting. The whole event, as much as he remembered of it, had been laid out in the report he'd dictated to the investigating officers. Then her last sentence registered, and her revelation started to take on an even more ominous light. "What did they want to look through?"

"Brian's case files. They asked whether he kept notes on any ongoing investigations and I said no. You know Brian left work at work.''

"What are they looking for?"

She gave a harsh laugh. "*Irregularities* is the word they used. Like he was a damn accountant or something. When I press for more information, they clam up. But every time they come around, they get pushier, and one of them threatened to get a search warrant.''

Although trepidation was circling in his gut, he made an automatic effort to soothe. "Don't worry about it, Carla. It's just I.A. on another wild-goose chase.''

She clutched his arm, her fingers biting. "I was a policeman's wife for eight years. I know what I.A.'s all about. Cops hunting other cops. They think Brian was dirty. They're investigating *him.*''

Looking into her liquid dark eyes, he couldn't find it in himself to lie to her. "What are their names?"

"Torley and Morrison. Do you know either of them?"

He shook his head. But then, he wasn't especially well-

acquainted with anyone from I.A. Because of their occupation, the cops he knew had a healthy disdain for that
department. Ferreting out corruption in the ranks was a
noble enough calling, he supposed, but good cops had a
way of getting dragged into their investigations, too. And
the taint of an I.A. investigation had stalled more than one
police officer's career.

Reaching into his pocket, he withdrew his wallet. It
took a moment searching the contents before he found
what he was looking for. He took out a card and handed
it to her. "I want you to get in touch with someone at this
number." She took the card and looked at it. "It's the
policemen's-rights committee. Tell them what's been going on and then follow whatever advice they give you."

Her jaw set in an expression that was all too familiar.
"I can't call them, Cade. It'd be like admitting there was
substance behind I.A.'s interest."

"It's an admission that you need help," he retorted,
"and with I.A. sniffing around, for whatever reason, you
do. Call them. I'm going to check in tomorrow to make
sure you did. Got it?" He waited until she gave him a
reluctant nod. "Good." Gathering her close, he patted her
back reassuringly. "Don't worry. It'll all turn out to be
nothing."

"You won't let them smear his memory, will you?"
For the first time her control seemed to waver. He could
feel the tremors working through her body. "He was a
decent cop. You said so yourself. I don't want my babies
growing up thinking otherwise."

The thought of his two dark-eyed godsons had his chest
going tight. At three and two, neither of them would recall
their father. There would be no memories of ball games
and barbecues, or fishing in the bayou. All they'd have,
all there was, were pictures and newspaper clippings. And

the stories their mother would tell them about their father's bravery. Living up to a hero's legacy could keep the boys on the right track all their lives. And living with a shadow over their name could send them hurtling down the wrong path.

"No." The word was torn from him without his conscious permission as he hugged his dead partner's widow closer. "I won't let them smear Brian."

# Chapter 2

"Shae, you're needed in I.C.U."

Shae looked up as Tim Pearson, the E.R. supervisor, strode into the examining room. "What's going on?"

He shrugged. "All I can tell you is that Martin Reeves called down and said to send you up to room six. We're not too busy right now. I'll take over for you here."

He reached for her clipboard, but Shae was slow to relinquish it. What would Martin Reeves, one of the hospital administrators, want with her? She'd rarely had occasion to even speak to the man, but when she did, it was in his office on the sixth floor, not on the intensive-care ward.

"Is it about one of my patients?"

He tugged lightly at the clipboard, and she released it. "He didn't say. Just asked if I could spare you for a few minutes, but you're using that time up pretty rapidly."

Given the number of times she'd rejected Pearson's invitations to go out together, she wasn't overly concerned with his brusqueness. He wasn't a man to accept rejection gracefully, but he was professional enough not to let it affect their working together. He was right about one thing—the only way to get her questions answered was to head to I.C.U.

"What do we have here?" Pearson asked.

A small smile tugged at her lips as she made to leave. A much bigger person wouldn't take a modicum of enjoyment from handing this particular case over to the man who had made such a pest of himself for several months before he'd finally given up on her.

But sometimes being small and petty could be so satisfying.

"Patient presented with severe pain due to an obstruction," she said blandly.

Tim's gaze shot up from the clipboard, took in the male patient positioned on his stomach, his hips propped up by several pillows. Next his eyes took in the utensils Shae had gathered, lingered on the set of forceps. His head swiveled to hers, the expression in his handsome face dismayed. "It probably wouldn't hurt if you were a little late upstairs. Just tell them you couldn't get free."

She was already moving away from the cubicle. "I don't think so. It doesn't pay to keep Martin waiting."

The small sense of pleasure she derived at the thought of Pearson's distaste for the task ahead of him had dissipated by the time the elevator doors slid open on the I.C.U. floor. It vanished completely when she stepped into room six and observed its four occupants. Reeves was there, his plastic public-relations smile firmly affixed to his plump face. With his solemn presence and unfailingly smooth tones, he'd always reminded her more of an undertaker than an administrator. A uniformed policeman stood next to the room's bed. But it was the patient in the bed that drew her attention. Jon LeFrenz.

With a thread of apprehension she swung her gaze to the man lounging in the corner. Cade Tremaine. He was again dressed in jeans, wearing a black T-shirt and black running shoes. Today he wore a shoulder holster, along with his shield. He didn't look any more rested than he had three days ago.

Annoyed that she'd made unconscious note of the fact, she stopped in the doorway, addressed Reeves. "You wanted to see me?"

"Dr. O'Riley, Detective Tremaine has asked for our cooperation while he speaks to Mr. LeFrenz. I assured him the hospital would extend him every courtesy."

It would have been difficult to miss the warning in the man's civil tones. Ignoring it, she asked, "Just exactly what courtesy is the detective requesting?"

"Me, Angel Eyes. I'm the one with the request." LeFrenz reached over to press the button that would raise the head of his bed. His other wrist was handcuffed to the railing. "I got no reason to trust Tremaine, but I said if you was in the room, maybe I'd answer a few questions for him." He grinned. Without the oxygen mask and pain twisting his features, it was apparent he was several years older than she'd originally thought. And equally apparent that he was taking great delight in drawing her into the drama between him and the NOPD.

She looked at Reeves. "I'm on duty. I don't have time to baby-sit."

The administrator's smile chilled but didn't disappear. "You can make time." Looking at Tremaine, he said cordially, "Dr. O'Riley is at your disposal, Detective. Please don't keep her too long. The E.R. is slow right now, but that has a way of changing suddenly."

"I appreciate it. If they page her, I'll send her right down."

Nodding, the other man strode from the room.

There was nothing quite so annoying as feeling like a pawn in a situation of someone else's making. Shae made no attempt to keep the irritation from her voice as she asked Tremaine, "Just what is it exactly that I'm here for?"

The detective shoved away from the wall he'd been leaning against, crossed to her side and cupped her elbow. "We can talk outside."

"Hey, where you taking her? Tremaine? Tremaine!" LeFrenz bellowed as Cade inexorably guided her resisting form to the hallway. "She's here because I said so. Bring her back. Now, Tremaine!"

Before they'd taken a dozen steps outside the room, Shae yanked her elbow out of the man's grasp and turned to face him. "Care to tell me what this is all about? I have patients downstairs to tend to."

The detective just gazed at her, his dark-green gaze inscrutable. "You have a patient up here, too."

"LeFrenz isn't my patient anymore. He's Dr. Lyndstrom's." Something about the steady intensity of his regard made her uneasy. Since no man made her nervous, not ever, she decided the reaction had to do with his occupation. Dealing with cops had always raised her stress level.

"I've been in to question him every day since he got out of surgery and he hasn't given me jack. The only thing he has said, more than once, is that he wants to see you." He gave her a mocking smile. "Apparently you made quite an impression on him, *Angel Eyes.*"

She gave an impatient shrug. "And this concerns me how?"

"Jonny hasn't been exactly cooperative up to this point. But he promised that your presence would change that. I thought it was worth a shot to see if he would be any more talkative with you in the room."

Giving an incredulous laugh, she said, "You mean, I'm a *bribe?* Drop dead, Tremaine." Turning, she walked toward the elevator.

He stepped into her path and she stopped, rather than risking running into him. "I wondered if there was a temper to match that red hair." His mouth quirked. "Now I know." As quickly as the humor flashed into his face, it was gone again. "Are you telling me you can't spare fifteen minutes to help the NOPD?"

She raised a brow. "Appealing to my sense of civic duty? Maybe that would have worked if you'd approached me first, instead of running to Reeves." Even as she said the words, she tasted the lie in them.

Cade shoved his fingertips into the front pockets of his jeans. "Reeves? Oh, you mean the suit. I figured you might need permission to leave the floor for a while. Yeah, okay, so I'm using you. I admit it. But I got a kid dead because of the sh—drugs that LeFrenz sold him. We're not so different, you and me. We both try to keep people alive."

Bitterness twisted through her at his words. Professionally, at least, his words were true enough. But personally... Tremaine would be shocked to discover just how far apart they were.

He moved closer to her, his head tilted intimately toward hers, his voice now low and persuasive. "C'mon, Doc. What's the harm?"

Startled, her gaze jerked to his. He had a smoker's voice, slightly raspy, with more than a hint of the South in it. She'd heard it hard, demanding, expressionless. But she'd never heard it sounding like this. That coaxing tone he'd adopted was pure sex, honey-coated temptation that issued its own beguiling invitation. She imagined there were few women who'd ever stood firm against it.

With new eyes she reassessed him, not as a doctor but as a woman. His long narrow face wasn't conventionally handsome, but it was strong, with its slash of cheekbones, straight nose and sensual lower lip. A lock of his dark-brown hair seemed permanently out of place, usually falling across his forehead. She'd noticed him shoving it away more than once. Coupled with those penetrating jade eyes and rangy build, his physical presence no doubt made it easy for him to persuade women to do just about anything he asked. The slight pallor he still wore would only make him more convincing.

He reached for one of her hands, held it in his as his thumb skated over her knuckles. At the touch, her eyelids lowered, her lips parted.

"Tell me something," she murmured throatily.

Although he hadn't moved, somehow he seemed closer. "Mmm-hmm?"

"Does this little act of yours usually work?" When he went still, she retrieved her hand, angled her chin and looked him squarely in the eye. She saw comprehension register there, followed by a flicker of amusement.

"Yes." There wasn't a hint of apology in his voice.

"Well—" her smile was brittle as she stepped away from him "—I'll have to readjust my estimate of women's intelligence."

He tucked his fingers in his pockets again and rocked back on his heels. "It was the hand holding, wasn't it. Too over the top for you? I was afraid so, but you're a tough one to read."

She didn't know whether to be annoyed or disarmed by

his matter-of-fact admission. It suited her to be annoyed. "Has it ever occurred to you to just be upfront about what you want?"

"Sure, I tried that first. Figured you for a more straight-forward approach. When that didn't work, I had to improvise."

Even as she was shaking her head at his blatant confession of manipulation, he was continuing. "You won't be in any danger in there, if that's what you're afraid of. LeFrenz can't get out of the bed, and if he could, the officer and I will be in there with you."

"I'm not afraid of him," she said automatically.

"You should be." His voice was grim. "He may look like a choirboy, but he's got a rap sheet as long as my arm. His juvie record dates back to when he was ten and mugged a homeless woman for her social-security check. He's one of the major drug dealers in the city now."

Despite herself, a chill chased up her spine. The detective was painting a picture of a hardened criminal. But she was painfully aware of the spin law enforcement types could put on people's pasts. She had no doubt that St. Theresa herself would be demonized beyond recognition if an ambitious prosecutor dug into her life.

It was that knowledge, rather than any real sympathy for LeFrenz, that kept her carefully noncommittal. "I don't know what help I'd be in there."

"You'll only be there to pacify LeFrenz." The detective's mouth curled. "The scumbag is being manipulative, but you're the only lever I've got on him. For some reason he's fixated on you. If he gets what he wants, seeing you, he might give up some information in return."

"He didn't seem about to give anything up in the emergency room a few days ago," she pointed out.

He shrugged. "I've got nothing to lose, do I? What do you say?"

Shae stalled by checking her watch. If she walked away as she wanted to, she'd certainly hear about it from the hospital administrator. But it would almost be worth it to avoid the detective.

He made her uneasy. Not nervous, but…on edge. She'd have to be dead not to be aware of the currents of energy that rolled off him. Her femininity might be dormant, but it wasn't dead. She didn't want to get involved in whatever mission drove the man hard enough for him to put his job before his health. She didn't want to get caught up with the police in any capacity.

As if her agreement was already determined, he started issuing commands. "When you go in the room, I want you to stand on the side of the bed he's cuffed on. Don't go too close. The officer will stay on the other side, and he'll stop him if he makes a grab for you."

"I hardly think I have anything to fear from an I.C.U. patient with only one hand free," she said dryly.

His expression was not amused. "Don't make the mistake of underestimating him. People who do that have a way of going missing."

He turned and headed back toward the room, leaving her to follow more slowly. Slipping her hand into her pocket, she brought out her beeper, as if she could will it to summon her back downstairs. But it remained stubbornly silent. With a sigh, she dropped it back into her pocket and entered the room.

"Angel Eyes." LeFrenz's gaze burned fever-bright. "Thought you might have decided not to join our little party."

"Me?" She kept her voice carefully expressionless as

she positioned herself near the side of his bed. "I wouldn't miss it."

"I was startin' to think you'd forgotten me down there." LeFrenz seemed intent on ignoring the policemen in the room. "Figured you'd at least come to check on me."

"As I explained to Detective Tremaine, there was no need. You're under Dr. Lyndstrom's care now. He'll do the follow-up visits."

"Dr. Lyndstrom don't have big blue eyes that a guy could drown in." LeFrenz looked her up and down with an insulting familiarity. "Don't have long legs like yours, neither."

When Shae had worked on LeFrenz in the E.R., he'd been just another patient needing her help. But now there was something revolting about that lascivious expression sitting on his cherubic countenance. Her flesh prickled. She experienced the same sort of revulsion by kicking over a rock and watching the disgusting creatures beneath scuttle for cover. "In the short time you'll be with us, I think you'll come to appreciate some of Dr. Lyndstrom's better qualities."

"That's right, Jonny." Cade strolled toward the bed. "You aren't going to be here long enough to get too attached. County lockup has a medical wing, and I'm betting they have a comfortable cot with your name on it. Can't promise you any good-looking nurses, but hey—" he gave a negligent shrug "—with where you're going, it's best you get used to not seeing women, anyway."

For the first time the patient pulled his gaze from Shae and looked at the detective. "You don't have enough to hold me, Tremaine."

Derision sounded in the detective's voice. "What are you, slow or something? I stood over that dying kid's body and he gave you up as the one who sold him the cocaine. I walk in on you in the middle of bagging your stash, you pull a gun on me and fire while attempting to flee. What part of that doesn't add up to 'enough' for you?''

Shae had the feeling she'd been all but forgotten. This was a private war, being fought between LeFrenz and Tremaine. The patient's voice was still cocky when he answered, ''Okay, so you'll get the possession with intent to stick. With the new sentencing laws in Louisiana, I'll be out in five. You can't tie the kid to me, though. With him dead, his naming me is hearsay. Ain't no jury in the world gonna convict on only your word.''

Tremaine's face remained remarkably calm. ''That might be true under normal circumstances. But that kid was the nephew of the mayor's wife.'' He waited for the news to sink in, noted with satisfaction that LeFrenz had gone a bit paler. ''Even you have to figure out what that means.''

The boy's death had already received more than the usual attention from the media. High-profile names in a police investigation always invited scandal, and scandal made for good copy. The political spin on this one was to turn the dead boy into an unwitting victim of a murderous drug dealer. The version was close enough to the truth to suit Cade, especially when resulting local sentiments were screams for LeFrenz's blood.

''Your only chance of surviving this is to tell me who's supplying you, Jonny.'' No one rose as rapidly as LeFrenz had in the illegal drug market without help. ''Give me the name and you become just another cog in the wheel. Cooperation buys a lot of leniency in the courts. Say the word and I can have the D.A. in here working out a deal.''

He knew he'd gotten to the man when he glanced away,

looked at Dr. O'Riley as if he'd read the solution on her impassive face. Despite his impatience at the delay, Cade could hardly blame the man for his distraction. The leggy redhead was difficult to ignore. Today her mane of hair was scraped back in some kind of fancy braid that hung to the center of her shoulder blades. The severe style showed off those high cheekbones, her short straight nose and her come-to-bed eyes. With the white examining coat and the shapeless scrubs she wore, it was difficult to guess at the figure beneath. But that didn't stop a man's imagination from filling in the details.

He'd never lacked for imagination.

"Whaddaya think, Doc?" Jonny's voice was conversational. If he'd been shaken by Cade's earlier remarks, he'd since recovered. "Think I can trust the detective here to play straight with me?"

A moment passed. Then another. Cade found himself hardly daring to breathe. Shae O'Riley had made no effort to hide her reluctance to be involved in this scene. But instinct told him that reluctance stemmed from more than her unwillingness to leave the E.R. There was something in her voice when she talked to him, something in her eyes that shouted distrust. Since he'd met her just a few days ago, he could only figure it was directed at all cops, not just him. And if that was the case, she was the last person in the world he needed advising his perp.

But her words, when they came, were noncommittal. "Seems to me you've been playing roulette with your choices for some time now. The question is, are you man enough to face the consequences?"

"Honey, I'm man enough for anything you have in mind." Cade sprang forward when LeFrenz reached for her with his free hand, but the uniform got to him first, restraining him. Jonny never took his eyes off Shae, just kept talking, his voice low and suggestive. "I'm looking forward to showing you that sometime. You and me, we could have us a real good time."

"Make your choice, LeFrenz." There was a slow burn in the pit of Cade's belly. Not a little of it was due to the way the punk kept looking at the doctor, as if she was starring in a pornographic movie reel playing in his head. "She can't help you with this. No one can. But you can help yourself."

"Maybe I can cooperate with this detective, Angel Eyes, whaddaya think?" LeFrenz's attention never swerved from Shae. "Maybe I can even tell him who put those bullets in his chest." Her breathing stilled. She stared back at the young man, noted the mouth curled in sardonic amusement, so at odds with the angelic face. How did he know about the detective's injury? She saw the same question reflected on the polished ebony face of the policeman at his side. But the man was too well trained to do more than look at the detective. Her gaze followed the direction of his, met Tremaine's. His expression was inscrutable.

"Think that would interest him, Doc?" There was a hard note of glee underlying LeFrenz's words. "I'm betting it would. I'm betting he'd arrange a pretty fine deal if I was to tell him where to look for the shooter."

"Don't change the subject, LeFrenz. You have one piece of information I want, and that's pretty simple. Just a name." Amazingly enough, the detective's voice sounded bored. "Make it easy on yourself and give it up. Then you can start planning for your retirement."

"He don't believe me," LeFrenz told Shae confidingly. "I'd think I would. We have something in common, me and him. We both know what it's like to have a bullet plow into us, to watch the blood pour out. 'Course, I don't know what it's like to watch my partner die on the sidewalk next to me." There was a stillness in the room that reminded Shae of an explosive waiting to detonate. "But then, maybe Tremaine don't care about none of that. Maybe his partner was as dirty as everyone's saying."

There was no warning of his intention. One moment Cade was standing there, face grim. The next he'd leaned down, yanked LeFrenz up with one fist on the neck of his hospital gown. "You'll show a little respect." The words were murmured almost soundlessly, but the warning in them sent a shiver down Shae's spine. Here was the control she'd sensed that first day from him, dangerously close to slipping. Here was the lethal intent that would drive a man from his hospital bed back to the streets much too soon.

And if LeFrenz was even half-right, here was the reason for that sense of purpose.

"A good cop is dead," Cade went on. "If you have anything to report on that, let's hear it. But don't even think about yanking me around on this, LeFrenz. Brian Hollister got a hero's funeral. No one in the city would even blink at the death of a two-bit drug dealer."

The two men's gazes did battle, while LeFrenz's face slowly flushed red from the stranglehold the detective had on him. When Tremaine showed no signs of releasing him, Shae put her hand on his arm.

"Let's give his wound a chance to heal before we inflict any further damage, shall we?" For a moment she didn't think the detective was going to respond. LeFrenz was turning scarlet. She exerted a bit of pressure on the detective's arm, and he slanted a look at her, the bitterness in it as sharp as a blade. Then in the next instant he released his grip, allowing the patient to drop down to the bed again.

"You're the doctor" was all he said.

The pent-up breath she'd been holding streamed out of her. "That's right. And I need to get back to the E.R. Let's end this."

"You tell the D.A. I got information on the shooting, Tremaine," LeFrenz said when he could speak again. "You tell him that's what I'm dealing. The name of a cop killer ought to trump a dead kid, right?"

"No one is going to believe you have something to trade on Hollister's murder." Shae listened in horrified fascination as the two men bartered. "Do you think you can just throw out some street gossip and beat a murder rap with it? You can't be that stupid."

"I got more than that, Tremaine. I got me a personal relationship with Freddie. You 'member Freddie, doncha?" Shae saw from the look on the detective's face that the name was all too familiar. "I've had me some…transactions with him."

"You mean you deal to him," Cade said flatly.

LeFrenz rolled his shoulders. "Don't matter how I know him. Just that he came to me that night in a big hurry. Had to get out of town and he needed some…supplies before he went."

Cade folded his arms over his chest. "Let me guess. You set him up with a quick fix. Easier to pump a junkie for details when he's just starting to reach for that high, isn't it? And Freddie must have been getting desperate by the time he found you."

"You never know when this kind of information is going to come in handy." One eye slid closed in a sly wink. "He was shook up, all right. Figured you both for dead. Had himself a wad of cash, too, so someone paid him off. Since cops don't deal in that kind of money, I'm thinking the shooters did."

The conversation was painting an all-too-vivid picture for Shae. She could almost hear the gunfire, see the bodies crumpled on the ground. But if the words were bringing back traumatic memories for Tremaine, it didn't show in his expression. That awesome control was back, and the rage that had briefly flared had been reined in, hidden. Somehow that evidence of his restraint was as fearsome as his temper had been.

"Where's Freddie now?"

Again LeFrenz shrugged. "Split, man. Guess it wouldn't be too healthy for him to stick around here. But before he left, he told me all about the whole thing."

Cade considered him for a long moment. "I'll run it by the D.A., see if he wants to deal. But your tip has to lead somewhere before he even considers trading for it. And we're still gonna need the name of your supplier, too, if you're hoping to slip out of a murder rap."

Her beeper sounded, an insistent reminder. Shae didn't reach for it. She was transfixed by the scene playing out before her.

LeFrenz laughed, an ugly sound. "Now who's blowing smoke? I give up a cop killer, they gonna give me the key to the city. You go on and call the D.A., Tremaine. Run this by him. He'll deal. I guarantee it." He looked at Shae then, clearly finished with the conversation. "So Angel Eyes, you gonna stay up here a while and keep me company? Fluff my pillows? Give me a sponge bath, maybe?"

"She needs to get back to the E.R. You've already wasted enough of her time, LeFrenz." The detective took her elbow and guided her of the room.

"You come on back and see me tomorrow, Doc," LeFrenz called after her. "You and me, we have lots to talk about."

Once in the hallway, she reached for her beeper, saw

the E.R. number. "I have to get downstairs," she said numbly.

"I figured." Tremaine was all business now. "Thanks for coming up today. There shouldn't be any reason for you to be here tomorrow. I think Jonny will jump at whatever bone the D.A. decides to throw him."

He walked her to the elevator, jabbed the down button. Shae cautioned herself to keep silent. This wasn't her business, none of it. But the questions whirling around inside her wouldn't be quieted. "Is what he said in there true?" When Cade only looked at her, she continued, "I mean about what happened to you and your partner."

The doors of the elevator slid open. Before they stepped inside, she was forced nearer to him to make room for people to exit. She chose the corner opposite his at the back of the compartment and leaned against the wall as she waited for his answer.

"It was close enough," he finally responded. "Whether he has any more than that remains to be seen. He might just be bluffing, trying to avoid giving up his supplier's name."

She studied him, but his profile could have been set in stone. No one would guess that he was talking about discovering the identity of the man, or men, who'd shot him. Who'd killed his partner.

Something compelled her to push further. "And if he does have information about your partner's death?" She waited for the detective's gaze to meet hers. "What then? Will that boy who died be ignored in favor of arresting a cop killer?"

"Unless you want to loan me that crystal ball of yours, I have no idea what the D.A. is going to go for. Whichever is the surest thing, I imagine."

The elevator doors opened to the E.R. floor. But Shae

didn't move. She couldn't. No more than she could prevent the bitterness from shading her tone. "So that's justice to you? The surest thing? Trading information for
freedom with scum like that the way kids trade baseball
cards?" There was a burning in her chest that was all too
familiar. A helpless hopeless fury that she could never
seem to completely dispel.

He stepped out of the elevator, his voice trailing over
his shoulder. "It might not pass for justice to you, Doc.
But sometimes it's the only thing we've got."

# Chapter 3

"I liked the monkeys best." The pigtailed six-year-old at Shae's side skipped a little as they made their way down the hallway back to her apartment. "Especially the ones with the rainbows on their bottoms."

"Those are baboons, honey." Shae smiled at TeKayla's description. "But they were funny, weren't they?"

The little girl nodded. "And I liked feeding crackers to the giraffes, too. Can we go back to the zoo sometime?"

Stopping before the girl's door, Shae rang the bell. "Maybe next month." Noting a sulk on the way, she reminded the girl, "You wanted to go to the alligator farm next, remember?"

TeKayla brightened just as the door swung open. "Momma, Momma, guess what?" She barreled through the doorway and wrapped her arms around her mother's legs. "Shae's gonna take me to a gator farm next."

"That sounds fine, baby doll." Weariness sounded in the woman's voice, showed on her face. She managed a wan smile for Shae. "Thanks for taking her to the zoo. I know she can be a handful."

"No problem. Did you get any sleep while we were gone?" Hapi Gleason worked two jobs, one of them third shift. TeKayla spent much of the time at home with a sitter when her mother could afford it, and alone when she couldn't. Shae knew Social Services were aware of the situation, but recent budget cuts had decreased their resources. So far, their involvement hadn't seemed to change things appreciably.

The door was already closing. "Had me laundry to do. Din't have no time for sleep."

"Well, let me know if I can—" the door closed in her face "—help." Staring at the raised panels, she sighed. There was no doubt in her mind that Hapi considered her an interfering do-gooder. But the truth was...

The truth, she thought, as she made her way to the elevator to go up to her apartment, was that fifteen years ago she'd have thought the same thing about anyone who tried to lend her assistance. She'd have viewed it with doubt and suspicion and sooner have spit on it than accept help, however well intended. At any rate, it was totally out of character for her to get involved like this. Her patients were her duty, her neighbors were not. Other than the Gleasons and the super, she had only a nodding acquaintance with the other people in her building. That had always been the way she liked it. Her hours didn't give her a lot of free time, and the time off she did have would be better spent on her own errands and chores.

When the elevator doors opened on the top floor, she went to her door and inserted the key. From the first there had been something about TeKayla's gap-toothed grin and puppy-dog friendliness that had charmed her. The child spent way too much time unsupervised on the stoop out front, even when her mother was home. Although this was a decent enough neighborhood, it was old and close enough to the projects to warrant exercising some caution.

She pushed open the door, dropped her keys and the mail she'd collected from her mailbox downstairs on the table beside it. Crossing to the closet, she hung up her coat and purse. There was no way she would have been able to afford this much space in a more exclusive neighborhood. The entire top floor had been converted to a loft apartment, with screens and throw rugs delineating the space. Upstairs, beneath a huge skylight, was a bedroom with an attached bath. It was simple, comfortable and private. It fit her needs precisely.

Walking to the kitchen tucked into one corner, she opened the fridge and took out a bottle of water. Twisting off the cap, she tipped it to her lips, drank.

"Quite a place you got here, Shae girl."

The bottle dropped from nerveless fingers as she swung around, her gaze sweeping the area for a weapon. She had her hand on the knife board before she recognized the voice. It was telling that even then, especially then, she had to force herself to release her grip on the weapon.

"What are you doing here, Da?" Her tone was flat, no welcome in it. She watched the tall handsome, man stroll down the spiral staircase from the loft, before posing theatrically at its base, arms spread.

"Shae, my girl, is that any way to greet your old man? Come over and give me a proper welcome."

A proper welcome would be something between a knife in his heart and a boot out the door. She settled for uncompromising indifference. "Most people use the doorbell. Mind telling me how you got in here?"

One well-manicured index finger to his lips, Ryan

O'Riley said, "Now, now. You know I never divulge my methods."

"You don't have to. You either broke in or bribed someone." She bent down, picked up the bottle she'd dropped and grabbed a towel to wipe up the water that had spilled. "Knowing your basic lack of ambition, I imagine bribery was your means of choice."

"You've grown hard, girl." An expression of sadness settled on Ryan's face as he heaved a sigh. "I blame myself for that."

Rising again, she tossed the wet towel in the sink. "There's plenty to blame yourself for, Da. By all means, don't stop there."

If age had caught up with Ryan McCabe O'Riley, it hadn't dared to show itself. His six-foot frame was still straight, his red hair as bright as her own. His unlined face looked a good ten years younger than its fifty years. It was amazing, Shae thought bitterly, what living without care or conscience could do for a person.

"I wouldn't say no to one of those bottled waters if you were to offer," he hinted broadly, leaning against the counter.

It was on the tip of her tongue to refuse. But spitefulness wouldn't solve anything, and it certainly wouldn't get rid of him. When he wanted something, her father could be amazingly thick-skinned. And he definitely wanted something, or he never would have shown up here.

She got him a water, slid it over to him. "I'm not giving you any money."

The stage had missed a born actor in Ryan O'Riley. The injured expression on his face was worthy of a Tony. "Can't I just stop by and catch up with my only daughter? My eldest and the dearest to her father's heart?"

Giving up, Shae propped a hip against the wall, watching him. There would be no rushing him. He'd take his own time getting to the point, and then use charm, guilt and familial loyalty to try to get his way. The combination had never worked on her, but he'd always refused to acknowledge that.

"I can't tell you how proud I am of you." Few seeing the beaming paternal look on his handsome face would doubt his sincerity. "My daughter, the doctor. I can't believe the little girl I raised is saving lives every day. The emergency room at Charity, right?"

She ignored his question, preferring to focus on his statement. "It would certainly be a stretch to claim you had any part in raising me. If we were to add up all the time you actually spent with your family, we'd probably come up with…what? Three years, total?"

His brows lowered. "Now, Shae, don't go blaming me for things out of my control. I did what I had to do to put food on my family's table, to provide for your mother, you and your brother. I know you always felt I could have done more, but—"

"You mean like hold a steady job? Bring a paycheck home? Be a father, instead of an occasional house guest?" With effort she kept her tone expressionless. Emotion was an ineffective weapon against him. He'd only wield it against her. "Any of those would have been a start. But you chose to take the easy route, running one scam after another in search of a quick buck."

"Those were legitimate entrepreneurial enterprises," he corrected her. "Each and every one of them."

"Of course. And the police take such a narrow view of entrepreneurs, don't they?"

"Apparently." Nodding, he took another swig. Sarcasm was wasted on him. It was only one of his annoying qualities. "Because I understand poor Liam got caught up in their net."

Rage, only recently tucked away, bubbled through her veins. "Poor Liam took a page out of his da's book and looked for the easy life. He was caught red-handed with an apartment full of electronics. Where do you suppose he learned his skill breaking and entering?"

"I won't be having you take that tone with me, Shae Kathleen O'Riley." Ryan's voice was stern. "I taught the boy better than that, just like I taught you."

As quickly as the fury had boiled over, it vanished, leaving desolation in its wake. "You should have left him with me after Mam died. We were doing fine on our own. He was in a good school and making decent grades. Living with you ruined him."

"Well, now, I know you've never forgiven me for taking him and leaving you alone, girl." With a neat twist, he turned the words back on her, distorting the truth. "But what kind of father would I have been to leave my son to be raised by his sister, and you only twenty yourself?"

The kind of father, she thought resentfully, who hadn't had his eye on the welfare check that could be applied for when an unemployed man had a dependent. She imagined the majority of it every month had gone to the track.

"We'd done well enough on our own for over two years." Not for the first time, she considered the futility of this line of conversation. Ryan would never change. She'd known that since she was eight. Arguing about it was pointless. She spent as much effort as necessary to avoid thinking about him most days.

"Why don't you tell me what brought you here today?" She hadn't even known he was in the city. She hadn't seen him since Liam's eighteenth birthday.

"Can't a father even…" Observing the stony expression on her face, he swallowed his words. "The truth is, darlin', your old man is in a wee spot of trouble." With the dimple winking in his left cheek, he looked like a mischievous rogue admitting to stealing a kiss from the neighbor girl. She'd seen the look too often to be swayed by it.

"Police or money?" she asked briskly.

He made a sound of dismay. "I believe the NOPD may be looking to have a discussion with me, but that's just a misunderstanding. However, there are some people I need to pay if I want in on a new venture. I think you'll agree that this is an opportunity I can't afford to pass up."

The buzzer sounded, which was just as well. Her temples had begun to throb, a sure sign that she'd been in her father's company too long. Crossing to the front door, she pressed the button on the intercom. "Yes?"

"Let me up, Shae."

She had no difficulty identifying the raspy tones, softened by a cadence of the South. But she did have difficulty responding to it. What could be so important that Cade Tremaine would seek her out here? That thought was quickly followed by another. She didn't want him here in her home. Didn't want to see him among her things, his presence stamping the area with an indelible brand that would be impossible to erase even when he'd gone.

"What do you want, Detective?" From the corner of her eye she saw the alarm cross Ryan's face, saw him push away from the counter.

"I'm not going to have this conversation standing in the street." His low smoky drawl was adamant. "Buzz me in."

"This isn't a good time for me."

There was a moment of silence when she wondered what he was thinking. But when he spoke again finally, he sounded no less determined. "Then I'll apologize for the inconvenience, but this won't wait."

"I'm afraid it's going to have to." She no more wanted to prolong this time with her father than she wanted Tremaine up here. And there was no way she could deal with the two men together.

She turned away from the intercom, fully expecting more demands. But it remained silent. Her father was staring at her, trepidation on his face. "What would a detective want with you?"

"It has nothing to do with you, Da." Abruptly a wave of weariness swept over her. The day had started in a relaxed-enough fashion, but stress was seeping in, one layer at a time. Seeing that her words hadn't wiped the worry from her father's face, she added, "It's something about work. A patient of mine. Let's get back to what brought you here."

Understanding had taken the place of concern in his expression. Understanding that, as it turned out, was totally misplaced. "You're not in any kind of trouble, are you girl? Take some advice from your da—keep your cons out of your workplace. It's cleaner that way."

For one of the few times in her life, she was speechless. She stared at him, shocked that he knew her so little. And then shocked at herself for being surprised by that. She shook her head, gave a grim laugh. "Yeah, Da, I'm running scams in the hospital. Got a little betting pool going on the wheelchair races on the fourth floor."

"Which brings me to why I'm here." Although she didn't quite follow his segue, she was glad he was finally getting to the point of his visit. Ryan reached for his bottle of water again. "I've got a chance to get in on a dandy little deal, and I think you can be a big help to me."

"No."

He went on as if he hadn't heard her. "All I need is a list of people in the city with the kind of money needed to be interested in what I'll be selling."

Shae picked up the lid to her own bottle, screwed it on with more force than necessary. "Didn't you hear me? I said no."

"Names, that's all I'm asking you for. Doctors have plenty of money and you must have contacts at the other hospitals, as well." His tone became wheedling. "It's not so much to give, Shae, to your dear old da you haven't seen in years." Pleased with his pitch, he tilted the bottle to his lips and drank. "Maybe you could arrange for an introduction or two, as well. I'll do the rest."

"I realize this is a difficult concept for you to understand, Da, but listen carefully. I'm not going to say it again." She leaned over the counter, shoved her face close to his. "No."

"You've got a streak of stubbornness in you, girl. Have to think you got it from your sainted mother's side, God rest her soul." Ryan did a quick sign of the cross, cast his gaze heavenward. "Can't help but believe she'd frown on the way you're treating your father right now."

"You've always had a talent for believing whatever suited your purposes." The irony in her voice was lost in the sound of her doorbell ringing. Her head jerked toward the door. She was the only occupant on this floor. It was rare for another tenant to come calling for any reason, with the occasional exception of TeKayla. Pushing away from the counter, she went to the door, looked out the peephole.

Somehow, the last person she'd expected to see there was Detective Cade Tremaine. She took a step back, and then another. But she couldn't avoid his voice. "Open the door, Shae. It'd be useless to pretend you're not in there."

Dimly she was aware that Ryan was rapidly making his

way to the staircase, ascending it. She could only assume
he was looking for a place to hide until the detective left.

"How about if I just pretend you weren't invited into
the building?" Temper snapped in her words. "Oh, wait,
that wouldn't be pretense, would it? I told you it wasn't
a good time, Detective."

"And I'm sorry about that."

There was that voice again, the same one he'd used
when he'd tried to convince her to help him with LeFrenz
in I.C.U. The smooth drawl coated his raspy tones like
thick sweet honey, designed to weaken the knees and el-
evate the pulse. But the fact that hers was pounding had
nothing to do with him, she told herself firmly, and everything to do with the stress of the past hour.

"I won't take up much of your time, Dr. O'Riley.
Shae." His voice dropped intimately on the last word, as
if caressing the single syllable. "Let me in. I don't want
to talk to you through a door and I'm not going away. I
can be very persistent."

She didn't need to be told that. Undecided, she threw
a look over her shoulder. There was no sign of Ryan, and
probably no reason to worry about him. He'd always had
an aptitude for dodging the police.

Making her decision, she unlocked the dead bolt, swung
open the door a few inches and surveyed him. "*Persistent*
isn't the word I would have used. Stubborn, maybe. In-
considerate. Pesky."

His mouth curved slightly. "Semantics. Are you going
to let me in?"

She didn't even need to think about her answer. "No."

"Okay." His easy acceptance didn't fool her. This
man's will was like forged steel. He propped himself
against the doorjamb, the position putting his face too
close to hers. She wasn't short, but he topped her five-

foot eight by a good four inches. "I looked for you at the hospital last night."

Wariness threaded through her. "I got off at five. I'm not back on again until tomorrow."

"That's what somebody said." He wore jeans again today, old sneakers and a white shirt under an open leather jacket. His eyes were a little bloodshot and he hadn't shaved recently. Either he'd gone on a bender last night or he hadn't slept at all. Intuitively she knew it was the latter.

"Why are you here, Detective?" she asked bluntly. The sooner they got this over with, the sooner she could send him on his way. And then focus on dispatching Ryan with the same speed. Just the thought made her tired again.

"Do you think I could have a glass of water?" When she only blinked, his mouth curved again. "Got a bit parched standing out front trying to wheedle my way in here."

"Since I didn't let you in, I'm assuming you wheedled one of the other tenants."

He gave a slow nod. "Nicest little old blue-haired lady. She had a mite more respect for my shield than you do."

"Look, Detective—"

"That water?" he prompted.

Giving up, she turned away and strode toward the refrigerator, yanked it open. Taking out a bottle, she rose, only to find him standing inside the apartment, the door closed behind him, his gaze sweeping the area. A burn began to simmer inside her. "Very clever. You're pretty adept at getting what you want, aren't you, Detective."

She could have told him that the innocent look he attempted was in vain. Innocence was one expression his warrior's face could never carry off. "All I wanted was a glass of water."

When she threw the bottle to him, he caught it in one hand. "Thanks." Taking his time, he removed the cap and drank, all the while surveying the space. "Nice place. I was a bit surprised at your address. I thought doctors lived in gated communities. By the lake or something."

"Maybe those are the doctors who've paid off their college loans."

"Maybe." His gaze landed on the two half-empty water bottles on the counter, lingered. "Did you have company?"

She'd never know what compelled her to lie. Experience had taught her that it paid to keep things simple. But the words tumbled from her lips before she'd had a chance to think them through. "No. I was just thirsty." He didn't speak, but neither did his gaze waver. And being the object of that intense jade regard was just as nerveracking as she'd feared. "I forgot I'd already opened one."

He crossed to the counter, leaned against it. After taking another swallow of water, he then set the bottle down, reached out a lazy finger and touched the one Ryan had left. "Still cold."

She snatched it away, took it to the sink and poured it out. "I have things to do, Tremaine. Let's get on with whatever it is that brought you here."

"Have you spoken to anyone from work today?"

The abrupt transition had her turning back toward him. "No, why?"

"Last night Jonny LeFrenz broke out of the hospital. Or rather," he corrected himself, "someone broke him out."

Gaping at him, she struggled to collect her thoughts, which had abruptly scattered.

"How... That's not possible. He was handcuffed to the bed. There was a guard at his door."

"The uniform had the keys to the cuffs."

"You mean he unlocked them?"

"No." Tremaine's expression was stony. "I mean whoever killed the guard got the keys from his pocket."

Abruptly in need of support, Shae leaned against a cupboard. "Someone killed that police officer?"

"Jabbed a hypodermic filled with a large dose of epinephrine into his heart. I'm told that would have dropped
him within seconds."

Horror washed over her. "It would have sped up the
cardioactivity until the heart was rendered completely ineffective."

"So I heard. The guard was summoned into the room
and attacked there. Once he was out of the way, it would
have been a simple matter to pull the covers up over
LeFrenz and wheel him out of the hospital, especially during shift change late last night."

She was shaking her head. "There'd be nothing simple
about it. Even on third shift, the hospital is full of people,
and a stranger is going to be recognized by somebody."
The detective's silence was its own answer, one she
quickly interpreted. "You don't think it was a stranger."

"Given the choice of weapon, the ease with which
LeFrenz got away, no, not necessarily."

Even while she attempted to grapple with this information, he dropped another bombshell. "What were you
doing last night, Shae?"

Her gaze flew to his steely one. Although she knew her
jaw was agape, it took a moment to summon the strength
to close it. "You think I helped LeFrenz break out of
police custody? That I killed someone to help him get
away?" Astonishment and indignation mingled in her
voice. "Are you crazy?"

"The entire staff is being questioned. I don't have to

tell you how serious this is. Another cop's been murdered, the second in the last couple months. Two different investigations, but the department is justifiably tense. So I'm going to ask you again, where were you last night?''

She swallowed, her indignation already fading at the thought of the silent officer she'd seen in the I.C.U. lying lifeless on the hospital floor. "I left the hospital at five, went to the gym…"

"Which gym?"

His question reminded her that he'd check her story. The whole scene began to take on a surreal aspect. "Women's Fitness on France and Tulane. I left there at six-thirty, came home and didn't leave again."

"Did you have any guests last night?"

"No."

Leaving the bottle of water on the counter, he pushed away, began to stroll around her apartment. She didn't know whether to be glad to be released from that unwavering gaze or to be annoyed as he picked up the book she was reading, looked at it, laid it down again. She decided she could feel both emotions at once.

"What time did you go to bed?"

She shrugged impatiently. "I don't know. Eleven. Eleven-thirty."

He looked over his shoulder at her. "Which was it?"

Stopping to think, she said, "Eleven-thirty. Conan O'Brien had just started." Looking past him, she noticed he'd picked up the mail she'd dropped on the table inside the door. Annoyance definitely took precedence now. "Do you mind?" Striding toward him, she snatched the pile from his hand.

Eyeing her soberly, he asked, "Has LeFrenz contacted you?"

"No. Why would he?"

The twist of his mouth was mocking. "I don't know, *Angel Eyes,* why would he?" When she remained stubbornly silent, he went on, "He's got a thing for you. He wanted to see you yesterday. That's why he made your presence a condition of cooperating. He's still in serious condition. He'll need a doctor's care. Pick a reason."

"No, he hasn't contacted me." Her tone was icy. "He'd have to be crazy to do so. He has no reason to believe I'd give him any help."

Tremaine studied her, as if looking for answers she hadn't given. "I can attest that he's crazy. He's also—" A small noise issued from the loft. The chill that came into his eyes then had her shivering. "Who's here?"

Her mind didn't seem capable of functioning. It had been too long since she'd last had experience lying to cops. And yet somehow not long enough. "No one."

Her answer had his mouth flattening. Turning, he began crossing to the staircase, drawing a gun from the back of his waistband. She could only follow helplessly,. "Detective. Tremaine. You don't have permission to invade my home like this." Her words didn't halt his progress. Taking the steps two at a time, she joined him in her bedroom, watched as his narrowed gaze took in the unmade bed, her nightgown tossed on top in a crumple of silk.

And then settle, as hers did, on the hinged set of bars swinging freely outward from the opened window. He went to it, looked at the pull-down fire escape that had been released to clatter to the ground. Then, his face hard, just a little mean, he looked back at her. "Your 'no one' just jumped out your window and went down the fire escape. Better start giving me a name, Doc. Or be prepared to come downtown so we can do this more formally."

# Chapter 4

For a moment Cade's metamorphosis to steely-eyed cop hurtled her back to the past, and she was twelve again, holding the line against the detectives who'd come to the door in search of her father. *No, he's not here. No, I don't know when he's coming back. And no, you can't search the house. Not without a warrant.* The memory of the bitterness and bravado she'd felt then was still fresh, a slice of the past that never seemed to lose its sting.

But she wasn't twelve anymore. With effort, she shook off the recollection. She didn't feel any particular compunction about protecting a man who'd never been much of a parent. But there was a very similar reaction to a cop, Tremaine this time, encroaching on her home and demanding answers.

She went past him, leaned out the window to retract the fire escape. Closing the window, she carefully locked it before shutting the hinged set of bars and turning the key to secure the lock on it. With a tinge of irritation, she replaced the key in the drawer of her bedside table, where her father must have found it.

When she turned back to Tremaine, she saw no lessening in the tension in his expression. "Come on, Detective. You can't honestly believe that I had Jonny LeFrenz in here. Or that a man who was still in I.C.U. twenty-four hours ago could be fit enough to scramble down a fire escape and race through an alley to make his getaway."

His tone was unrelenting. "All I know is you didn't want me in your apartment and you lied about being alone. If it wasn't Jonny LeFrenz who jumped out your bedroom window, who was it?"

Still unwilling to answer that question, she countered, "Why would you think I'd help the man, anyway? From everything you've said, he's a dangerous criminal. What possible reason would I have for allowing him up here?"

The shrug he gave was anything but nonchalant. "Maybe you didn't have a choice. Maybe you knew him before he showed up in the hospital. Or maybe you're just one of those women who have a things for bad boys." His gaze turned speculative. "Unless you have another explanation for that letter downstairs from the Louisiana Federal Penitentiary."

Her fingers curled into fists. It took more effort than it should have to keep them at her sides. She'd known as soon as she'd seen the long brown envelope in his hands that the return address wouldn't have escaped him. She felt a surge of resentment, so sudden and fierce it nearly choked her. She didn't owe this man anything, least of all an explanation. She wasn't in the habit of airing her family's dysfunctional secrets for the entertainment of strangers.

And that was exactly what Detective Cade Tremaine was. Although he'd recently been popping up in her life with unsettling frequency, the fact remained that she knew nothing about him. Except that he was a cop. He was in her apartment uninvited. And he was asking questions she'd much prefer to leave unanswered.

He must have read the obstinance on her face. "You don't seem in too big of a hurry to give me answers, Doc. Maybe I'm gonna start drawing my own conclusions."

"Go ahead," she invited, tossing her head. "Start with the conclusion that I don't want you here. That I resent your intrusion into my life and my home, and the way you seem to assume you have the right to demand answers to questions that are none of your damn business."

A shutter seemed to come down over his eyes. "Somehow your privacy doesn't stack up all that high against a dead cop and a drug dealer back on the street, instead of the cell where he belongs. One way or another, I *will* get answers to my questions." He bared his teeth in something less than a smile. "But if I have to get uniforms here to canvass the neighbors, I'm not going to be near as patient as I've been so far."

Shae had never much cared for the helplessness that came from dealing with cops. And she'd always hated the man responsible for putting her in those situations. But there was another part of her, an equally strong part, that recoiled from having policemen talking to her neighbors about her. The one thing she'd always been careful to maintain since she'd been an adult was her privacy.

"I haven't seen Jonny LeFrenz since you questioned him that day," she said flatly. She walked past Tremaine to the staircase. She'd much rather be having this conversation downstairs than in her bedroom. Turning back, she saw that Tremaine didn't seem in any particular hurry to follow her. He remained where he was, standing too close to the side of her unmade bed for her peace of mind.

"Have you had any contact with him at all since then? Has anyone talked to you about him?"

She responded to the rapid-fire questions succinctly. "No and no."

It was impossible to tell from his expression whether he believed her. It didn't matter. All that mattered was finishing this and getting him out of her bedroom. "And the man who left through your window?"

"What makes you think it was a man?" He didn't blink, just looked at her with that implacable stare. Suddenly she tired of this whole scene. She released a breath, and with it, some of her stubbornness. "It was my father."

Although he still didn't change expression, she had the feeling she'd managed to surprise him. She had no doubt that he'd be even more surprised by what a phone call to headquarters would no doubt elicit on the subject of the man. With a note of futility sounding in her voice, she invited him to do just that. "Dodging the police is an art form for Ryan O'Riley. You can call it in if you don't believe me."

There was a pang in her chest when, without a word, he reached for the phone on her bedside table to do just that. But before she could examine that emotion, it was quickly followed by dismay as he sank down on the side of her bed after placing the call.

Amidst the tangle of her lace-edged sheets, he appeared utterly foreign, utterly male. His lean hard frame should have seemed out of place in the deliberately feminine decor she'd chosen, but instead, he looked as if he'd just risen from that very bed after spending a particularly restless night. As if he'd just sat down for a moment after dressing to say goodbye to the woman he'd left sleeping there.

Her cheeks burned at the inescapable mental image. She

didn't do morning-afters, not ever, so it wasn't experience that had supplied that particular picture. It was Tremaine himself. He seemed a little too comfortable in the intimate setting, enough so that he didn't spare a glance for the slip of nightgown she'd left carelessly heaped in the center of the bed. Or for the pile of clothes she'd slipped out of last night, the black bra and scrap of matching panties, lying much too close to his feet.

After a brief conversation, he hung up the phone, rose to face her. "If your father is Ryan McCabe O'Riley, there's a warrant out for his arrest."

"What a shock." This time she did leave the room, not waiting to see whether he'd follow. She was already seated on the couch, legs crossed, when he descended the stairway to survey her.

"You don't seem surprised."

"The police have always displayed more interest in my father than I have." She made a lazy gesture. "If the uniforms hurry, they may be able to pick up a trace of him before he disappears."

"He's wanted for fraud, the desk sergeant said." Tremaine crossed to the couch and sat next to her, instead of choosing a chair several feet away, as she would have preferred.

"He has difficulty distinguishing the fine line between businessman and crook." She shrugged as though it didn't matter. Wished it didn't. "And before you ask, I couldn't give you any information on him even if I wanted to. Today was the first time in four years I've spoken to him."

He glanced toward the loft, then back at her. "In that case, I should apologize for my timing."

Rather than the speculation she'd expected, there was genuine sympathy in his eyes, in his voice. Uncomfortable with it, she rose. "Well, we can't all grow up with Ward and June Cleaver. Now if you're satisfied that I'm not harboring your runaway gangster, I have a ton of things I still need to do today."

As a hint, it was far from subtle. But it failed miserably. He stretched his arms out along the back of the couch, giving the appearance of a man who meant to stay awhile. "I'll admit that you don't have LeFrenz hiding in your bedroom. I'm even willing to bet that you spent the night just as you claim. But there's still the little matter of Jonny's fixation on you."

He must have read the impatience and frustration on her face, because he went on, "You may not know him, but I do. He's a two-bit dealer who has always managed to avoid hard jail time."

"I've treated dealers before, Detective. I've also worked on murderers and child molesters." Her voice was stony. "We provide care to anyone who needs it, whether they're upstanding citizens or not. I've never had one of them contact me outside the hospital."

"After last night, the stakes are even higher for LeFrenz," he countered. "Besides the death of that kid he sold drugs to, he's going to face life or execution. The State of Louisiana doesn't take well to cop killers. So he's automatically more dangerous, because he's got more to lose than usual if he gets caught. He also has a very powerful friend. It took money to arrange that escape. You have to wonder who wants him out of police custody and why."

"This is all very interesting," she drawled, in a tone that said it was anything but. "But it has nothing to do with me. If LeFrenz has that much at stake, the last thing he's going to do is come out of hiding to contact me. I was cooperating with your interrogation. He's got no reason to trust me.''

"You're thinking logically, in terms of what makes sense to you. You're not thinking like a man who has always taken everything he's ever wanted. One who sees no reason to deny himself anything.'' He gave her a moment to digest that before adding, ''And based on the way he acted at the hospital, what he wants right now is you.''

She rubbed her arms, where an involuntary shiver had prickled her skin. Tremaine was reaching, she told herself firmly. He had no evidence to suggest such a thing, only supposition. But she couldn't shake the idea that twice today she'd had unwelcome visitors in her apartment. If LeFrenz wanted to, what would prevent him from being the third?

As if he'd read the thought, Tremaine said, ''You need to call a security consultant and take a few extra precautions around here.''

"I will.'' She meant it. And if the extra precautions kept her father from entering her apartment illegally, she'd consider that a bonus.

"Good. You need to be careful at the hospital, too. Do you drive?''

"Of course.''

"Start taking taxis. It'll be more expensive, but at least you won't have to worry about having a stowaway waiting for you in your back seat or about having to cross a dark parking lot at night.'' His tone was brisk, as if handing out such stark advice was commonplace for him. ''Don't go anywhere alone, and when you're home, don't let anyone in. I'll still be working the case, so I'm not going to be able to look out for you around the clock.''

"That's okay, I'll…'' His meaning hit her then, and she

swung around, narrowed her gaze at him. "Who asked you to look out for me?"

"No one. But I'm going to be sticking close, in any case. I'm betting that sooner or later, LeFrenz is going to come looking for you. And when he does, I'll be around to nail him."

The sheer audacity of the statement had her gaping at him, while a little sprint of alarm tore up her spine. "If you think I'm going to live my life under armed guard because of some crazy intuition of yours, you're seriously deluded."

He gave her a crooked smile, further distracting her. It softened his face, lent it the charm she knew he was capable of and almost diminished the resolve in his expression. Almost. "Relax, it won't be for long. Just until LeFrenz is picked up again."

"No," she pronounced firmly, with a sense of déjà vu. Was it only twenty minutes ago that she'd been telling her father the same thing? "I'm not going along with this, and there's no point, anyway. I'm rarely home. Even if LeFrenz did come calling, he probably wouldn't find me here."

"Your father did."

Her mouth opened, snapped shut again. The irrefutable logic of the remark elicited a snarl of feelings best left untangled. Steering clear of them, she reached for calm. "Look, if LeFrenz is as smart as you claim, he's got to realize that you'll be expecting him to show up here. Which means I'm the one person he'll steer clear of."

Judging from the unyielding expression on his face, he remained unconvinced. "I didn't say he was smart. But he is an arrogant punk who's gotten away with murder. He'll contact you all right, eventually. And when he does, I'm going to be here."

His words and the accompanying visual image sent a sneaky blade of panic slicing through her. It was ironic that that the thought of being accosted by an escaped suspect had less impact than did the thought of spending days in Tremaine's presence. "That won't be necessary. If I should hear anything from LeFrenz or see anything suspicious at all, I'll call you right away."

He couldn't possibly know just how huge a concession that was for her. Certainly he didn't appear impressed by it. Folding his arms over his chest, he merely arched his brows. "Good. Your cooperation will make my job easier. You probably won't have to look hard to find me, though. I don't plan to be too far away."

There was no reason his words should have sounded so much like a threat. Should have felt so much like one. They shredded her control, already frayed from the events of the day. "I'm not going to live my life in fear, Tremaine, either from LeFrenz or from the police." Movements made jerky by agitation, she rose again, strode to the door. Yanking it open, she stood next to it in an unmistakable message, one she was almost surprised that he seemed to read.

Slowly he stood, followed her to the door. But he didn't go through it. Not yet. Instead, he stopped much too close to her and said soberly, "I'm going to put two plainclothes policemen on you until we have LeFrenz in custody. Don't worry," he continued as she opened her mouth to protest. "You won't know they're there, and hopefully neither will LeFrenz. We want to draw him out, not scare him off."

His proximity made her want to rear back, to maintain a safer distance between them. Pride stiffened her spine, making it impossible. "Nice to hear that using me as bait doesn't interfere with your high-minded ideals to serve and protect. But then, I've never known a cop who wasn't willing to do whatever it took to solve a case.'' The words were no less than the truth, and they had an immediate effect on him. His face hardened, and once again he was the steely-eyed cop from the trauma room.

"Then you won't be surprised when I tell you that I'm determined to track LeFrenz down. It's just a matter of time. But you're wrong if you think I'll risk you to do it.''

Once again he'd managed to surprise her. She stared at him for a moment, wide-eyed, and he took a step closer, brought his face nearer.

"He was wrong about one thing, you know,'' he murmured. "LeFrenz.''

Shae could only look at him, fighting the urge to flee, the temptation to move closer. He continued speaking, his shaman's voice as soft and sensuous as rumpled velvet. "Your eyes aren't blue, they're gray. The color of the sky right before dawn. But you do look like an angel. Just not the saintly kind.''

Then he moved past her out the door, leaving her to stare blankly at the wide expanse of his back as he walked away. It took far longer than it should have for her to close the door behind him. And even longer to remember to secure the locks again.

Once he got to his car, Cade lost no time calling in the order to the station. He'd been dead serious when he'd told Shae he wasn't going to take chances with her safety. But he'd never fooled himself into thinking it would be an easy sell to his lieutenant, who was heading up the task force hunting for LeFrenz and his accomplice.

"I don't know, Cade. Tying up two men, hoping LeFrenz is going to show up eventually to see this woman doesn't sound like a sure thing. We don't really have the manpower to spare.''

"I'll explain when I get to the station,'' Cade responded tersely, starting the car and pulling out into the traffic, the cell phone to his ear. "But this is solid, Lieutenant. It might not be today or tomorrow, but he will try to contact her. I'd stake my shield on it.''

"Come in and we'll discuss this further. Then we'll see.'' Cade had heard that noncommittal tone in Lieutenant Howard's voice before, had often seen the expression to match on the man's mahogany face. It wasn't going to deter him.

"Put the men on O'Riley now. If you're not convinced after our conversation, you can always reassign them.''

There was a silence, then a long-suffering sigh. "You'd better be on your way here right now.''

It wasn't triumph Cade felt at the small concession, but relief. He didn't think he was overstating his certainty that O'Riley was going to be their key to catching LeFrenz. Or his concern for her. "I'm on my way.'' He broke the connection.

He hoped his lieutenant was going to be easier to convince than Shae had been. He'd barely been certain of her cooperation. If ever there was a woman who shouted No Trespassing, she did. Cade had no difficulty reading the signs. Hell of it was, he'd never been one to follow them. He was intrigued by her, had been from the start. She was a study of contrasts, starting with her occupation. He knew of plenty women doctors, but few who chose to work the adrenaline-pumping ER field.

With a quick look over his shoulder, he changed lanes, edging into a narrow opening in the traffic. Then there was the woman's looks. Hair the color of flame, eyes that could go glacial in the span of seconds. Fire encased in ice, her frosty demeanor was designed to ward off the most determined man. Cade was just obstinate enough to be fascinated, instead. Years of police work had taught him more than he'd ever thought to know about human nature. He couldn't help but wonder what was behind that guard she wore like armor. Couldn't battle the temptation to try to bridge it.

His cell phone rang again, abruptly shattering that wholly inappropriate line of thought. "Cade?" The woman on the end didn't identify herself. She didn't need to. He recognized Carla Hollister's voice, even layered as it was with defiance and fear. "Can you come over right away?"

"What's wrong?" But even as he asked the question, Cade was scanning the street, searching for a way to change course. He pulled into an alley and stopped.

"It's Torley and Morrison. They're here again and, Cade—" her voice hitched once, then evened out "—this time they have a warrant."

His priorities abruptly shifted. The conversation with his lieutenant would have to wait. "I'll be right there." Cade eyed the traffic behind him, backed out into a narrow opening and, with a screech of acceleration, headed toward the Hollister home, fury and resolve mingling in a hard knot in his belly. The police shrink would have said the feeling stemmed from survivor's guilt, for being alive when Brian was dead. Shrinks had all kinds of psychobabble to explain things that really needed no explanation. Things like loyalty. Friendship. And a determination to keep his partner's memory from being irrevocably stained.

The nondescript blue sedan parked in front of the Hollister town house was instantly recognizable. Not because Cade had ever seen it before, but because it was the type he figured I.A. suits would choose. Dull, stolid and lacking in imagination. As he ascended the porch steps, Carla opened the front door, rushed out with Richard squalling in her arms.

"Thank God you're here, Cade. I can't get them to tell me anything, and they're totally trashing our home. Can they do this? Can they just walk in and..."

He pushed aside his own anger and resentment at the men's tactics and schooled his voice to soothing. "I'll see what I can find out, okay?" He reached out and took the screaming toddler from her. "Hey, big guy, what's the problem, huh?"

Richard quieted to hiccuping sobs, his big dark eyes liquid with tears. Cade murmured nonsense to the toddler in a low lilting tone, his gaze sweeping the house's interior as he entered. His mouth flattened. Carla's description wasn't too far off the mark. The place wasn't a shambles, but the I.A. team was being methodical and none too careful, judging from the gaping drawers and cushionless furniture. Pictures had been taken off the wall and not replaced, and one officer had the vent unscrewed and his arm inside, searching. Another was seated on the floor, Richard's floppy teddy bear on his lap, the seam ripped open. Apparently Richard had taken offense at the indignity his toy was suffering. Cade could appreciate the sentiment. "Maybe if you boys told us what you were looking for, we could help you out."

The cop in front of the vent glanced up. "Just stay out of the way, buddy, and we'll..." Cade flashed his shield and a modicum of arrogance faded from the other man's voice. "Sergeants Torley and Morrison have the warrant. They're around here somewhere."

"I'm sure they are." Cade rubbed Richard's back in slow rhythmic circles as the boy took a deep breath, popped his thumb in his mouth and laid his head on

Cade's shoulder. "Question is, what corner are they skulking in and how far have you already violated the contents of the warrant?"

The man got to his feet, eyed Cade warily. "Why don't I go find them?"

"Why don't you?" Cade said agreeably. "Tell them Detective Cade Tremaine is here."

As the man hurried out of the room, Carla moved to his side, Benjamin's hand clasped tightly in hers. "Maybe I shouldn't have called," she said in a low voice. "I don't want to make any trouble for you."

"You know me." Cade smiled down at her with an amusement he was far from feeling. "I never could resist trouble."

"Now that just might be the most interesting bit of information we've turned up here so far."

Cade turned at the voice, saw the officer had returned with two plainclothes cops. With his face carefully averted, the third man brushed by them and returned to his search, leaving Cade to study the newcomers. "I'm Torley," the speaker continued tersely. Jerking his thumb at the other man, he said, "This is Sergeant Morrison. Lucky for us you stopped by. Saves us a trip."

"Yeah, I'm all about saving you guys some work," Cade said with mock politeness. The two men were about the same height, a couple of inches shorter than him. But their similarities ended there. Torley was thin and angular, with a low forbidding brow above deep set dark eyes. Morrison was beefier, with a build that suggested muscle going soft. He wore his light hair in a buzz cut and his blue eyes were puppy-dog friendly.

"Sorry about your partner," Morrison said. "We offered our condolences to Ms. Hollister."

"Before or after you shoved a warrant at her?"

"This is going to be hard enough without you copping an attitude, Tremaine," Torley put in. "Wouldn't kill you to throw a little cooperation our way."

"Maybe I'll do that. Provided you show me that warrant so I can judge how much cooperation you deserve."

"Ms. Hollister got served the warrant. We don't have to show it to you."

Morrison put his hand on his partner's arm, stemming the man's words. "I don't think it'll hurt to show Tremaine." He reached into his pocket and took out the folded sheets, handed them to Cade. "I'll think you'll find everything's in order."

Scanning the document, Cade's mouth twisted. "You guys are taking a few liberties, aren't you?" At their silence he looked up. "Case files, bank records, computer software…is that what you think you're going to find in that stuffed animal over there?"

Morrison flushed, but Torley shot back, "There's no telling where we'll find any of it, you should know that. Maybe you narcs have x-ray vision, but the rest of us poor saps have to be more thorough."

"Hey, I know the timing here isn't so hot," Morrison said placatingly.

"You think?"

"But we talked to Ms. Hollister a few times before it got to this point. You can ask her."

Cade turned to Carla and handed her the baby. "Why don't you take the boys out back for a while?" he suggested, his gaze never leaving the two men in front of him. He waited until she'd left the room before speaking again, and when he did, every ounce of civility had vanished from his voice. "So tell me what had the two of you sniffing around Brian before he was even cold. Most cops have a little more respect for their colleagues than that, but then—'' he bared his teeth ''—you're really not cops, are you.''

"There's no reason to make this adversarial, Tremaine." With surprising agility, Morrison shifted his weight so he stood between Cade and Torley, who'd clenched his fists. "You have your job, and we have ours. Truth is, we didn't know you were back on the job until recently. We have every intention of speaking to you about the way things played out."

"That's real fair-minded of you," Cade said evenly. "But that's going to be damn hard when I don't even know what 'things' we're talking about." He looked from one man to the other. "You suspect Brian of being on the take, is that it?"

"Interesting how that immediately popped into your mind," Morrison said blandly.

"Well, I'd claim it was because of my brilliant powers of deduction, but since you're looking for a bank book, it didn't take much detective work." There was a vise in his chest, squeezing viciously. He'd graduated academy with Brian; been the best man at his wedding. While the man had had his faults, lack of integrity had never been one of them. These two men were strangers, worse yet, desk jockeys, passing judgments on a man who'd been a better cop than either of them could ever hope to be.

"Look, this isn't the time for this conversation," Morrison said. "Why don't we make an appointment to get together, informally, have you answer a few questions, how's that? You know Paddy's on Canal Street? What do you say we meet there tomorrow. We can—"

"I don't think so," Cade said.

"Don't make this difficult, Tremaine." Torley slanted a glance at the officers still searching the room beside them. "You're going to have to talk to us sooner or later."

"Sure. But when I do, it will be done formally. At the station, after you make a request to my lieutenant." The two sergeants exchanged a look and Cade smiled grimly. "Damned if I'm going to let you hide what you're doing to Brian's name in a dark bar or behind closed doors."

Although Morrison looked chagrined, Torley merely lifted a bony shoulder. "Makes no difference to us. You might want to reconsider your attitude before our discussion, though. I'd think you'd want to get to the bottom of this even more than I.A."

"Really?" Derision dripped from the word. "And why is that?"

"The way I hear it, you're the one with three bullet holes in your chest." The man swiped at an imaginary piece of lint on his sleeve. "Seems like you'd have more than a passing interest in why. And whether or not it was your partner's fault that you were almost killed."

# Chapter 5

"You need to calm down."

Cade stopped pacing the narrow confines of Lieutenant Howard's office to lance his superior with a bitter look. "Calm down? Those two I.A. humps are lucky I left them upright. They have a helluva nerve, overturning Brian's house, his widow right outside, and laying all the responsibility for his death on him." Resentment surged anew, threatened to boil over. "Easy enough when they ride a desk all day to throw mud at decent cops and see what sticks. Hell of a lot easier than chasing any of the scumbags on the street."

"I'm not disagreeing with you." The calm in Howard's voice did nothing to dissipate Cade's anger. "But tangling with Internal Affairs isn't going to clear up Brian's investigation. If anything, it'll convince them to dig deeper."

Turning to stride across the room again, Cade said, "They don't need any encouragement to do that. I don't

know where they got this crazy idea about him or what
they think they have for evidence, but the two I.A. jerks
I talked to already have their minds made up. Especially
Torley.'' He crossed to the lieutenant's desk and placed
his palms on the edge, leaning toward the man. ''You
could do something about this. Get the investigation dismissed. Call in some favors. Go higher up.''

''That's the last thing I'd do,'' Howard said bluntly.
''And if you'd sit down and relax, I'll tell you why.''
Ebony gaze battled with green, before Cade pushed away
from the desk. Hooking a foot around the leg of a nearby
chair, he dragged it over and dropped into it. The sitting
part was accomplished easily enough. Relaxing was impossible.

Lieutenant Howard settled his spare frame back in his
chair with the air of a man about to impart some unpleasant news. ''I did pull a few strings,'' he began. His eyebrows shot upward when he read the surprise on Cade's
face. ''You're not the only one who can feel outrage that
a good cop—a dead cop—is having his name dragged
through the dirt. And everything I've managed to find out
indicates that I.A. is on more than a fishing expedition
with this investigation.''

Rage torched a hole through the pit of Cade's belly.
''So you're ready to hang Brian out to dry, too?''

Howard held up a hand. ''Not even close. I didn't get
details. I.A. doesn't trust me any more than they do any
of us. But I do have it on good authority that they're
following a trail of evidence that is…disturbing at best.''

Cade's eyes burned. ''Nice to know how much trust
you put in the detectives in your squad, Lieutenant.'' He
launched himself from the chair, prepared to leave.
''Maybe you call that standing behind your men. I'd call
it something else.'' He headed toward the door.

"Tremaine, sit down."

The command barely registered through the red haze of fury fogging Cade's vision. His hand reached for the doorknob. Twisted it.

"I said sit down!"

Looking over his shoulder, Cade saw that the usually unflappable lieutenant had risen from his seat, his hands braced on the desktop. And the thunderous expression on the man's face was unusual enough to cool a bit of Cade's ire.

"What the hell good is it going to do Brian to antagonize the investigators on this case?" Howard demanded.

Stubbornly remaining silent, Cade slowly lifted his hand from the doorknob, returned to his seat. "What good is it going to do him to sit and let I.A. build a phony case against him?" he countered.

"If you think I'm going to let that happen, maybe it's time you transferred to a new command. Trust is a two way street, and you obviously don't feel it."

The statement had Cade shifting his gaze. "I've never had cause to distrust you," he muttered. Silence stretched between them, the tension palpable.

"Well, that's something, I suppose." Howard smoothed a hand over his receding hairline as he dropped back into his chair. "You said you looked at the warrant. Did you happen to see the signature on it?" When Cade nodded, he asked, "Did you recognize the judge?"

"Just the name."

"Well, I know her. And she's as big an ally as this department has. The fact that she signed it tells me that I.A. has something solid." When Cade opened his mouth to protest, he held up a hand again. "I'm not saying their allegations are true, just that they'd have to show good cause to her before she'd have signed that warrant. We have just as much to gain from this search as they do.''

Slouching down in his chair, Cade propped an ankle on the opposite knee. ''Don't see how.''

''If they don't find what they're looking for, it's going to take a little steam out of their case.''

Cade shook his head wearily. ''Or make them more determined to find it elsewhere.''

''And the longer they look without collecting more evidence, the less credibility their investigation has.''

''You're talking about playing a waiting game with them. Let this drag on for weeks, months maybe, until it fizzles out. In the meantime Brian's rep is completely destroyed.'' A helpless sense of bitterness burned through him. ''You know as well as I do that the stench of an I.A. investigation alone is enough to smear a cop's name. So they don't find anything. It's the suspicion that people remember, not the fact that nothing was proved.''

''We'll just have to make sure he's cleared,'' Howard said evenly. He waited for Cade's startled gaze to meet his before going on, ''You're right. We can't depend on I.A. to broadcast his innocence. If we're convinced they're wrong about Brian, we owe it to his memory to make sure the world knows it.''

Finally the man had said something he could agree with. ''Okay. What do you suggest?''

Howard picked up a pencil and began tapping it against the desktop. ''You're going to be in the best position to gather information about their investigation. I.A.'s going to want to talk to you. Only natural, to see what you noticed. You might be able to tell from the direction of their questioning what they've got.'' He leaned forward suddenly, fixed his unblinking gaze on Cade. ''Use them, dammit. The same way they try to use cops to give up dirt on other cops. Beat them at their own damn game, and we'll see who ends up with the proof about Brian Hollister.''

Approvingly Cade surveyed his superior. He was all but being given permission to conduct his own inquiry. Department policy prohibited him from being on the investigative team looking into the incident that had resulted in his own shooting and his partner's death. But he could nose around and try to find out what I.A. had on Brian. And then do his damnedest to find another way to explain it. Because he had an unshakable faith that the man he'd loved like a brother wasn't capable of defiling the oath he'd taken to protect the people of New Orleans. That was the thing with faith. It didn't require proof. It just was, welling from the heart.

The law would require evidence.

Giving a curt nod, he said, ''All right. I'll cooperate with I.A. and somehow manage not to put my fist in Torley's ugly mug.''

''I know how big a sacrifice that will be for you,'' Howard said dryly. ''Keep me posted. Together we'll figure out their angle and decide where we go from there.''

Cade nodded. ''How's the investigation of Brian's death coming? Ryder and Sanover turn anything up yet?'' The two homicide detectives from Fifth Precinct had been assigned to the case. He'd talked to them several times during his recuperation.

''There's nothing new. Except that they're now working in conjunction with the narcotics task force.''

''What?'' The news had Cade straightening in his chair. ''Why?''

''Apparently they think the dealer you were tracking is a big fish, and the task force always wants credit for the flashiest cases.'' Howard waved a hand. ''That was unprofessional. Forget I said that. The party line is we're all cops and what does it matter who solves the case as long as it gets solved?''

Cade grinned. The earlier touch of territorial sarcasm reminded him of why he respected the man so much. Despite the fact that he was administration, he was also a cop and hadn't forgotten everything that meant.

''At least the case will have more manpower this way.'' He didn't give a damn who found the killer, as long as he was found. He'd concentrate on clearing his partner's name. He owed the man that much. He owed his widow.

As if reading his thoughts, the lieutenant asked, ''How's Carla holding up?''

Cade gave a shake of his head. ''The investigation coming on top of Brian's death is really taking its toll. I suggested that she leave the city, go stay with her folks in Baton Rouge for a while.''

''Good idea. This thing has got to be stressful for her. She's going to need all the support she can get.''

They were all going to need support, Cade thought grimly. Trying to do an end run around I.A., in addition to working the LeFrenz investigation, was going to going to mean keeping long hours. At least he wouldn't miss the rest. Sleep had been elusive ever since he'd opened his eyes and seen his partner's blank stare. Ever since he'd watched his own blood eddy out of him to pool with the river streaming out of Brian.

''You sure you're up to this? Physically, I mean?'' The other man's words shook Cade from his grim reverie.

''I'm up to it.''

The fact that the man didn't push nudged Cade's respect for him up another notch. He'd had enough of people fussing and poking at him during his recuperation to last him a lifetime. His little sister had been the worst offender of all, although his entire family had felt free to share their disapproval of his decision to return to work so soon. They hadn't understood his need to get back to the same streets that had robbed his partner of his life. Only another cop would understand that.

"What was your feeling about LeFrenz's claim to know something about Brian's death? Do you think there's a real link there?"

Cade shook his head at the question. "It seemed a little too convenient, you know? Like something he'd throw out to rattle me or just to get me off his case about naming his supplier. But his knowing Freddie makes sense. Maybe he did meet with him after the shooting. When we find him, I guess we'll discover for sure if Freddie told him anything."

"And you still think that our best chance of finding him is by watching this O'Riley woman?"

"I'm certain of it." Again he outlined LeFrenz's obvious fascination with the doctor and his machinations to get her into his room during the interview. "I'm positive he'll attempt to contact her."

"But you don't know when."

"No, of course not, but—"

"I'm not saying you're wrong." Cade braced himself for the *but* he heard coming. "But we don't have the men available to keep an around-the-clock guard on the woman on the off chance he visits her. We need to focus on LeFrenz's usual haunts, his known acquaintances…hell, you know the drill as well as I do."

Cade did. He could also predict where this was going. "Of course we're gonna work the case, but I don't expect LeFrenz to show up at any of his usual places. The guy's no rocket scientist, but he's not that dumb. And even if he is, whoever's behind him has brains and money."

''I'll give it a couple days,'' the lieutenant said with finality. He held up a hand to stem any further argument Cade might have made. "That's as long as I can afford to waste two officers. Even that's pushing it."

Cade knew when not to press his luck. He'd wait to see what turned up by the end of that time and deal with it then. "Thanks, Lieutenant."

The man waved him from the room. "Don't thank me. Just go make the case. Both of them."

They exchanged a glance, unspoken understanding between them. Finding LeFrenz was going to be simple compared to what it would take to clear Brian's name.


Shae pressed the pamphlet into the woman's uninjured hand. "Just read it," she urged evenly. "Take some time before making your decision."

The blonde blinked, both eyes ringed with a rainbow of bruises, swollen half-shut. "Decision. What decision? I told you I fell. Tripped over a step stool." When Shae said nothing, just looked at her, the woman rushed on. "I'm clumsy like that. Always banging into something."

"Shattering your nose. Dislocating your shoulder. Breaking your arm." Shae nodded at the new cast she'd put on the woman. "I've read your file, Nancy. No one is that clumsy. Whoever is doing this to you, you need to stop covering up for him. Because one of these days he's going to kill you."

"He'd never do that," the woman said automatically. Then, as if realizing what she'd admitted, her gaze slid away from Shae's. "You don't understand. We love each other."

Tamping down her rising frustration, Shae said, "I see this kind of *love* all too often. I know what I'm talking about. Just go to a shelter for the night. Take some time to think about your options. They have counselors there who can help you.''

''Dr. O'Riley, you have a phone call.''

''Take a message.'' Shae didn't take her gaze off the huddled woman on the examining table. Now was the time to press her case, when she could sense the woman's resolve wavering.

But the nurse persisted. ''He's refused to leave a message the dozen times he's called today. I can stay with your patient if you want to take it.''

''I don't.'' She rarely received phone calls at work, and never since Liam had been sent to prison. Which meant that the caller was either Cade Tremaine or her father. Neither prospect was especially tempting. She was still smarting from the detective's insistence the previous day. And despite the fact she hadn't seen or heard from him in nearly thirty-six hours, she didn't doubt that he'd been serious about his vows to be back. He didn't strike her as a man who made empty promises.

Aware that the nurse was still watching her, Shae aimed her a look, raised her brows. The woman sighed and left the room, and Shae shifted her attention back to her patient.

''I don't want to go to a shelter,'' Nancy blurted out, chewing her lip. ''I just wouldn't be comfortable going there on my own and all.''

''I can admit you here for the night,'' Shae offered. ''Keep you under observation for possible damage to your occipital nerve. Internal injuries.'' It wouldn't be much of a stretch, she rationalized. And if the ensuing time had Nancy finding the courage to leave her abuser, she'd say it was money well spent, and to hell with the HMOs.

''Dr. O'Riley.'' It was the same nurse again. Shae

swung around, her eyes narrowed. The woman held up her hands placatingly. "You're wanted at the desk."

Nodding in resignation, Shae turned back to her patient. "Just take some time and think about it. I'll be back in a couple minutes and we can discuss it further, okay?"

Nancy ducked her head, her hair covering her features. But she nodded, a short jerk of her head, and Shae laid a soothing hand on her shoulder for a moment. "It's going to be okay. I'll help you in any way I can." When the woman failed to respond, she turned and hurried to the hall.

She approached the desk, expecting to see Tim Pearson waiting impatiently to talk to her. What she didn't expect to see was Cade Tremaine leaning a shoulder against the wall, watching her approach, his green gaze intent.

She faltered for a moment. His lean jaw was shadowed with a day's growth of beard. And although his eyes were alert, he looked as if he could use a few hours of sleep. Or a few days' worth.

Shae caught herself before the observations could soften into concern. It was second nature for her to immediately size up a person's appearance as she tended to their health. Tremaine wasn't a patient, of course, but at the rate he was going, he could be. He wouldn't be the first to drop from sheer physical exhaustion. She knew intuitively that he wouldn't appreciate her reminding him of that.

"Dr. O'Riley." His low drawl made her name sound like an endearment whispered in the still of the night against dark satin sheets. "I came to escort you home."

"I've been finding my own way home since I was five. I don't need an escort."

Amusement laced his voice. "It's no bother. No need to thank me."

"Look." She strove for patience and, with it, logic. "It

doesn't make sense for you to hang around here on my account. I keep odd hours and I can't just leave when you show up."

"You've been off duty for forty-five minutes. The E.R. isn't especially busy, so there's no real reason for you to stay." He surveyed her critically. "When's the last time you ate something?"

She tried, but couldn't remember. The rotation that day hadn't been so much slow as routine. A baby with croup, a couple of sports-related injuries, a few broken bones and a ruptured appendix. Memory kicked in. Between the sprained ankle and the appendix she'd had a handful of jelly beans off the admission's counter. "One o'clock," she said triumphantly.

"Candy snitched out of a desk drawer or lunch in the cafeteria?"

Because it was less galling than telling the truth, she changed the subject. "I'm capable of feeding myself, as well. Go home, Detective. Get some sleep before we have to admit you." She spun around to return to her patient, half-surprised that he didn't protest. But she didn't spend much time wondering about his easy capitulation. Not when she went back to the trauma room where she'd left Nancy, only to find it empty.

She went back into the hallway. "Gayle." She stopped a nurse who was hurrying by. "What happened to the woman in Room 5?"

"The broken arm? She just left."

"Just now? Was she alone?"

Gayle shook her head. "She left with some guy. Come to think of it, he's the one who signed her out."

The nurse continued down the hall, leaving Shae wrestling with a surge of frustration. So her patient had chosen to return home with her abuser. Again. And all she could do was hope that the next time something set the man off, he didn't kill her.

Working her shoulders tiredly, she went to the locker room and retrieved her coat. Nancy had been her last patient. Now that she'd gone, there was no reason for Shae to stay. As she opened her locker and exchanged her stethoscope for her purse, she tried not to let the woman's choice weigh too heavily on her. Trying to grapple with things that were out of her control was fruitless and frustrating. There were enough of those instances daily in the E.R. to keep her humble.

But the woman's behavior was an all-too-poignant reminder of her childhood. Ryan O'Riley hadn't physically abused Shae's mother, but she'd exhibited the same blind faith that Nancy did. An unshakable belief in whatever their partners told them. That someday the man they loved would change. That someday things would be different. Watching that never-ending cycle had turned Shae into a skeptic by eight. A cynic by twelve.

And by thirty-two she'd become an expert at guarding her emotions.

As she headed toward the exit, someone fell into step beside her. With a sense of shock she saw that it was Cade Tremaine. Had she been thinking about it, she would have realized he was unlikely to give up so easily. As it was, she faced straight ahead and wished futilely for the power to make him disappear.

"My car's right out these doors," he offered.

"That's okay. I can call a cab."

"There's no need. I'll take you home. We need to talk."

Shae drew a deep breath and stopped short. "Listen, I'm sure you thought I was dodging your calls today, but the truth is, I was busy. And I really think we've said everything that needs saying, unless you're here to tell me that LeFrenz has been caught.''

Cade was studying her speculatively. ''He hasn't. And I didn't call you today.''

She immediately felt foolish. ''Oh.'' Why had she leaped to that conclusion? Because, she immediately justified, the man had bulldog tendencies and had made it clear she hadn't seen the end of him. Aware that his gaze hadn't left her, she looked away ''It must have been my father.''

''Only way to know for sure would be to answer your calls once in a while,'' he said.

''I have a job to do.'' She continued walking, lingering embarrassment propelling her faster. ''I don't have time for personal calls.''

''What about a personal life?'' Cade inquired as he strolled along beside her. It was irritating to note that, as long as her strides were, he kept up easily His legs were longer than hers, and encased in soft denim that showed their lean muscular form to perfection.

She jerked her gaze, and her thoughts, off his body and focused on his words. ''What about it?''

''I was wondering if you had time for one.'' He dug in his pocket and pulled out a set of keys. ''Seems like I've mostly found you at the hospital.''

''Why should that interest you?'' She made no effort to couch the words civilly. It was bad enough that the detective seemed intent on barging into her life at whim. Commenting on just how uneventful that life was was downright insulting. She could have told him that the very ordinariness of her days had been long sought and were prized highly. When she was a kid, her household was constantly in upheaval. As an adult she craved stability.

Demanded it. She wasn't a woman to appreciate the unexpected.

"It makes my job a little easier, actually. A jealous
boyfriend might take exception to my hanging around
you."

"*I* take exception to you hanging around," she said as
he pushed open the double doors and they stepped out of
the hospital. "That doesn't seem to stop you."

"My car's this way." The hand cupping her elbow,
exerting the slightest pressure, was just gentlemanly
enough to almost make her follow him. Almost. She
stopped, forcing him to halt beside her.

He looked down at her, quirking a brow. "How many
hours did you put in today?"

Nonplussed, she thought for a moment. "I don't know.
Twelve or so."

"That's a long time to be on your feet." He dropped
his hand and rocked back on his heels a little, surveying
her. "Is it really worth it to wait another twenty minutes
for a cab when I could have you home in that amount of
time?"

Put like that, refusing his offer seemed almost churlish.
Still, she was loathe to accept. Prolonging the day a bit
while waiting for a taxi would be infinitely preferable to
allowing him to have his way again. At some point he
would have to accept the fact that she wasn't going to let
him rearrange her life to suit himself.

With a sigh, she decided that particular battle should be
fought sooner, rather than later. "All right." She gave in
with ill grace. "And on the way home you and I are going
to get a few things straight."

His lips curved, a quicksilver glimpse of a rare and
wicked smile. "I stand warned. Give it your best shot."

The words sounded more like a dare than an invitation,

but she'd never lacked fortitude. "You haven't asked if I've heard from LeFrenz."

They'd resumed walking to his car. It was annoying to observe that he'd shortened his strides to match hers. "You haven't."

"No." Her brows came together. "How did you know that?"

"You would have told me. At least that was what you promised the last time we spoke."

"I didn't promise. Exactly." When he slid a sideways gaze at her, sharp despite his lazy stance, it was all she could do not to squirm. "I just said I would." She wasn't in the habit of making promises. Not to anyone. Words were such fragile things, really, to bear the weight of the hopes which were inevitably pinned to them. She'd always found it far better to keep things simple. Free of expectations and recriminations.

"It's right here." His words jolted her back to the matter at hand. Looking past him, she saw a sleek midnight-blue sports car. She knew nothing about luxury cars, but even in her ignorance she could tell it was fast, powerful and expensive. Looking from it to him, she asked blandly, "Police issue?"

Amusement laced his words. "Borrowed it from impound." He pulled some keys from his pocket and clicked a button on the keyless entry. She heard a quiet snick as the locks released. Reaching past her, he opened the door, held it for her.

Shae looked into the dark interior, then back at him. For some reason she was strangely reluctant to slide into that confined space with him. "Look." Her fingers tightened over the strap of her purse. "I told you he wouldn't contact me, and I think this proves I'm right. It's a waste of your time to be hanging around me, thinking otherwise.

You'd be better off doing…whatever it is cops do to investigate a case."

"How about if we make a bargain?" he suggested. Although he hadn't moved, he seemed to loom closer. "I won't tell you how to do…whatever it is that E.R. doctors do. And you won't tell me how to do my job." While her mouth was still hanging open at those words, he'd handed her into the car and gently shut the door.

Shae's mouth snapped shut. Okay, fine. Obviously he was sensitive about taking suggestions. Unfortunately for him, she'd never been one to tiptoe around a man's fragile ego. "Look," she snapped once he'd gotten in the car, "I didn't realize you were so touchy. I'm just trying to point out that you could be spending your time more productively."

"It's not a problem." He turned the key in the ignition, and the engine roared to life. "These days I don't have much of a personal life, either."

Which was totally beside the point, and she was certain he knew it. Even more, it was surprising. Cade Tremaine didn't look like the type of man to spend too much time alone, at least not by choice. She could only believe that his convalescence, coupled with the investigation he was involved in, were the cause of his state. While hers was more due to choice.

But then all other thought was chased out of her mind. She had only a moment to secure her safety belt before the car leaped forward and out of the hospital parking lot. The high-performance engine sounded a muted roar as they headed in the wrong direction.

"This isn't the way to my apartment," she said automatically.

"I'm hungry, too. I thought we could pick up some sandwiches on the way home."

She cast a glance at him. *On the way home.* The phrase sounded a little too cozy. A little too intimate. As if it was a place they lived together, one that bore the stamp of both their personalities. The idea sent a chill skittering down her spine. Shae enjoyed having her own space entirely too much to welcome the thought of sharing it with anyone.

"What happened to your patient?"

His words jerked her attention back to the car and the man who looked all too natural driving it. "What patient?"

"Back at the hospital you said you still had a patient to tend to. But it was only ten minutes or so before you headed for the doors."

The reminder had Shae's mouth turning down. "Oh." She lifted a shoulder. "I was hoping I'd convinced a woman to spend the night at a shelter. Or at least let me admit her overnight."

"But she bolted?"

The memory of her earlier frustration and helplessness came flooding back. She leaned back into the soft leather seat and rested her head against the backrest. "Someone signed her out. Probably the same guy who put her in that cast and blacked both her eyes."

"And you're afraid she'll be back."

The accuracy of his statement, its matter-of-fact delivery, turned her pensive. "I'm afraid she *won't* be. I'm afraid next time she'll go straight to the morgue."

He was silent a long time. When he spoke, he uttered none of the platitudes that were so useless, so annoying. "Yeah, those are some of the toughest ones. Used to run into them frequently when I was on a beat, answering domestic calls. Most often the woman wouldn't press

charges, so we know the guy was going to spend his night
in jail and go home again, maybe be even worse.''

Of course, she hadn't considered that. As a cop, Cade
would have run into many situations like the ones she
encountered in the E.R. Shae had even heard once that
cops and emergency-room personnel were attracted to
each other because they were both adrenaline junkies.
She'd always thought that was a bunch of bull. People
chose their careers out of personal need and preferences.
And most often chose their partners out of weakness.

Shae made it a point to never be weak.

''It's the kids who always get to me the most,'' he
murmured, surprising her. She opened her eyes, turned to
look at him. His profile was shadowed, all planes and
angles. In the darkness he looked more than a little dangerous. Untamed. ''When there are kids in the house, and
you can just about bet that something violent is going on,
but no one's talking. So I have to turn around and go back
to the car, knowing in my gut that I've just turned my
back on them in more ways than one. Even though I have
no other choice. I'd rather take a blade between the ribs.''

He stopped abruptly then, but not before his words had
struck a chord. He'd see things in his line of work to rival
what she experienced in hers. He'd have some similar
frustrations when his assistance proved too little or too
late.

She looked away, shaken, gazing sightlessly out the
window. It would be unwise to allow herself to feel an
affinity for the man beside her. Unwiser still to let herself
feel anything at all. He exuded a sexy masculine confi-
dence that would be all too appealing under normal circumstances. Circumstances where she could set the
boundaries and control the situation. A casual no-strings

relationship that could be entered into and exited from under her terms.

Nothing about Tremaine struck her as casual, and he certainly didn't appear to be the sort of man who let anyone else take control. Recognition of this kept her wary. That, coupled with the fact that he was a cop, should be enough to keep temptation firmly in check.

Just the acknowledgment that she was tempted was disturbing enough to have her welcoming his change of subject. But her reaction was shortlived.

"You seem pretty certain that your caller today was your father."

"He hasn't changed much. He doesn't like to take no for an answer. Something the two of you have in common."

He ignored the dig to continue contemplatively, "There's another possibility, you know." The note in his voice filled her with trepidation. Although she hadn't considered it until that moment, she knew what he was going to say. "Maybe it wasn't your father who was calling you today at all. Maybe it was LeFrenz."

# Chapter 6

Everything in Shae recoiled from the thought. "You're reaching, Detective. LeFrenz isn't going to contact me, and even if he did, the last place he'd try is the hospital."

"How do you know?"

Cade's blunt response had her scrambling for logic. "Because...it's too risky."

He made a sound that might have been a snort. "Nice try. What's the risk—that someone might recognize his voice? That the police would tap the hospital phone lines? Think about it, Shae. There's nothing stopping him from contacting you in just that way."

She forced herself to consider the possibility before rejecting it again. "I'm still unconvinced. And it's futile to debate it."

"There'll be nothing to debate if you start answering your calls. Want to prove me wrong?" The hint of dare in his voice had her turning her head to look at him. "If you get more calls tomorrow, answer them. Then we'll know for sure.''

He pulled into the parking lot of a small restaurant lit by a garish neon sign proclaiming it the location of the city's best po'boys. "I guarantee their sign is as much truth as advertising. What do you want?''

She shook her head. "Nothing.'' She was both surprised and relieved when he got out of the car, leaving it running, and jogged to the building. Any appetite she might have had earlier had abruptly dissipated at Cade's suggestion about the origin of her calls today.

It was totally unlikely, she thought stubbornly. Possible, maybe, in a broad stretch of the word, but unlikely. The sheer volume of the phone calls suggested someone bent on talking to her, and the man she knew with that kind of perseverance wasn't a threat to *her,* just to her peace of mind. Ryan O'Riley would continue to pester her until he got his way or was convinced of the futility of his quest. She knew from experience what it would take to convince him. The task was distasteful, but hardly alarming. And she wasn't going to allow Tremaine to see specters of LeFrenz behind every perfectly normal detail in her life. She wasn't going to fall into that pit.

By the time Tremaine had returned to the car with a sack in his hand, she'd quelled her initial apprehension. The man wanted to capture the escaped suspect so badly he was grasping at straws. Or else he was deliberately trying to frighten her, to make her more *pliable* and co-operative. She gave a small smile. He'd soon find that pliable wasn't a description that fit her at all.

But when she sought to continue the discussion where they'd left off, Cade leaned forward, turned on the CD player. After fiddling with an array of buttons and knobs, a blues tune filled the air, a saxophone wailing a mournful note. He'd left the volume on a shade too high, just loud enough to make further conversation difficult. Shae settled back in her seat, resigned. The issue of LeFrenz would be resolved tonight, despite his machinations.

It was that intent that kept her silent once they'd reached her apartment. She didn't protest when he insisted on accompanying her up to her apartment, although she did throw him a narrowed look when he brought along the sack he'd gotten from the restaurant. But that inner peace began to dissolve rapidly when he entered her apartment ahead of her and set the bag of food on her kitchen counter.

Skirting the center island, he walked into the kitchen and started opening cupboards. "Where do you keep your plates?"

Brushing by him, she barely restrained an urge to send her elbow into his stomach. The man redefined the term *pushy*. "I could give you a paper plate and you could take the sandwich to go."

Taking napkins out of the holder she had next to the stove, he said, "I wouldn't want to leave you to eat alone."

When she turned back to him with a plate in her hand, he reached past her to withdraw another from the cupboard she'd just closed. "I bought you a sandwich, too. You said you hadn't eaten today."

"I never said—"

"You never admitted it, but I concluded. I do that a lot. Draw conclusions, I mean. That's why I'm a detective." When she only looked at him, a corner of his mouth quirked. "Come on, we're only sharing sandwiches. How frightening can that be?"

"*Annoying* is the word I'd use," she snapped, snatching the plates from his hands and marching back to the kitchen counter. "And in your case, the answer would be extremely." He proved the description particularly apt when he rummaged in her refrigerator and withdrew two bottled waters.

"Would it make you feel better to discuss the case while we're eating?" The look he threw her was deceptively innocent.

"It would make me feel better if you were eating alone in your car on the way home. To *your* home." Resigned, she watched him unwrap food and arrange it on plates until the counter looked like a cozy arrangement for two. Abruptly the situation took on an intimacy she was anxious to deny. "Look, Tremaine—"

"Sit down." He used his foot to push out the chair next to him and picked up his sandwich. "I make it a point never to eat with a woman who calls me by my last name. Bad for the digestion."

"Given your behavior, I'm betting you get called a lot worse." He might have smiled at that; it was difficult to tell around the sandwich he was biting into. Shae's stomach growled. The tantalizing aroma of the food was a vivid reminder of just how long it had been since she'd eaten a real meal. She took another moment to weigh hunger against stubbornness. Hunger won.

Sitting down beside him, she reached for the sandwich he'd put on her plate and bit into it with more than a modicum of frustration. As the spicy flavor exploded on her tongue, it was all she could do not to close her eyes in pleasure. Besides, she rationalized as she took another bite, he was right about one thing. She had to eat.

It didn't embarrass her in the least that she was shoving her empty plate aside while Cade still had a quarter of his sandwich left. A glint of real amusement was in his eyes.

"I like a woman who doesn't get all coy and delicate when she eats."

Shae nearly laughed. "There's nothing coy or delicate about me, Detective. I'm mercenary enough to take a free meal when it comes my way, even knowing that you're not going to like the outcome of this evening."

He didn't seem particularly bothered by her words. "I'm not? Why?"

"Because I'm going to contact your superior officer and insist that he call off all officers assigned to watch me." She paused a beat, before continuing meaningfully, "That includes you."

He seemed to contemplate that while he finished eating. Then he wiped his mouth with his napkin and reached for his water. "Fair enough. I appreciate you telling me your plans up front."

Something about his easy manner alerted her. "You don't believe me?"

Bottle tilted to his lips, he nodded. Lowering it, he said, "Oh, I believe you. It just isn't going to do you any good."

The feeling of well-being that had come from filling her stomach and forming a strategy abruptly vanished. Shae glared at him. "If I insist, the police will have to shift their investigation elsewhere..." Something in his expression alerted her. "Well, I'm certain I can convince your boss that he's wasting manpower by concentrating on me."

"He wouldn't be hard to convince," Cade surprised her by saying. "But even if he does reassign the two men we have on you, I'm not going to be so easy to get rid of. Especially after those phone calls you got at work today."

She closed her eyes in sheer frustration. "How many times do I have to tell you it was most likely my father?"

"Maybe we can make sure of that." He nodded toward the answering machine at the end of the counter. Following the direction of his gaze, she saw that the light was blinking. "Why don't we see if anyone left messages for you today."

Shae stared at the winking light for a moment, an unfamiliar sense of paralysis attacking her. Moistening her lips, she made no move toward the machine. Cade reached past her, held down the replay button. They listened in silence to the automated invitation for callers to leave a message. There was a string of clicks, as callers declined, then a man's voice filled the air between them. "Shae girl, you're a tough one to get hold of. But I'm still interested in that transaction we discussed. Call me at this number." Her father rattled off a cell-phone number she had no intention of calling. The rest of the tape elicited only several more clicks.

When the machine fell silent, Shae released a breath she hadn't realize she'd been holding. She damned herself for allowing him to raise her anxiety. With arched brows, she asked, "Satisfied?"

It was plain from the expression on his face that he wasn't. "Do you always get that many calls and hang-ups a day?"

Exasperation filled her. "Telemarketers are responsible, not your nefarious criminal."

"I'm surprised you have many telemarketing calls with that thing." He nodded to the small device she had sitting next to her phone. "I heard they were pretty effective at decreasing calls from phone banks."

"So it was my father. You heard him. He wants me to call him."

"Maybe." The word was laced with doubt. She'd pay it no heed. This apartment had been the first real home she'd had since Liam had gone to live with their father. She was comfortable here, and she wasn't going to allow Tremaine to ruin that. She'd spent her entire childhood afraid to answer the phone or the door. Police hadn't been the only people looking for her father. His dealings with bookies, loan sharks and other low lifes had resulted in shady characters showing up at the house far too often. It was one more reason to despise the man. What kind of father would put his family at risk that way? The answer was plain.

She got up and cleared the counter. Despite Cade's reservations, she wasn't going to start jumping at shadows, especially in the one place she could call her own. Her apartment suited her needs exactly, except for one thing: he was still inside it. "It wouldn't hurt for you to go home and grab some sleep. From the looks of you, you could use it."

"Anxious to get rid of me?" He shook his head sadly. "Chauffeurs are so unappreciated these days."

He'd managed to make her feel small and she fought the reaction. "I do appreciate the ride. And the meal. But I won't be needing either from you in the future. I'm in no danger from LeFrenz. I'm convinced of that, even if you aren't. I'm not letting you disrupt my life any more than you already have."

Cade surveyed her, his head tilted to the side. "Used to arranging things to suit yourself, aren't you."

Releasing an incredulous laugh, she jammed a hand into her hair. "Said the pot to the kettle."

"Okay, then." But still he made no move to leave. "Have you contacted a security company yet?"

"Yes," she said, relieved to forego another safety lecture. "I've already signed a contract."

"Good. I'd like to look it over."

Shae nearly ground her teeth. "Why?"

"Because I want to be sure they're going to do everything I'd recommend. Who'd you end up going with?"

"McNulty."

He nodded approvingly. "They're good. Decent response time. Pricey, but they're worth it." He waited expectantly and finally she crossed to a desk against one wall, and withdrew the written agreement from a drawer. With little grace, she slammed it into his hands. Anything to get him out of here.

The phone rang as he began skimming it. She froze for a moment, then looked at him, saw he'd noted her reaction. Spine straightening, she brushed by him to answer the phone, damning him for the nerves that had reared at the sound. She wasn't going to be afraid in her own home. She'd worked too hard for her tranquil existence to allow anyone to disrupt it.

Her voice was a little more brusque than usual when she answered it. "Hello?" When she heard her brother's familiar voice, the nerves evaporated completely to be replaced by a familiar mixture of love and regret. "Liam. It's wonderful to hear from you."

Aware of the man beside her, she deliberately turned away. With a discretion she wouldn't have credited him with, Tremaine moved to the recliner and sat down to read the contract she'd handed him, giving her a modicum of privacy.

"How are you? I'm still planning to come see you this weekend." She hated the stilted note in her voice, the way her mind frantically searched for something to say to him, for some piece of normalcy. Nothing had been normal between them since he'd been sentenced two months ago. And there was certainly nothing normal in those awkward prison visits, with other inmates and guards looming nearby, a sense of hopelessness permeating the space. There had never been anything quite as painful as sitting across from her brother, both of them trying so hard to be positive for the other's sake. Both of them dying a little inside.

"Is there anything I can bring you?" Hearing her brother's request lightened something inside her a fraction. "I've never been much of a baker, but I think I can manage chocolate-chip cookies. I remember you're a connoisseur." They had a few more minutes to talk before his allotted time was up. It took several more moments for Shae to compose herself, to steel herself against Tremaine's inevitable curiosity. But when she finally turned to look at him, she didn't face a quizzical expression and a barrage of questions. He didn't say anything at all. He was asleep.

The sheaf of papers rested against his chest, still clutched in one hand. His head was turned to the side, his breathing slow and even. His face wasn't any softer in sleep, but it was less guarded, the fatigue apparent. Shae had the feeling few were allowed to see the man this way. Sheer exhaustion had to be the cause for him exposing this unusual vulnerability. An exhaustion that made her strangely reluctant to awaken him.

She stood watching him, undecided. He looked entirely too at home in her chair, in her apartment. His pose infused the place with a sense of intimacy she wanted violently to reject. He'd be more comfortable at home, she rationalized. She started toward him with the intent of shaking him awake. They'd both be more comfortable with him at his own place.

But when Shae stood next to the chair, her hand stretched out toward his shoulder, something prevented her from following through. It was easiest to blame her reluctance on the physician in her. She was all too aware of how sleep-deprived he was. Given his recent trauma, rest was a vital part of his complete recovery. Her hand hovered in the air for a moment, then dropped to her side.

She looked around the room, nonplussed. What did she do while he slept? Going to bed herself while he was still there was out of the question. She was hoping he awoke long before then. She finally crossed silently to the desk and sat down to pay bills. The task would keep her hands and mind busy. And off the man snoozing in her living room. With any luck he'd doze for a half hour or so and then awake on his own. At least she hoped so.

It was close to three hours before Cade moved. And when he awoke it was with a return to awareness that was as fascinating as it was startling. His eyelids opened abruptly and his green eyes were instantly alert. The only remnant from his earlier slumber was his sleep-roughened voice. "You should have woke me."

Shae reached up and removed the headphones that had kept the television from bothering him. "I figured you could use the rest."

"Yeah, well…it'd be better to get it at home, right?" If he'd been anyone else, she'd have sworn she read embarrassment on his face. The notion would be ridiculous, but for the haste with which he was getting to his feet. He shoved his free hand through his hair, which was more unruly than usual. His effort was in vain. The same lock of hair fell forward again.

He glanced down, seemed surprised that he still held the sheaf of papers in his other hand. "I read through this. Sounds pretty solid, but I'd feel better if there was a mention of security measures for that skylight in your bedroom."

"It's going to be hooked to the alarm system, too," she said. She was unwilling to put bars over it. Sleeping beneath it, being able to look up at the stars, gave her a sense of freedom that would be irreparably marred if the skylight was altered. The alarm would be enough.

Nodding, he crossed to the desk and replaced the papers, then continued on to the stool by the counter where he'd left his coat. "Well, I'll take off so you can get to bed. When do you go to work tomorrow?"

Unsure what else to do, Shae followed him to the door. "Seven."

Cade paused in the act of shrugging into his jacket. "In the morning?"

When she nodded, he winced. "All the more reason you should have kicked me out of here hours ago. I wouldn't have minded. I don't make a habit of falling asleep in pretty doctors' apartments."

"I'm not in the habit of allowing it." The words, stark with truth, escaped her before she could think about them. She would have done anything to call them back.

His expression was arrested. "Why did you?"

Shae forced a shrug, walked past him to open the door. "From the looks of you, I wasn't sure you were getting sleep anywhere else."

He trailed after her slowly. "So it was an act of mercy?"

"Something like that."

He paused at her side, looking down at her, an odd expression on his face. "Then I guess I should thank you." Before she could guess his intention, he cupped her face, lowered his head and brushed her lips with his. Shock held her still. He hesitated, his mouth barely touching hers, their breaths mingling. Then with a barely audible groan he deepened the contact, his lips moving firmly, persuasively against hers.

There was nothing tentative about this kiss or her response to it. She knew he was capable of charm and of an awesome control. If he'd used either, she could have resisted. But it was surprisingly difficult to summon resistance to this hard reckless plundering, one that spoke of urges unchecked. Of a control unleashed.

She opened her mouth beneath his and his tongue swept in. She tasted it, enjoying the jolt of pleasure as his dark dangerous flavor imploded on her senses. One of his hands threaded through her hair while the other wrapped around her waist, pulling her closer until she could feel his heart thundering, echoing hers, beat for beat. Teeth clashed as her mouth twisted beneath his, both battling for another angle, as the kiss grew deeper, wilder, hotter.

Heat combusted within her, spreading a fire that was as heady as it was unfamiliar. She scored his full bottom lip with her teeth, pleased to feel him shudder. Sex with Cade would be like this—a wicked wild ride, careening from sensation to sensation before the culmination of shattering pleasure. It could be as simple, as uncomplicated as that, as long as she set the pace. She didn't indulge in sex indiscriminately, but when it happened, she chose the man, the place and the time. He was making it impossible not to choose him. Here. Now.

Shae tore her mouth from his, then gasped as his teeth went to the cord of her throat, leaving tiny stinging bites that he soothed with his tongue. "You don't have to leave yet." Her voice was more breathless than she would have liked, her vision, when she managed to drag her eyes open, less focused. "We can continue this upstairs."

She felt the arm around her waist tighten reflexively, and there was a flash of hunger on his face that had her knees turning to water. But in the next moment the expression was followed with one of regret, which had her senses mourning even before he rested his forehead against hers. "You have to work early tomorrow, remember?" he murmured, frustration rife in his voice. "And if I stayed, you'd get damn little sleep tonight."

It was on the tip of her tongue to tell him he wouldn't be staying, at least not beyond an hour or so, but he was already moving away from her, his movements jerky with checked desire. "I'm gonna hope like hell that you issue the invitation again another time. Believing that is about the only thing that's gonna get me out of here."

He paused in the doorway and it was only then that Shae realized the door had been open the entire time they'd been in each other's arms. Giving her a quick hard kiss, he muttered, "Lock the door after me." Then he was gone, striding down the hallway to the elevator, his spine straight, his shoulders rigid.

Not wanting to be caught staring after him, Shae stepped back on shaky legs, swung the door shut and locked it. Then she leaned against the panels, her limbs too weak to hold her without support. It was for the best, she thought, and tried to believe it. Although Cade Tremaine didn't seem the type to seek sticky entanglements, neither did he appear to be the kind of man who relinquished control easily. Would he be satisfied with the little she had to offer, or would be push for more?

The question wouldn't be answered tonight, and on one level she was grateful he'd left when he had. There were too many unknown facets about the man. She'd do well to be more certain she could control all aspects of any relationship between them before she entered into one, however briefly.

But hormones operated on a different level from logic,

and those hormones were still putting up a disappointed chorus when she made her way upstairs and got ready for bed. As she slipped between the sheets and closed her eyes, she was welcomed by a mental scrapbook of images—ones of Cade, sleeping in her living room, grinning over a sandwich, looking at her with his face stamped with arousal.

Issuing a groan, Shae flipped over, punched her pillow into a more comfortable position. She had a feeling her sleep would have been a lot more restful had Cade accepted her invitation.

Surprisingly, she slept. Not a deep slumber, but one dominated by a green-eyed man with a lazy smile and a lethal air. She didn't know what brought her awake at first. She opened her eyes, disoriented, her gaze going to the alarm clock on the bedside table. Three a.m. Then the phone rang again and she reached for it automatically. She wasn't on call, but it wouldn't be the first time she was asked to come in to cover for another physician.

"Hello?"

"Angel Eyes."

The blood slowed in her veins, forming layers of ice. The voice was instantly recognizable, and dread mingled with disbelief as she sat upright in bed. Sweeping her hair out of her eyes, she said, "Who is this?"

"You know who it is, Angel Eyes. Sorry to wake you up, but you're a hard one to get hold of." LeFrenz's voice was conversational. "Guess you doctor types don't have time to answer the phone, but it seemed a little rude to me, ya know." There was a pause, one that seemed filled with menace. "I'm trying to believe you weren't just avoiding me by not answering."

The words, in light of the man's actions, seemed particularly incongruous. "I didn't know the calls were from you," she replied as evenly as she was able. "Why didn't you give your name?"

"I knew I'd catch up with you eventually. You knew it, too, dincha, Angel? I could tell, that time in my room, you were feeling the same thing I was. You had to know you and me weren't finished."

No, she thought sickly, she hadn't known. Hadn't believed it. But Cade had. He'd been right the entire time. She shuddered, drawing the covers up over her shoulders. But her voice was steady when she said. "I heard you killed a police officer. How did you get out of the hospital? You had to have help." Hearing his voice in the darkness made him seem all too real, all too close. With her free hand she reached out, snapped on the lamp.

"That don't matter. They ain't gonna find me. And it ain't gonna stop the two of us from getting together." His tone went low and intimate. "We're gonna have us a time, Angel Eyes. Bet you know lots of ways to pleasure a man, you being a doctor and all. I'm gonna let you show me all of 'em. Then you're gonna find out what a real man is like. You're gonna love it, too."

Revulsion snaked down her spine. But rather than stating it, screaming it, she said, "You're seriously injured. You should be under a doctor's care. You need medicine and possibly rehabilitation if you're to recover. Where are you?"

"Now that's real nice." Satisfaction laced his words. "You worrying about me. It's okay, I got everything I need. Still have to take it easy for a while, but I didn't want you to think I'd forgotten about you, Angel Eyes. Didn't want you to forget about me."

Her throat was dry. She had to force the words out to respond, "I haven't forgotten. But if you tell me—"

"All you need to know is I'm gonna be around, Angel. And when the time is right, I'm coming for you."

The line abruptly went dead. It was a moment before she could unclench the fingers that clutched the receiver so tightly. Another before she could force herself to return the receiver to the cradle.

Reaction set in, a dizzying spiral of emotion that hammered her insides with brutal pummeling fists. Somehow, despite Cade's certainty, she'd never believed LeFrenz would contact her. Why would he? She'd barely spoken to the man. How could Cade have picked up on something she'd been so blithely unaware of?

Chills skated over her skin, and she rubbed her arms. She was forced to believe it now. LeFrenz had left her with no illusions about his plans. She'd treated enough rape victims to know what was in store for her if the man succeeded catching her alone.

The alarm that twisted in her stomach was matched by the response that came from her next thought. With this proof that Cade was right about LeFrenz, she needed the detective now in a way she was loath to accept. In a way that made her vulnerable and dependent on him.

She didn't know which of the prospects frightened her more.

# Chapter 7

Cade pushed open the door to the lieutenant's office, sending a curious glance toward the stranger in the room. "You wanted to see me, Lieutenant?"

"This is Detective Quentin." The tall dark-haired man rose, proffered a hand. "He's heading up the narcotics task force that took over Brian's and your investigation."

Interest sharpening, Cade shook the other detective's hand. "You guys come up with any good leads?"

Quentin was tall and broad, with a face that would look more at home on a magazine cover than on the street. The regret in his voice sounded real enough when he said, "Wish I had better news. We aren't close to an arrest yet, but we've narrowed down the supplier you guys were looking for to a couple names. Lucky Reggau or Justus Davies. Haven't been able to close in on either one of them yet, but it's just a matter of time."

Cade's brow creased. "Reggau? He's always been two-bit. He wouldn't have had the financing or the brains to put together an operation the size of the one we were looking at.''

Quentin shrugged. ''Our sources are pretty good. Reggau was in the pen a couple years ago. He could have made contacts there. And Davies just moved here last year from Chicago. He's affiliated with the Trax gang and started his own operation down here. Ever run into him?'' When Cade shook his head, he went on, ''The CPD suspect him of several drug-related killings, but they've never been able to come up with enough to make the charges stick. We're hearing both these guys' names on the street as ones to talk to. I like Davies better than Reggau for it myself. Putting out pure stuff is a Trax tactic. They use it to issue warnings to troublemakers thinking to get a piece of their territory.''

''I don't know.'' Cade was unconvinced. ''Taking out a couple of cops is pretty ballsy, even for a gang member. And neither of those names came up during the course of our investigation.

''Lips loosen when something as big as a cop killing goes down. No offense,'' Quentin said quickly. ''Informants start coming out of the woodwork when they smell big money to be had. Makes it hard to sift through to the real leads, but we're still working on it. These two names represent the best leads so far. Unless you've remembered something that wasn't in your earlier report.''

Cade shook his head. ''It was all there. I hope you're right and you're close to nailing this guy. It'd be nice for Brian's widow to be able to get some closure on the whole thing.'' After a quick glance at Howard he asked, ''Did Jonny LeFrenz's name ever come up from one of the informants?'' The question had been nagging at him since the punk had professed knowledge about Brian's shooting. The guy had been expanding his drug territory pretty rapidly. It was enough to make Cade wonder whether LeFrenz's information was firsthand or had come from Freddie.

Quentin leaned back in his seat, crossed his leg over his other knee. "The guy who took out the uniform at Charity?" Cade nodded. "His name comes up in a lot of our investigations. He's a scumbag, but nothing we've gotten so far points to his involvement."

Which didn't explain whether he'd been blowing smoke when he'd claimed to know something about it. The only way to be sure, Cade reflected, was to track down Freddie and LeFrenz and determine for himself.

After a few more minutes Quentin rose, shook hands with the lieutenant. "I know what it's like to lose a man. I'll keep you posted."

"I appreciate that," Lieutenant Howard said.

The man looked at Cade. "Sorry about your partner. But if it's any consolation, I'm not going to rest until someone gets put away for his death."

"Thanks."

When the man had left the office, the lieutenant said, "Well? What'd you think?"

Cade lifted a shoulder, sat down again. "Davies and Reggau sound like small fish to me. Everything we were looking at pointed to someone with a lot of power, someone who generated a lot of fear."

"Well, you know how it works," Howard said. "Maybe one of these guys will lead us to a bigger cog in the chain."

Yeah. Something tightened inside Cade. He definitely knew how it worked. He also knew precisely how many unsolved murders there were in New Orleans. He was determined Brian's wouldn't be one of them. "What was

Quentin doing here, anyway? I thought Ryder and Sanover were keeping you posted on the investigation.''

"They were. Apparently I.A. had some questions about what the investigation has turned up and Quentin fielded them.''

At the mention of I.A., the omelette Cade had devoured that morning turned to lead in his stomach. "Speak of the devil…Torley and Morrison should be set up in the coffee room now.''

"When's your appointment with them?''

Glancing at his watch, Cade replied, "Ten minutes ago.''

Howard smiled a little. "You've made your point. They've been kept waiting long enough. Go see what you can find out about what they're up to.''

That advice was easier to suggest than follow, Cade reflected as a half hour later he sat across a battered wooden table from the I.A. sergeants, a tape recorder situated conspicuously between them. The two men took turns asking a series of cagily worded questions that had Cade getting more and more frustrated. Apparently he wasn't giving them the answers they were looking for, because a few minutes after a question was asked, one of them would rephrase it. "Were you there when Hollister set up the meeting with his informant?''

Slouching down in his chair, Cade replied with exaggerated patience, "No. I just got done telling Torley a few minutes ago that I didn't hear the conversation. So it would follow that I wasn't there when the meeting was set up.''

Morrison looked up from the tape recorder in front of him. "So Hollister came to you and said he had a guy he wanted you to meet…''

As interrogation techniques went, his was blatantly obvious. By subtly twisting Cade's earlier response, he was attempting to bait him into agreeing to something he could use as a contradiction later. "No, I told you twice already. We'd both been working our informants hard, digging for a lead. Either no one had anything, or they weren't talking. People on the street knew we were looking for information. Freddie contacted Brian, said he might know something." Cade shrugged. "We weren't even that excited about it. He's just a junkie snitch, trades information for enough cash to get high. We doubted he'd have anything worthwhile, but figured it was worth listening to. It wasn't like we had anything else to go on."

"So Hollister said Freddie contacted him?" This from Torley. He had a habit of looking up from the pad he was scribbling on without lifting his head, making his brows look more forbidding than usual. Cade had the unkind thought that the man looked like a young Frankenstein without the build.

"That's right."

"But you can't verify that, because you…"

"…didn't hear the conversation." Cade made a point of checking his watch. "You guys might have all day, but I've got a job to do. Maybe we could hurry this along by you just asking me the same question twice, instead of half-a-dozen times."

"The reason we're asking is we have no record of Freddie calling Hollister," Morrison put in. "We've got his phone records. He didn't call Hollister at home, the district or on his cell."

Cade released an impatient breath. "So he didn't make the call from his place. Big deal." He didn't see the significance of that particular point, but the I.A. officers exchanged a meaningful glance.

''What we do have is a dozen calls from Hollister's cell to Freddie's number.''

''So? I told you we were shaking all our usual snitches for any information we could get from them. Brian called all his informants. So did I.''

''Twelve times?'' Torley asked. He worked his angular shoulders as if he had an itch between his shoulder blades.

''As many as it took to make contact. Probably had a hard time catching up with him. Junkies don't keep regular hours.''

Morrison leaned forward across the table, buddy to buddy. ''See, the thing we don't get is, you said the two of you had been working on your case for two weeks. But these phone calls spanned a month or so.''

Although the news took Cade by surprise, he took pains to hide the fact. ''And? We work lots of cases. And we use informants on all of them.''

''There was nothing in the log that indicated Hollister had paid this guy for information during that time. Nothing written in any reports that made note of it, either.''

'''Cause Freddie didn't have anything worthwhile to offer?'' Cade suggested blandly. ''Where you guys going with this?''

Rather than answering that question, Torley switched to another subject. ''How well do you know Carla Hollister?''

Instantly cautious, Cade responded, ''Pretty well.''

''Brian ever complain about her spending habits? Like maybe she had expensive tastes he couldn't afford?''

Disgusted, Cade folded his arms over his chest. ''No.''

''Never talked about how hard it was to raise a family on a cop's salary? His wife didn't work, did she? I thought she said she stayed home with the kids.''

"She did. And Brian never complained about money. He liked being a cop."

"Yeah, according to his jacket he'd racked up a few commendations along the way," Morrison said. "So have you." Cade said nothing. "But a family can't eat commendations and awards, can they?"

"Thousands of cops are raising families on their salaries. You gonna suggest they're all on the take?"

Morrison looked up then. "You keep bringing that up. But we've never said anything about Hollister being on the take."

"You didn't have to. All this questioning about money is pretty self-explanatory. You guys want to go fishing, you should take a vacation."

Torley glowered. "We're not on a fishing expedition here, Tremaine. We have reason to believe that Hollister was supplementing his income, and as his partner, you might have some information on that. Unless you have a reason for not talking."

Dropping his arms, Cade leaned forward. "Yeah, my reason is there's nothing to say. If you've got some hard evidence to go on, you wouldn't be talking to me. You wouldn't need to. Struck out with that warrant, didn't you?" He made a mock pitying sound. "Too bad. But I told you before you were wasting your time."

"Who says we struck out?" Torley shot back. "If you're telling us the truth about what you know, it might be that you're the one who didn't know Brian Hollister as well as you thought. Ever think of that?"

Cade's chair clattered as he abruptly rose from his seat and leaned across the table on clenched fists. Morrison rose, too, his voice placating. "Okay, let's bring it down a notch. We all have a job to do here. You might not care for the way we do ours, Tremaine, but we want to get at the truth as much as you do.''

But Cade had heard enough. ''If you have anything else to ask me, do it now. Because I'm—''

The door opened and the desk sergeant stuck his head in.

''Tremaine, you had a call. I took a message and figured you'd want to know right away.'' When he turned, the man entered and handed him a folded slip of paper. Cade unfolded it, read it and felt his blood congeal.

With little preamble he headed toward the door. ''I'd like to say it's been a pleasure, boys. If you need anything else, we'll have to reschedule.''

Torley rose, as well, as if to prevent him from leaving. ''Wait a minute, we're in the middle of an interview here. Where the hell do you think you're going?''

''I'm going out to work a case.'' Reaching the door, Cade looked over his shoulder at the two men, saw the men wore matching scowls. ''I know that's something you desk jockeys wouldn't understand, but it's what real cops do, not sit around rooms assassinating good cops' reputations.'' With no little satisfaction, he went through the door, closed it on the two Internal Affairs sergeants.

He grabbed his coat and took the time to stick his head in Lieutenant Howard's office. ''I'm heading over to Charity Hospital. I just got word that LeFrenz contacted Shae O'Riley last night.''

Howard looked up. ''The woman we've had detail on? I thought she was cooperating. Why'd she wait so long to let you know?''

That question, along with a few others, were burning a hole in his gut. Grimly Cade said, ''That's exactly what I'm going to find out.''

But the answers to his questions weren't immediately forthcoming. The E.R. was filled with people, noise and no little chaos. He could ignore all those, but it was the smell that had assailed him upon entering through the double doors that had the skin on the back of his neck prickling. He'd spent more time than he cared to remember in this place, flat on his back, wounded both emotionally and physically. Just the aroma of disinfectant was enough to elicit a reaction.

Forcing it aside, he went to the desk to ask for Shae and found it difficult to even get someone's attention. Finally he stepped in front of a woman in a lab coat hurrying by and said, "Have you seen Dr. O'Riley?"

"Exam room three." The woman sidestepped him and went on her way, preventing Cade from asking directions. Memory kicked in and he headed down the hallway in the opposite direction from the one he'd taken when he'd accompanied LeFrenz to the hospital. Following the sound of earsplitting obscenities, he walked into room three, found it jammed with people. He heard Shae before he saw her, giving orders and talking to the patient in the same even voice.

"He's been altered since he was brought in?" A medic nodded and Shae said, "Call Follett for a psych consult." A dark-haired orderly went to the wall phone and picked it up, sending Cade a curious glance. The filthy bearded man on the cart stopped his screaming abruptly and began singing "Be Kind to Our Web-Footed Friends" in glass-shattering tones. "Sir, can you tell me where it hurts?"

The man continued to bellow off-key.

Content for the moment to watch her at work, Cade leaned a shoulder against the wall. Something inside him, something he hadn't even realized had knotted, released slowly. He identified the feeling as relief. Stupid, really.

If Shae had been hurt, she certainly wouldn't have been able to call in the message to the district. Seeing her now, well and unharmed, melted his concern, leaving only irritation in its wake.

She looked competent, calm, if a little harried at the moment. Her patient, a homeless man from the looks of him, had three people restraining him and they could have used a fourth.

''I'm going to need that coat open to do an examination, sir,'' she said. As her hands went to struggle with the buttons on his filthy trench coat, the man stopped singing and heaved himself upward, throwing off the nurse who was restraining him on one side. Cade shoved away from the wall, springing to her side, but he was a moment too late. The homeless man flung out his arm as Shae opened his coat, and suddenly the room was filled with feathers and fluttering wings.

Pigeons. Realization hit Cade as he helped the attending personnel wrestle the patient to the cart again. The man had had three of four of the birds inside his coat. How the hell he'd coaxed them in there in the first place was something to be considered at another time. The panicked birds were swooping and flying around the room. One hit the tray of sterilized instruments next to the cart, upsetting it and sending the utensils clattering to the floor.

''For God's sake, hold him down.'' It was the first time Cade had ever heard Shae raise her voice. The patient was fighting with the strength of six men, making it a struggle to restrain him. Cade wondered if he was ''altered'' by mental illness, drugs or a combination of the two. He and the orderly grabbed the man's shoulders, pressing him back against the cart, while the nurses held his arms against his sides.

Cade saw the flash of a needle and turned his head in

time to see Shae swiftly inject the man with what he fervently hoped was a sedative.

He ducked to avoid a gray-and-white pigeon flying toward his face and saw the man's eyes go wide, then roll back in his head. Moments later he was still.

There was a shriek as the dark-haired nurse jumped away from the pigeon that had grazed her shoulder. With a sheepish grin at Shae, she muttered, "I'm not a nature lover."

"This scene's for the birds for sure," the orderly said, and laughed.

"This guy isn't going to give us any more trouble. Julie, why don't you get the wrist restraints as long as he's out. And then call security." The woman moved to obey Shae's command.

Cade let go of the patient. The curtain that separated the room into two compartments was bunched into a wad against the wall. He waved the birds into the far end of the room, then jerked the curtain closed, effectively caging them in the smaller area. "Better tell security to bring a couple of nets." Then he looked at Shae, really looked at her, for the first time since the freakish bird escape, and concern bloomed anew. "Looks like he clipped you a good one when he got his arm free." Moving to her side, he took her jaw in his hand.

"You're going to have a shiner, Doctor," the orderly said.

"I'm fine."

Cade couldn't tell whether it was stubbornness or embarrassment he heard in Shae's voice. Despite her attempts to free herself from his grasp, he kept her face cupped in his hand, turning it toward him so he could see the injury better. He frowned. "You're already beginning to bruise."

A faint bluish mark marred the creamy skin on her right

cheekbone. He wasn't the medical person here, but he'd been on the receiving end of more than his share of fists. He didn't think she was going to have a black eye. But she was going to have a hell of a bruise.

Julie turned away from the phone and winced when she saw Shae. "He's right. Why don't you go take care of yourself and I'll check this guy out."

"That's not necessary."

But Cade had already slipped an arm around her waist and started guiding her toward the door. "Good idea. Let's go get something to put on that mark."

"Anything I need can be found in this room," she reminded him in a voice that was a little too even.

"So can half the pigeons from City Park." He knew if she wasn't forced to, she wouldn't stop to tend her injury for hours, if at all. She didn't like to show weakness, and especially not in front of him. Although he understood her behavior, it did nothing to stem his concern.

As they stepped out into the hallway, a man strode up to them. "What's going on in there, Shae?" the man asked. His brows skimmed upward when he noticed her face. "Some patient take offense at your bedside manner?"

"Just a mentally unstable vagrant with a penchant for feathered friends." She waved off his next question. "Security's on the way, Tim. It's under control."

The man's gaze swung to Cade, then dropped pointedly to the arm he still had around Shae's waist. It was easy to figure out the guy didn't like to see him touching her. Either he had a claim on her or he thought he did.

Deliberately Cade resisted Shae's subtle attempts to free herself. "I figured she probably ought to see to that bruise."

"You're right. Do you need any help?"

"I'm fine, Tim." Shae's tone managed to be civil. Just.

"I'm going to grab an ice pack." She and Cade moved away, leaving the man staring after them.

Cade remained silent until they'd entered a small room filled with locked cabinets and shelves. Then, accepting the slight nudge she gave him with her elbow, he stepped aside. She went to a small freezer on the far wall and took out an ice pack, put it to her face. "You know, this really isn't necessary."

"The ice pack? I'm not the medical expert here, but I always heard ice keeps swelling down."

She shot him an irritated glance. "No, I mean this…concern. I've had worse, believe me. And I can't afford to be gone too long. The E.R. has been wild since I got in. Full moon last night."

"I've been concerned since I got your message today," he replied steadily.

For a moment, remarkably, she looked blank. Then when comprehension filtered in, she glanced away. "Oh. You mean LeFrenz."

"Yeah, I mean LeFrenz." He had to restrain himself from reaching out and shaking her. Or to haul her into his arms. To avoid doing either, he shoved his hands into his pockets. "How long after I left did he call?"

"It was about three." In an expressionless voice she recounted the conversation to him. With each sentence of the retelling, Cade could feel his blood run a little colder.

"He threatened you," he said flatly when she'd finished.

"Not…" She glanced at him, her eyes widening when she saw the expression on his face. "You were right." The words sounded as though they pained her a great deal. "I never believed he'd get in touch with me. I still don't understand it."

Being right had never felt less satisfying. Cade had an

urge to bury his fist in the plastered wall at his side. Or preferably in LeFrenz's smug face. "What's to understand? He has a habit of taking what he wants."

She whirled around to face him. "But why me? I have nothing to do with all this. Why would he fixate on me when it would be smarter, safer, to stay as far away from the hospital personnel as possible?"

"LeFrenz doesn't care about being safe or smart. He's cocky enough to believe he can beat the odds. As for why you—" Cade swept her with a glance he couldn't hope to keep objective "—you've got mirrors in your apartment. You can't be that unaware." But in the next instant he doubted his own words. She looked embarrassed by his remark, but still a bit uncomprehending. As if she was unused to seeing herself as men might. Like temptation encased by ice, promising to blister the skin and confuse the senses of any man daring to touch. To taste.

The errant thought brought lightning memories of less than twenty-four hours ago when he'd done both. And there hadn't been a hint of ice or her frosty reserve when he'd had her in his arms. What there had been was steam, plenty of it, and a torrent of desire that had been so sudden, so savage, it had stripped his mind clean.

He forced the mental replay aside for the moment and took her over the conversation again, word by word, making her search her memory for nuances, inflections, anything that would glean more information about LeFrenz's location. When he heard her tell how she'd tried to get the man to divulge exactly that, he felt a flicker of respect. Although he was certain nothing could force her to admit it, she had to have been rattled by the call. Frightened. Yet she'd still had the foresight to try to elicit information that would help them.

"I checked the caller I.D. and last-number redial. Both said the number he'd called from was unavailable."

Cade shrugged. He hadn't expected it to be otherwise. LeFrenz wouldn't be that careless. "I've already got an order in with the telephone company. They'll be able to place the number."

She looked doubtful. "You don't think he'd call from where he was staying, do you?"

"It'd be nice if it were that easy, but probably not. Still," he continued, noting his answer had her tensing up again, "someone might have seen him in the vicinity of the phone he did use. They might remember something. This could be the break we've been waiting for." It was turning out just as he'd promised his lieutenant. LeFrenz contacting Shae might be the best break they'd had in this case yet.

Sometimes he really hated his job.

If he hadn't been watching her so closely, he might have missed the rigidity of her shoulders before she relaxed them. "Well, great." The words were brittle. "Glad to be of help."

"Why didn't you call me about this last night?" It took more effort than it should have to make his voice as expressionless as hers. To keep the focus of the question on the case and not on feelings that stemmed from a far more personal level.

The shrug she gave tried for nonchalant, didn't quite make it. "When I found there was no number on the I.D. box, I knew there was nothing you'd be able to find out until morning. There was no use interrupting your sleep."

Something in what she wasn't saying alerted him. Trying to sort it out, he said slowly, "You seem overly interested in my getting sleep. How much did you get after LeFrenz called?"

When she didn't answer, he muttered a curse. "You should have called me right away."

"There was nothing you could do."

"I could have come over." He could have been there with her. He didn't like to think of her there in her apartment, frightened and alone, sitting awake in the darkness with LeFrenz's voice sounding in her head. She wouldn't have gone back to sleep after hearing his threats. She wasn't that cool, despite the impassive mask that had slipped over her features. He wondered savagely if it was designed to reassure him or herself.

"I was fine." Her tone was dismissive. He held her gaze long enough to make her look away. "Okay, I admit, I was a little shaken up. But not anymore. I've got the security company there today to do the work I contracted for, and even if LeFrenz does intend to follow through with his plans, he's going to be too ill to try anything for a while yet."

The matter-of-fact way she discussed when, not if, the man would come after her had his throat closing. "You're still under surveillance," he managed. "And the phone company is tracking down the number from the incoming call you received last night." The lieutenant wouldn't be able to dispute the fact that Cade's hunch had been right. But the realization brought him no satisfaction. The threat to Shae was too real and, despite her words, too immediate to be downplayed.

"Maybe you'd rather not return to your apartment." The words were uttered before he'd really thought. But once he heard them, they made perfect sense. "We could arrange a secure place for you to stay."

She lowered the ice pack from her cheek to stare at him. "No."

Although he recognized the steel in her voice, he

pushed further. "I'll make sure you're safe no matter what you decide." He didn't question where the need to reassure her came from. It was just there, primal and undeniable. "But maybe you'd be more comfortable somewhere else."

"Because he already knows where I live?"

Gray eyes battled green. He respected her enough to be honest with her. "Probably. If he doesn't yet, he will."

She took a breath, released it. "He's not going to drive me out of my own home. I'm not going to live in fear."

The fierceness in the words made him wonder what other emotion was behind them. But he wasn't going to push. Not right now. As long as he could keep her safe in her home, she could stay there. And the minute he thought her safety was compromised, she'd leave, even if he had to carry her out himself.

"I don't want you taking taxis anymore." He wasn't going to take the chance of LeFrenz grabbing her while she was waiting for a cab. "Someone on the detail will escort you to work and back home again each night. And anywhere else you want to go."

She skirted his gaze, folding the ice pack and replacing it in the freezer. "Like I said, I really don't expect him to come after me. Not anytime soon, at any rate."

He never knew what made him cross to her, turn her around and tip her face up to his. "He's not going to get you," he said firmly. It was a promise, both to her and to himself. And for reasons he didn't completely understand, it was imperative that she believe him. "A copkiller warrants a lot of attention. We're going to catch up with him. I won't let him near you."

"I can take care of myself," she started.

A smile played across his mouth. "Yeah, you look pretty tough. But if it's okay with you, the NOPD might just hang around, anyway, in case you need any help kicking bad guys' butts.''

A faint sheen of pink stained her cheeks, as if she was unused to such teasing banter. "I just meant—"

"That you're self-sufficient." He didn't need her explanation to know that much. "You're not used to letting anyone do anything for you. You like to keep everyone at a distance, and the police at a greater distance than most. Yeah, I've figured that much out."

Her brows skimmed upward and that detached mask descended over her features. "What I can't figure is why that matters to you."

Her tone was so honestly baffled that something in him lightened. And made it easier to recognize that he'd been asking himself that very thing almost since he'd met her. "I'm a cop. It's my nature to be curious about people. And there's something about you," he murmured, brushing his thumb across the angry mark on her cheek. "Something I can't explain. But the harder you push me away, the closer I want to get. And I don't think that can bother you half as much as it does me." The flash of panic on her face called him a liar. "Guess we're just both going to have to get used to it."

# Chapter 8

Cade had a two-o'clock meeting with the team assigned to the LeFrenz investigation back at headquarters. Glancing at his watch, he figured he had just enough time to go by the man's apartment once more and do another walk-through. The place had been thoroughly searched by the backup team Cade had called for, while Cade had accompanied LeFrenz to the hospital. Upon his escape from the hospital, it had been searched again. And although they had an officer staking it out, Cade doubted very much that their suspect planned to return to it. Even if he was that stupid, it was a good bet his accomplice was not.

The place was a walk-up a couple of blocks off Bourbon Street, situated above a seedy tavern. He didn't doubt that LeFrenz could have afforded better, but the locale he'd chosen put him near a ready source of customers, none of whom would raise any eyebrows as they entered and left his place at odd hours of the day and night.

The detective in the car across the street was a sixteen-year veteran from Cade's district. They chatted for a few minutes before Cade entered the building. Police tape still crisscrossed the doorway to the apartment, and a padlock had been affixed to the door to secure it. Whatever locks had previously been in place had been rendered useless when Cade had kicked the door in to apprehend the man.

He experienced a sense of déjà vu as he entered the place and surveyed it. The kitchen table where LeFrenz had been sitting when he'd entered was still standing by the wall. The man's first instinct had been to lunge out of his seat and go for his weapon.

Involuntarily Cade's gaze went to the wall at his side. The two bullets LeFrenz had fired had lodged in the plaster, to be retrieved by the investigative team. His own single shot had taken the punk down.

With his hands shoved in his coat pockets, Cade moved around the small space. He'd busted LeFrenz two other times before the shootout that had wounded the man. The first time Jonny had only been sixteen and had avoided doing real time by hiring a slick lawyer who'd gotten him tried as a juvenile. Three years later Cade and Brian had brought him in with a solid case. The week of the trial, their star witness had suffered a convenient lapse of memory. The trial had progressed, but without the eye-witness testimony, LeFrenz had been acquitted. The memory of the smug look on LeFrenz's face when he'd sauntered out of the courtroom still burned.

But he was no longer the two-bit punk they'd brought up those last two times. Cade crossed to pick up a remote, flipped the power switch. The big-screen TV in the corner developed into a three-foot picture of a bikini-clad blonde on a white-sand beach. He flipped it off again. Next to the TV was a state-of-the-art entertainment center that looked like solid pecan. Jonny had come up in the world in the past couple of years. Due to lucrative business decisions or a more highly placed supplier?

The apartment itself wouldn't cost him much, but its furnishings must have. Having an eye for the finer things himself, Cade recognized the authentic Italian leather, the craftsmanship of the wood. If he stepped into the next room he'd find a closet filled with expensive, if gaudy clothes and a large bed covered with leopard sheets. Money could buy just about everything but taste.

LeFrenz would relax right there, in the big double-wide recliner situated a few feet from the TV. Eyes slitted, Cade imagined the scene. A lamp and the remote would be within easy reach. A small fridge sat next to the chair to save a few steps to the kitchen. Memory told Cade it was filled with bottles of imported beer.

He crossed to the chair and sat, releasing the mechanism so it would recline. He could almost see LeFrenz there, everything he needed to run his little empire within arm's reach. He'd feel satisfied at the way he'd managed to surround himself with the finest things money could afford. He'd beaten the cops. That was what the punk would have thought. They'd tried but hadn't been able to touch him. His territory was expanding, and he could afford to buy just about anything he wanted. He must have felt like a king. One who could lift his finger and have just about anything he wanted.

And now he wanted Shae.

Cade's eyes snapped open. He was already on the run from the NOPD, facing a long stretch in prison for his client's overdose. Facing death if it could be proved he'd been an accessory to his police guard's murder.

There was little more dangerous, Cade knew, than a man with nothing left to lose.

While LeFrenz was free, Shae was in jeopardy; he was

more convinced of that than ever. If he were LeFrenz, he'd have run long and hard. He could never hope to continue to operate in New Orleans undetected again. But from his conversation with Shae, it had sounded very much as though he was still in the vicinity. And that meant something important was keeping him here.

Cade concentrated fiercely, trying to think the way the other man would. Was it his physical injuries that had him hanging around? Because from the conversation Shae had relayed, it sounded as though he was intent on staying put, at least for the time being. What would convince a man to stay in the midst of the hunt going on for him right now?

Not a woman, Cade thought. They would come too easily to LeFrenz for him to value one that much. That lead had already been exhausted, at any rate. They'd interrogated every female he'd ever been seen with, and none claimed to know his whereabouts. Right now he was fixated on Shae, but would he risk his life to follow through on his plans for her?

Money was usually a powerful motivator. But LeFrenz's store of drugs and cash had been removed from the safe they'd found in his bedroom closet. Noticeably missing had been any list of business contacts, dates or transactions. He was a very careful man. The place had been turned upside down twice, and no records had been found. He must have had them stashed elsewhere.

Questions without answers continued whirling in Cade's mind. His gaze fell to the floor as he considered the possibilities. It was a moment before he noticed the ballpoint pen there. It had probably fallen off the table during the search.

Reaching down, Cade retrieved it, went to set it back on the table—then his hand froze in midmotion.

*Everything LeFrenz needed was right here.*

A quick glance around reaffirmed that earlier thought. The easy chair, the lamp, the remote, the fridge. There was no traditional phone service to the apartment, but with a cell phone the man could sit right here and control his little empire. It didn't make sense to keep his paperwork somewhere other than his apartment. Like most businessmen, LeFrenz had records to update. The most secure place for him to do it would be here.

Interest sharpening, Cade sat up, looked around with new eyes. Everything in the room pointed to a man who enjoyed his creature comforts. Someone who sat in his own little throne while he enjoyed his ill-gotten gains. Launching himself from the chair, Cade went to the table, running his hands over the wood. Maybe the top lifted, to reveal a shallow compartment. He was unable to pry the top up, however. And a more thorough examination of the wood revealed no mechanism that would release it.

Rocking back on his heels, Cade's gaze skated to the chair. In the next moment he was beside it, turning it upside down, to carefully check the springs and mechanism. Minutes later he was just as convinced it wasn't concealing what he was looking for.

Undeterred, Cade reassessed. The more he thought about it, the more certain he became that he was on to something. But he found nothing beneath the carpeting nearby, nor did an examination of the drywall yield anything.

Which left the mini refrigerator. Taking out his pocketknife, he extracted the utensil that doubled as a screwdriver. Within minutes he had the back off the appliance to reveal…only dust and electrical coils.

Muttering a curse, he opened the door, surveyed the interior balefully. The molded plastic that covered the

back and sides didn't provide any clues. Which only left
the door. There were two buttons on the interior side of
the door. One would secure it when it was closed. The
other…Cade pressed it, heard a tiny click. Quickly he ran
his fingers over the front testingly, trying to move it. And
was rewarded when he was able to slide the panel upward.

He released a breath. Jackpot. The false front revealed
a fat black notebook. Flipping through it, he found notations of names and transactions, complete with each customer's preferences, dating back three years. The only
other item in the compartment was a cell phone.

So the punk hadn't used his own cell to call Shae. He'd
either used a conventional telephone or one belonging to
someone else. Either way, they were going to get some
valuable information once the number was traced. Extract-
ing the cell phone from the fridge, he flipped through the
numbers LeFrenz had plugged into its memory and
grinned as one after another was displayed. With any luck,
this discovery was going to lead them to LeFrenz even
sooner than he'd hoped. Before the man could follow
through on his plans.

Before he acted on his promise to Shae.


"Nice work, Tremaine." Lieutenant Howard's face
wore an uncustomary smile. The dozen officers working
the LeFrenz case would have filled his office to overflow-
ing, and so they were sitting in the coffee room. The notebook Cade had discovered in the apartment was being
passed around the table.

"I can't believe we missed this," Josh Birtch, the
rookie detective on the squad, muttered. "I went over the
fridge myself three times."

"Maybe your attention was on the beer inside," Joe
Pascan, a six-year veteran, joked. The other men laughed.

"I missed it myself the last time through," Cade said. And it would be a long while before he'd forgive himself for that mistake. "But we've got it now, and the records and cell phone should give us plenty of new leads." He knew he wasn't the only one in the room feeling an increasing sense of urgency on this case. It was a well-known fact in police work that if more than twenty-fours had passed since the commission of a crime, the chances of its being solved decreased dramatically. Allowing LeFrenz to get away with murder, literally, wasn't an option.

In a few succinct sentences, Cade informed the rest of the men about the phone call Shae had received.

When he'd finished, Howard said, "The phone company called a few minutes ago with the location LeFrenz called her from." Looking around the table, he ordered, "Pascan, Rollins, LeGrand and Pearce, you check out the contacts in LeFrenz's book. Lloyd and Manden, see where the cell phone takes you. Those on stakeout will continue. Tremaine, you and Birtch follow up on the origin of that phone call." He took a slip of paper from his clipboard and handed it to Cade. "Here's the address."

Cade made a point of keeping his expression blank, while everything inside him rebelled. He had nothing against the kid, Birtch. Someday he might even be a hell of a cop. But he hadn't partnered with anyone since Brian was killed. It wasn't that he hadn't thought he would again someday. He just hadn't been prepared for someday to be now.

He looked at the paper, then at his superior. "I was planning to set up the trap and trace for O'Riley's phone. Do we have the court order for that yet?"

Howard nodded. "You can do that, too. I want everyone reporting in at end of shift today with whatever you've gotten so far." He stood. "That's it for now." The men got up and started drifting from the room. "Tremaine." Cade stopped in the act of rising. "I'd like another minute."

The lieutenant waited for the last officer to leave the room before shutting the door and turning back to face him. "What went down with I.A. this morning?"

Just the thought of the earlier meeting was enough to make Cade's gut clench. "They didn't give up much of anything. It's for sure they think Brian was taking kickbacks from someone. Since we've been working narcotics, it goes to figure they're thinking he was either dealing or allowing others to. They seemed awfully interested in his phone calls to Freddie over the couple of weeks before he died."

Howard lowered himself back into a chair. "You mean they thought the junkie was somehow connected to dealing? He only used, didn't he?"

Cade shrugged. "He might've sold small amounts when he had plenty, but no, he wasn't into anything big. If I.A. thinks Freddie was paying off Brian, they're on the wrong track completely."

"Forget what I.A. thinks," Lieutenant Howard ordered. "What do you think?"

"The only thing Freddie dealt in that was worth a damn was information," Cade said flatly. "And according to Brian, even that was suspect half the time. That's the only explanation I can think of for their communications."

"But Brian never mentioned anything the man had told him before the meeting in the park?"

Shaking his head slowly, Cade admitted, "No. But that doesn't mean anything, either. I didn't tell him every time I worked a snitch, especially if they didn't have anything important to give." His words sounded more certain than he felt. Because those phone calls to Freddie did bother him. A lot. Brian had made it sound like the man wasn't particularly reliable. So why would he have hit him up for information as often has he had? It didn't make sense. But it sat a hell of a lot more easily than considering I.A.'s assumption—that Brian had been corrupt.

"Still no sign of Freddie on the street?"

"I don't expect him to hang around. LeFrenz claimed he advised him to get out of town. That he gave him enough supply to hold him awhile. Ryder and Sanover told me they've notified departments around the area, sent his picture. If he's seen, he'll be grabbed."

Howard grimaced. "Since he hasn't been found yet, he's probably long gone."

"Probably. But he did get a wad of cash for giving us up to the shooters," Cade reminded him. "That could buy him plenty of dope and a place to stay until the money runs out."

"Who knows? When we catch up with LeFrenz, we might learn something about Freddie's whereabouts from him."

"I keep wondering about that last conversation with him in the hospital." Because he thought better on the move, Cade rose to his feet to pace. "I figured at the time he was probably claiming to know something about the shootings just to get at me. He had to have realized we'd check out his information before offering him a deal. But naming his supplier would only buy him a reduced sentence, while giving up a cop killer might just get him off scot-free, with protection to boot."

The lieutenant frowned. "So?"

Cade stopped pacing and arrowed a look at the other man. "So who do you think would be more interested in getting LeFrenz out of police custody? His supplier? Or the guy responsible for the shootings?''

Howard stared hard at Cade. ''So now you're thinking his information might be on the up-and-up?''

Giving a grim smile, Cade said, ''I'm considering three possibilities.'' Holding up his hand, he ticked them off one by one on his fingers. ''LeFrenz lied about what he knows, which wouldn't have taken us long to prove. Or he only had secondhand info from Freddie, which wouldn't buy him dick from the D.A.''

The lieutenant was following his line of thought. ''Or he had firsthand knowledge of the shootings.''

''I'm not saying he was one of the shooters.'' Forensics had told them there'd been at least two. ''But yeah, he might have been involved on some level. A person would be pretty motivated to keep that kind of information from coming to light.''

''Motivated enough to kill the cop at the hospital.''

Cade nodded, his mind working furiously. ''And if it was the guy responsible for the shootings who helped him escape, LeFrenz would have had to know and trust him to go along. Which means somehow he's connected.''

Howard pondered that for a moment. ''When you asked Quentin if the shooting investigation had turned up any connection to LeFrenz, he said it hadn't.''

''Yeah.'' That was troublesome. But then again, Cade hadn't been convinced by either of the names Quentin had mentioned, either. He looked at his superior. ''So I guess there'd be no reason to share this conversation with the task force.''

His chair squeaked as the lieutenant leaned back in it. ''It's just supposition at this point.''

''Exactly what I was thinking.'' But his thoughts belied

his bland tone. A great deal of police work stemmed from gut instinct. And that instinct was screaming at him now.

"Maybe a conversation with LeFrenz would shed some light on the I.A. investigation into Brian, too."

"Maybe." Cade's voice was noncommittal. He still remembered the glee in the man's tone when he'd addressed Shae in the hospital. *Maybe his partner was as dirty as everyone's saying.* He wouldn't trust that scumbag to tell him the truth about Brian, even assuming he knew anything about him. He wouldn't trust I.A., either. The only way to find out what really happened leading up to the man's death was to ferret out the facts for himself. It was the least he could do for the man who'd been like another brother to him. The man who'd died, leaving Cade with three holes in his chest and a helluva lot of questions.

As if reading his mind, the lieutenant asked, "What are you planning to do next about I.A.?"

"Our meeting this morning was cut short, so they'll want to do a follow-up." The plan that was already forming in his mind had knots twisting in his stomach. "I could maybe reach out to Morrison. He's not as big a jerk as Torley. See if he'll meet me more informally and go from there." The man would be suspicious of the offer, but he'd meet him. Cade was sure of that. And maybe one-on-one he stood a better chance of learning what I.A. had on Brian.

"Keep me posted."

Cade nodded and they both headed toward the door. When they reached it, though, Howard said, "Don't forget about taking Birtch out with you today."

He didn't turn around. He couldn't. There was no mistaking the reason behind the lieutenant's reminder. No denying the need for it.

Turning the knob, he went out to the squad room, tossed

a look at Josh, who was sitting at his desk. "Well, come on, Birtch. I would have thought you could have had the car warmed up by now, at least."

With undisguised eagerness, Josh jumped to his feet and grabbed his coat. "Want me to drive?"

There was a hitch in Cade's stride. Brian had always driven, not because there was any truth to his assertion that he was better at it, but because Cade had the sharper eyes when it came to watching the streets for their quarry. In the next instant, however, he'd recovered. Snagging the leather jacket off the back of his desk chair, he asked, "Got your permit yet?"

"Funny."

The two of them walked out of the squad room, the way he and Brian had done thousands of times. The way they never would again. "What the hell." Cade tossed the younger man the keys, feeling as if he was throwing away a bit of his past. "Knock yourself out."

He waited until Birtch had pulled out of the parking lot, raising his gaze skyward when the man cut off a taxi. While the cab's horn blared after them, he looked at the slip of paper in his hand. "Head over to Tenth and Algiers. The call to Shae came from a pay phone outside a Quik-Mart there."

Birtch angled the car over a lane to prepare to take the next exit. "There's not going to be much chance of people hanging around in that neighborhood at that time of night," he observed. "At least not the type to want to talk to us."

"Maybe someone inside saw something," Cade said with more optimism than he was feeling. The neighborhood they were heading for had a high crime rate, with a corresponding low incidence of cooperation with the police. "Those Quik-Marts are open twenty-four hours, right?"

"Yeah."

"So maybe we'll catch a break." Cade needed to believe that. It was past time they had some luck on this case. He didn't think for a moment that LeFrenz would be content with only one phone call before trying to meet up with Shae. He'd call again. And again. Stretch out the anticipation, the game. Because that was how the creep would see it. A game of intimidation in which he set the rules. While his prey got more and more panicked. Wondering where he was. When he would strike.

But LeFrenz didn't know Shae at all if he thought his tactics would be successful. The knowledge brought Cade a measure of satisfaction. Whether through sheer determination or old-fashioned stubbornness, Shae wasn't about to cave in to his manipulations. Cade had bumped up against her resolve often enough to be certain of that.

"So is she good-looking?"

Cade grabbed for the door handle as Birtch narrowly missed sideswiping a car. "Who?"

"That doctor. O'Riley."

He sent an irritated glance at the man beside him. "What difference does that make?"

Birtch shrugged. "I was just wondering. You've been doing a lot of the legwork on this case, and so you must have talked to her a few times." He paused for a moment as he slammed on the brakes to avoid running into the car in front of him. "Besides, you called her Shae."

There was sweat beading his brow. Cade resisted the urge to wipe it away. It'd be a hell of a note if he'd survived three slugs to the chest, only to die on the New Orleans city streets with a kamikaze detective at the wheel. "I did not," he denied.

"Yeah, you did."

Cade thought back through the last couple of death-defying near misses to his earlier words. Had he? He'd been thinking of her as Shae for some time now, but he was surprised, and not a little displeased, to hear that his professional guard had slipped. He'd be no good to her if his judgment was clouded.

"So is she?" At Cade's blank look, Birtch repeated, "The O'Riley chick. Is she good-looking?"

"Chick?" Cade slouched further down in the seat and surreptitiously checked the security of his seat belt. "What are you, seventeen?"

"Nope." The other man turned the corner without bothering to slow down. If Cade's seat belt hadn't been tight enough to cut him in two, he'd have been thrown against the door. "I'm twenty-seven."

How the hell could someone only five years younger than he was manage to make him feel so ancient? "So you're old enough to have had a couple years' driving experience. What a relief."

Josh tossed him a grin. "Don't like my driving?"

"Only slightly less than your questions."

"Hey, I was just making conversation. You know. Establishing rapport. Breaking the ice."

Cade's eyes slid shut, partially in self-defense. He figured it would be better if he couldn't see the near misses. "I like ice. Leave it the hell alone."

An injured silence followed, one that didn't last nearly long enough. "Okay, no problem." Josh started whistling tunelessly in a manner only slightly less annoying than his chatter had been. But Cade found it infinitely preferable to fielding his questions about Shae.

It'd be useless to pretend, to himself at least, that Shae O'Riley was just part of a job. He shifted uncomfortably.

He wasn't quite sure when she'd started becoming more. Certainly before he'd taken her in his arms and the taste of her had nearly torched his control. And sometime after he'd talked his way into her apartment and found himself oddly reluctant to leave.

The timing, he reflected, was lousy. He had a case to work. A vow to keep to his partner's widow. One to keep to himself. But just as strong now was the need to keep Shae safe. It was useless to question it. But he couldn't deny the fact that it complicated everything.

"This it?" Josh's voice interrupted Cade's thoughts.

He opened his eyes. Birtch had been right about the neighborhood. The Quik-Mart stood like a shiny brave soldier amidst a field of walking wounded. Nearby buildings were boarded up, with others sporting bars over the windows and doors. They got out of the car and Cade turned, located the public telephone a few yards away on the corner. The glass was broken out of it, and it was little more than a shell, but miraculously the phone was intact. The one LeFrenz had used to terrorize Shae.

Jaw clenched, he joined Birtch and approached the Quik-Mart. A sign on the door announced that the place had less than fifty dollars in the cash register at all times. It was obviously no deterrent. Cade knew junkies who'd knock a place over for a fourth of that.

Cade pushed the door open and approached the clerk at the front desk. Flashing his shield, he reached into his coat pocket and pulled out a picture of LeFrenz. "Excuse me, ma'am." The frizzy-haired older woman behind the counter eyed them suspiciously. "Were you working here last night?"

"Nope. I don't do night hours. I told that worthless manager it ain't safe around here at night for women alone." She crossed her arms as if to protect her virtue.

"He still tries to schedule me once in a while. I don't know how many times I gotta tell him, I'm not taking them kind of chances for six bucks an hour. It ain't worth it. You wouldn't believe the kind of weirdos we get in here in the middle of the night. Why, I heard tell of one time there was this guy who—"

"You know, ma'am, I think you're wise to stay away from this area at night." Cade interrupted the woman's monologue with a smile. "Would you happen to know who did work, though? The midnight shift?"

When the woman shook her head, Cade slid the picture across the counter. "How about this guy? Ever see him in here before?"

She leaned over to put her face close to the photo. Studying it for a moment, she said definitively, "Nope."

"You're sure?" Birtch said.

The woman glared at him. "I said no, didn't I? I ain't blind. Besides, a guy that looks like that, no one's gonna remember him, anyway. Too normal. You should ask me about some of the weirdos that come in here. Why, just yesterday there was this guy—"

"Do you have the manager's number?" Cade asked, sweeping the interior of the store with his gaze, lingering on the security cameras mounted near the ceiling around the store.

"Yes." She rattled it off from memory.

"Get him on the phone." Throwing a look at Birtch, Cade said, "I want him down here in fifteen minutes with the name and address of whoever worked here last night." The other detective nodded and reached for his cell phone. Cade moved away to look at each of the cameras in turn, his gaze tracing the path each lens would capture. With a quick surge of disappointment, he realized that none of them would have a range beyond the interior of the store.

He went to the front and out the door, hoping that a place with as many holdups as this one had would have cameras outside, as well as in. Looking up to the roof overhang, he noted the narrow openings near the top, indicating cameras secreted inside. Measuring the distance between the storefront and the phone booth, a grim smile settled on his face. Maybe one of those outside cameras had caught LeFrenz's late night appearance less than twelve hours before. And if they had any luck at all, it'd yield even more—like a companion they could I.D., or a car that could be traced.

Propping a shoulder against the window, he waited impatiently for the store manager. And for what he fervently hoped would be a break on this case.

# Chapter 9

When the buzzer announced a visitor out in front of her apartment, Shae gave serious thought to not answering it. She'd just stretched out on the couch, her favorite blues band filtering through the stereo speakers, a sweet white wine poured and just within reach. After the workers from the security company had left, she'd showered, thrown on some comfortable clothes and looked forward to an evening of, if not inner peace, at least quiet.

The buzzer sounded again. Heaving a sigh, she picked up her wineglass and crossing to the intercom mounted next to the door right above the shiny new alarm keypad, she pressed the button. "Yes?"

"It's Cade."

The sound of his voice sent an immediate suffusion of heat spreading beneath her skin. The reaction was involuntary, and as such, completely unwelcome. Her hand hesitated, hovering above the intercom button that would allow him entry. It had been a long day already, and she wasn't up to a verbal wrestling match with the persistent detective. Given the craziness in the E.R. today, coupled with dealing with the workers in her apartment when she got off work, she'd successfully kept thoughts of LeFrenz and his late-night call at bay. Something told her that would change as soon as Cade stepped foot in her apartment.

Putting the glass to her lips, she sipped, refusing to consider the action as fortification. Resolutely she buzzed him in. She'd never been a coward. Never been one to take the easy way out. Regardless of how distasteful thoughts of LeFrenz were, she was anxious to know what further actions the police were taking. What actions, if any, she needed to take herself.

When she pulled the door open to admit Cade, her brows arched. "Please tell me that's not your porn collection."

One corner of his mouth quirked up. "Smart-ass." He walked by her and set the box of videotapes on her counter. "Didn't want to leave these in the car in case some punk went by and decided a few movies were worth the risk of breaking in."

"More likely they'd go after your car stereo in the trunk."

"Which can be replaced. These couldn't be."

"What are they?" She moved to stand beside him, gazing into the box curiously.

"We got the trace back on the call LeFrenz made to you last night."

Everything inside her stilled. To give herself something to do, she took another drink, then found she couldn't force the wine around the boulder that had lodged in her throat. "And?"

"It came from a phone booth just outside a convenience

store. I've got another detective going over the recordings from the interior CCTV. There may be a chance we could identify a customer last night who saw him as they entered or exited the store.''

It was easy enough to read what he wasn't saying. "You mean, the clerk in the store didn't see anything," she said flatly.

Cade's gaze was steady. "No."

"And these?" She gestured to the carton of tapes with her free hand.

"The store hasn't completely switched over to closed circuit yet. Their exterior security is still done by video cameras. The help is none too organized when it comes to changing the tapes. I'm hoping one of these caught him on video around the store last night."

A chill prickled down her spine, along with a healthy dose of frustration. "How is that going to help us? Seeing him make the call isn't going to get us any closer to him." A dart of something all too close to helplessness threatened to lodge in her chest. With effort, she shoved it away. Helplessness was typical of a victim, and although Le-Frenz's interest in her had made her a target, she'd be damned if she'd be a victim. But there was little in this situation she had control over. And she despised that circumstance most of all.

As if following her train of thought, Cade said, "We've got a dozen officers working on this case, following a lot of different leads. There's nothing for you to worry about."

"That's easy for you to say." Jerkily she turned and went back to the table where she'd left the wine bottle. Picking it up, she filled her glass again. "You're not the one having her life turned upside down on the off chance this slimeball decides to call again."

"About that…"

Although her back was to him, something in his voice alerted her. Suspiciously she looked over her shoulder, silently commanding him to continue.

"We're ready this time. When he calls again, we'll have his location nailed in a matter of minutes."

She stilled, comprehension flashing through her mind, before whirling around to accuse, "You tapped my phone?"

"Not exactly."

"Then what? Exactly?" Old memories stirred, igniting her temper. The thought of having some faceless, nameless policemen listening in on every conversation, poring over every number that contacted hers was as distasteful as it was infuriating. The feeling of defenseless indignation had been all too familiar during her childhood. Having to stand silently by while a couple of policemen, enacting a warrant, tore the house apart looking for her father. Watching as they carelessly dug through her things, a girl's secret treasures, clothes and underthings tossed aside in a quick and thorough search for anything that would lead them to Ryan's whereabouts.

The memory alone had her free hand clenching into a fist. "I don't want this. Not any of it." How had she managed to get dragged into all this? How could someone who'd gone to the trouble she had to avoid complications in her life be catapulted into such a mess of someone else's making?

His voice became low and soothing, like a smooth heated stroke over bare skin. "We have to do this to protect you. I want to make sure we pick up LeFrenz before he gets any braver than a phone call."

Stubbornly she resisted the persuasiveness in his tone. "I never consented to this."

"You don't have to. We didn't tap your line—that would take a warrant, and it isn't necessary, anyway. All we did was put a trap-and-trace device on your line so we have a record of the incoming calls. Given the level of cooperation the phone company has promised us, that will allow us to get a quick fix on his location next time." He considered her with eyes that saw too much. "Were you afraid your dad might call? Because we're not interested in him."

"No." She could feel her face flame, the curse of a natural redhead. Ryan could take care of himself. She'd never fallen into the trap of trying to protect him. Even as a child she'd recognized that her family was in need of protection from him, emotionally at any rate. She lifted a shoulder, the movement oddly jerky. "I just don't relish having my privacy violated this way." She could understand the need even while she hated the reality of it. Despised feeling like every ounce of autonomy she'd achieved was slipping away, a fraction at a time.

"Maybe there's someone else you're trying to spare, then."

Startled, she glanced at Cade and was fascinated to see that his eyes had gone hard and almost as cold as his tone. He shrugged, the nonchalant gesture at odds with his flinty expression. "Last time I was here someone called you. Someone you were making plans to visit."

Liam. She remembered the call immediately. The awkward search for conversation, the effort to gloss over all the things neither of them dared say to the other. She'd thought Cade had been asleep for most of that call, but it was obvious that he'd heard at least part. And wondered about it.

"It was my brother." She was amazed at herself for offering him the explanation. And intrigued by the arrested look in his eyes when he heard it. "I'm planning to visit him this weekend."

She could almost see the tension seep from his limbs, but before she could wonder about it, he said, "I'll see if I can arrange it. How far away does he live?"

Her heart stopped for a moment. "Why?"

"If it's not far, I can arrange for someone to accompany you." Because he'd gone to dig in her refrigerator, he missed her reaction at first. But when he closed the door again, turned toward her with a bottled water in his hand, something in her expression must have alerted him. "You can't seriously believe that I'd let you go on your own when LeFrenz is out there, just waiting to get to you."

Why hadn't she considered that? The boundaries being drawn around her life, boundaries not of her making, began closing in and threatened to choke her. She hadn't for a minute thought about how this situation affected people around her. Not only was there Liam to think about, but TeKayla, as well. What if LeFrenz followed her on her outing with the little girl? Shae shivered at the thought. If this situation put anyone else's life at risk, she'd never forgive herself.

Cade twisted the top off his water, watching her carefully. "I'm not suggesting keeping you prisoner. There's no reason you can't go about your life within reason. We'll keep you under surveillance." His voice was expressionless when he offered, "Or if you prefer, I'll go with you."

"No." The next moment she realized he might misconstrue her vehemence. She sought to temper it. "I'll just postpone my plans until…this is over." The thought of Cade going with her to the Louisiana Federal Penitentiary had her chest going tight. And the thought of introducing one of New Orleans's finest to her younger brother made it worse.

Frowning, she paced the room. Her relatively simple life had become suddenly fraught with complexity. It was her nature to tackle obstacles head-on. With Ryan as a father, with his penchant for using their front door as a turnstile, someone had needed to bring order to their chaotic lives. Since her eighth birthday, that someone had been Shae.

"All right. What can I do to help?"

If Cade was surprised by her sudden offer, he didn't show it. He tipped the bottle to his lips and took a long pull of water. When he lowered it, he asked, "Do you have a cell phone?" She nodded. "Let me see it."

Shae went to the table near the front door where she'd set her cell, and brought it back to him. Setting his bottle down, he studied the phone for a moment before tapping in some numbers. Then he clicked the power off and handed it back to her. "Keep it turned off. If LeFrenz should somehow get that number, I don't want him to be able to use it."

"And that number you just put in my cell memory?" she asked dryly. "The local pizzeria?"

His lips twitched. "Not quite. It's my cell. Twenty-four-hour service, though, and I do make deliveries. Satisfaction guaranteed."

Flames licked through her veins. Cade Tremaine on her speed dial. The ability to summon the sexy detective at the press of a button. Deliberately she put the glass to her lips. The thought was more provocative than it should have been.

"I want you to keep the cell phone with you at all times. If he calls again, just hit my number to alert me. I'll tip off headquarters and we can get the trace running."

"Maybe it won't come to that." She was tired of waiting around for something to happen. The need for action propelled her to suggest, "I've got a VCR. Let's watch those tapes now and see if we can see anything useful on them."

She couldn't imagine what she'd said to put that look of wariness in his eyes. "I was going to do that later. At my place."

Striding past him, she went to the box on the counter. Reaching in, she took out a handful of tapes and headed toward the VCR. "So you'll watch them here, instead. What's the difference?" She'd quickly grown tired of waiting on the sidelines while decisions were made that affected her. She was ready to do something—anything— that might speed the process along.

Shae knelt in front of the TV and put a tape into the recorder. After pressing rewind, she said over her shoulder, "It should go pretty fast. You said these were from the camera filming outside the store, and we can fast-forward through the film with daylight on it. We'll be able to quickly see if—" Her words abruptly halted and she narrowed her gaze at him. "What?"

His head was tilted to the side, and he was watching her with an all-too-male expression of appreciation on his face. She was instantly aware of the clothes she'd thrown on before she'd realized she'd be entertaining the detective that evening. The gray yoga pants and matching ribbed tank top had been chosen with comfort in mind and left only her arms bare. But the outfit was snug enough to call attention to her shape, a fact that didn't seem to escape him.

Her pulse whipped a faster beat. When it came to Cade Tremaine, the cop, she was certain of one thing: she wanted this case closed so she could go about her life again. She was so eager for that to happen that she'd supply him with whatever help she could. But Tremaine, the man... A cluster of butterflies fluttered in her stomach. She wasn't so anxious to see the end of him. Not until she'd explored that dangerous control of his. Not until she'd discovered what it took for him to set the cop aside and unleash the primal male animal that lurked beneath.

Shae was neither coy nor indiscriminate when it came to sex. When it came to choosing the time and the man, her major consideration was how easily he could be extricated from her life when the time came to part. That was why she never dated colleagues. Cade didn't qualify, but there was still an unknown quality to him. As a detective he was used to being in control. He might not be as easily dispatched as other men.

He gave her an easy smile, one designed to disarm. "I wasn't staring. I was just admiring your...ah...technique with the VCR."

The machine had finished rewinding, drawing her attention away from him. A man didn't get to be that charming, she reflected as she pushed the play button, without a great deal of experience. And given his lack of ties, she could safely assume he liked it that way.

As she rose, he said, "I was going to do this at home. It'll be tedious work."

"I need to be doing something," she retorted grimly. "You can watch them here just as easily, can't you?" As she went in search of the remote, he sat down on the couch and shrugged out of his jacket. When she rounded the couch again, remote in hand, he'd toed off his battered running shoes and stretched out on the couch. It hadn't taken long to convince him.

Shoving his feet off the couch, she made space for herself in one corner and sat, gaze trained on the TV. When she saw that the date on the tape matched the day before she'd gotten the call, she fast-forwarded through the grainy street shots until she got to the night segment on the tape. Slowing the speed, she leaned forward to better study the scene on the screen.

She glanced at Cade and found him unfastening the top button of his shirt and pushing up his sleeves. Her breathing hitched and her brows arched. "Making yourself comfortable?"

"Definitely. Like I said, this isn't going to be a short process. As a matter of a fact, you might want to call out and order a pizza or something."

She looked from him to the TV, then to the box he'd carried in. "How many tapes did you say there were?"

"Three dozen or so."

Comprehension began to filter in. "All unmarked."

He propped his feet on her coffee table and crossed them at the ankle. "That's right. And three different cameras."

His bland tone invited a response, one she wasn't going to give him. She did settle back more deeply into the couch, however. From the looks of him, he fully expected this to take a while. If he thought that was going to deter her, he was mistaken. As boring as the task ahead of them was, it marked the first time she'd taken an active role in the case that had so inexplicably ensnared her. That alone was enough to guarantee her interest.

Three hours and a dozen tapes later, Shae's vision was beginning to blur. To give her burning eyes a rest, she got up to remove the nearly empty pizza box from the coffee table before Cade's feet knocked it to the floor. She went to the kitchen, threw away the box, then got a soft drink from the refrigerator. The wine hadn't done much for her ability to focus on the TV screen, so she'd put the bottle away a couple of hours ago.

They'd rapidly arrived at a sort of routine. With three cameras and six-hour tapes, they could quickly discard the ones with times and dates that didn't match that of Le-Frenz's phone call. But when they came on one of the tapes from the night in question, Cade insisted they watch at least an hour of it—before the time of the call until after—hoping for a glimpse of LeFrenz. So far they'd been disappointed. Although they'd watched a few illicit drug transactions and one instance of a minor paying someone to go in and buy beer for him, there had been no sign of LeFrenz.

"So after handling this kind of excitement all day, what do you do for an encore at night?" she asked.

Cade scrubbed his hands over his face, then refocused on the TV. "Paperwork, usually, to document my glamorous days of routine jobs just like this one."

"Those bullet holes in your chest would suggest otherwise." She felt a tug of something suspiciously close to concern. Although he'd somehow managed to convince his attending physician, he'd never make her believe his job wasn't fraught with danger. "Have you worked narcotics long?"

"Five years, on and off. I worked undercover before I made detective. And then a couple of years ago Brian and I volunteered…" His words stopped abruptly. Brian, she thought, his dead partner. Sympathy stirring, she crossed back to the couch, watched him lean over to pick up the remote.

"There was an opening and we both had experience. We took it." The remainder of the explanation was delivered expressionlessly, with none of the emotion she suspected churned within him at the memory.

"Do you believe LeFrenz really knows something about what happened that night?" The question had been lurking in her mind ever since that scene in the man's hospital room.

"Hard to tell at this point. But I sure intend to ask him about it when I catch up with him."

Frowning, she attempted to remember the exact wording of the conversation. "He said that people were saying your partner..." She paused, trying to think of a diplomatic way to put it.

"That he was dirty?" Bitterness laced his words. "Jonny might have just picked that up on the street. There's an Internal Affairs investigation that's tearing into Brian's life now. Making life hell for his widow."

Shae dropped any pretense that she was watching the tape he was rapidly moving through. "He left a family?"

Cade nodded. "A wife and two little boys." He fast-forwarded through the daylight portion. "These investigations are long and they get ugly. Lots of times when the smoke clears, there's no hard evidence, but the stench of the inquiry clings to a name forever. I'm not going to let that happen to Brian."

It was oddly disconcerting to hear him talk about a detective being the focus of such intense scrutiny. And it caused memories of Liam, and the evidence against him, to come hurtling back. It was still deeply disturbing to realize that her faith in him had been unjustified. And that his pleas of innocence, made so fervently and tearfully, had been just as false. "Sometimes the best-kept secrets are held by those closest to us."

"Brian was my friend." There was a warning in his eyes. "I knew him as well as I know my brothers. I.A.'s wrong about him."

"I hope so." And she did for his sake. Because it was

easy to guard against being hurt by the ones most likely to let you down. There was little her father could do now that would touch her emotionally. But the little brother that she'd watched over, fed, helped with home-work…there was a special kind of pain that struck when one was blind. Unsuspecting. She hoped with every fiber of her being that Cade wasn't in for that kind of heartache.

"Date's not right on this one," he said in an obvious attempt to shift topics. Wordlessly she got up to exchange the tape for another from the pile of those they hadn't watched yet. She recognized the No Trespassing note in his voice. She'd perfected the technique herself. And so she'd respect it, although their conversation had yielded more questions than it had answered.

The next three weren't a match, either. When she saw the date on the next one, blazoned across a night scene, hope flickered once again. Cade forwarded to the time they were looking for, and again disappointment welled up. "You can't see a pay phone from this angle, either."

"It's possible none of the cameras reach that far."

"What?" Her head swiveled toward him.

"I'm just saying, I don't know what the range of the cameras are. Maybe we won't be able to see the booth. But we still might see him approaching or leaving the scene."

He backed up the tape and stopped it at 2:30 a.m. The amount of activity on the street at that time of night sur-prised her. Cade had said the Quik-Mart was in a rough part of town, and she could see that from the customers that frequented the place and those who loitered in front of it.

"Given the locale and the clientele, I can't understand how a place like that can stay in business," she remarked.

He reached over and stole one of the pillows near her

to cushion his head as he slouched lower on the couch. "You see a steady stream of customers, though, don't you? If they weren't making money, they wouldn't take the risk. Probably sell mostly beer and smokes this time of night."

"And the last guy who came out with some looked like he had a gun in his coat pocket," she retorted.

"Yeah, well, places like that really hose you on the cigarettes."

That surprised a laugh from her. The innocent tone, at odds with the wicked look in his eyes, had her stomach abruptly hollowing out. Here lay the real danger of Cade Tremaine. It was simple to resist the steely-eyed cop. But that issued its own seductive invitation. It made him all too approachable. All too irresistible.

That thought was sobering. She was immune to charm. Ryan exuded buckets of it, and while it had worked on her mother until her death, it had always been wasted on her. She'd never failed to be surprised when people couldn't see beneath her father's slick surface to the empty, self-involved con man beneath.

She firmed her lips and directed her attention back to the screen, where two scruffy-looking characters were circling each other, exchanging obscenities. In the next moment one of the men lunged at the other. What followed was a quick and vicious knife fight that ended only when a car slowed in front of the store, preparing to turn into the lot. One of the men looked up and the other took advantage of his distraction to dart forward, his blade glinting in the darkness.

Sickened, Shae asked, "Do you suppose this got reported? Is there any way you can check? Because that guy on the sidewalk had to have required medical attention." At Cade's silence, she looked over at him, struck by the expression on his face. "Cade? Do you recognize one of them?"

"No." He rewound the tape to the beginning of the fight. "But I recognize the driver of that car going by. See him?" He leaped off the couch to tap the screen.

She frowned, straining to see around his finger to identify the person in the grainy film. And when she did, her mouth suddenly went dry. There were only a few seconds on which the man's face appeared on screen, and that only in profile.

But it was long enough to identify Jonny LeFrenz.

# Chapter 10

The tape was wound and rewound, and each time he watched it, Cade was more certain of the driver. The camera's angle didn't take in the phone booth. Seconds after the car appeared on the screen, it disappeared into the parking lot. Ten minutes passed before it appeared pulling out of the lot again and back onto the street.

"Outsmarted yourself, didn't you, you little bastard," Cade muttered. He was sitting cross-legged on the floor, his face inches from the screen. "You were careful enough to go out looking for a phone that couldn't be traced to you, but you didn't even think about winding up on film."

"You can see part of the license number there... Wait—right there." Shae tapped the screen. "SR...something. Is that an O?"

He played the tape back and paused it several times before finally saying, "It looks like a *U*, but I can't make out the numbers that follow. We may be able to enhance the image back at headquarters, but chances are this will be enough to go on.''

Dubiously she looked back at the TV. ''Really?''

Cade got up and walked to the chair he'd laid his jacket on. Taking his cell phone from the pocket, he pressed the number that would connect him to headquarters and waited. When the night sergeant answered, he said, ''It's Tremaine. I need a check on a partial Louisiana license-plate number.'' He recited the first three letters. ''Midsize, early-nineties model. Black or navy, maybe a Lumina or Monte Carlo. Driver's door dented.''

Shae's head whipped back to the screen as if to check for herself. Her finger found the area on the screen. ''As many times as we played it back, I never even noticed that,'' she murmured.

''It's probably going to be quite a list,'' the sergeant warned.

''Yeah, I know. Call me back.'' Cade set his cell phone on the coffee table. ''We'll get a list of cars fitting that description from the Department of Motor Vehicles and go from there.'' Shae didn't look particularly encouraged. ''Hey, this is a good thing. We're one step closer to LeFrenz.''

''What if it's not his car?''

So that was what had been bothering her. He hesitated before saying gently, ''It's not.'' When her face fell, he cursed himself for sharing that with her. But she wasn't the type of woman who would allow coddling. ''But that doesn't matter. It may lead us to someone who has talked to him or seen him. Nine times out of ten, this is how police work is. One thing links to another, then another...'' He shrugged. ''You can't tell me things are always black and white at the hospital.''

She shook her head. One long strand had escaped from

the knot she'd pulled her hair into, and it curved along her jaw. Cade wanted, more than was comfortable, to brush it away. To allow it to curl around his finger, and to see for himself if it was as soft as it looked.

"No, not always. Occasionally a patient presents with symptoms that have us spinning our wheels trying to figure them out."

She got up from the floor and he reached out, gave her fingers a friendly tug and pulled her down on the couch. "So then what do you do?"

Although she looked a little surprised at his pressing, she said, "Run some tests. Maybe get another opinion. Start eliminating possibilities."

"Kinda like police work." He nodded, hoping the conversation would distract her from the concern he'd seen on her face moments before. "You narrow down the possibilities until you nail it, then you act."

She made a wry face. "Okay, so I'm looking for a quick end to this. I'm used to running my life to suit myself."

"No kidding" was all he said, and earned himself a pointed look.

"You strike me as a man who likes to arrange things to his own liking, as well."

"Who doesn't? But sometimes fate has a way of barging in and upsetting things, regardless of our plans." He thought of the time he'd spent flat on his back, drifting in and out of consciousness. The long arduous weeks of recovery, pushing himself to heal faster so he could get back on the streets. It had seemed the least he could do, since Brian wouldn't be going back to the job at all.

"I don't want this to go on so long that it ends up affecting someone else in my life," she surprised him by saying. At his look, she smiled wryly. "It's the oath they make us take. First do no harm. I don't want anyone hurt because some crazy is fixated on me.''

Not for the first time, he marveled at the contrasts in her. A woman who surrounded herself with a force field of defense, who'd chosen a career of helping others. He'd seen her treat patients. Remembered how frustrated she'd been when one of them had left with her abuser. Although she was an expert at keeping her distance, she wasn't detached. Her complexities were intriguing. "Do you have any other siblings besides...Liam, is it?''

His hope of drawing her out a bit more was doomed with that question. Her face shuttered. "No. It's just the two of us.''

Cade knew better than to press further. Instead, he stretched out again, propping his feet on the coffee table. She hadn't kicked him out yet, so that was a good sign. "I've got two brothers,'' he said, "one older, one younger. And a little sister who was more trouble than the three of us put together.''

"I feel compelled to point out that your perception is probably dictated by your gender.''

"If that's a polite way of calling me a male chauvinist, I'll deny it. Half the folks in Tangiphoha Parish would agree. And the other half just can't see beyond Ana's blinding smile. Those of us who know her best realize that her cute exterior masks a streak of sheer deviousness. Took all three of us to keep her in line when we were growing up.''

"Something tells me she didn't thank you for your efforts.''

There was a smile in Shae's voice, although it hadn't made it to her face yet. Encouraged, he went on, "She's always been quite vocal about her lack of appreciation for our...protective tendencies.'' Though that was the most

that was the most polite thing Ana had accused her brothers of, and it had been true enough. "She's married now,
so her husband inherited that job, poor slob."

"You don't approve," she observed shrewdly. "Is it
marriage in general or her choice of husbands?"

He slanted a surprised glance at her. He was certain
there'd been nothing of his mixed feelings in his voice.
"Marriage is great for those in the market for it. As a
matter of fact, there's a lot of it going around in my family
lately. One of my brothers, Sam, is engaged."

"And you like his fiancée," she prodded, humor still
evident in her words.

He thought of Juliette, soon to be his sister-in-law. It
would be hard to dislike the dark-haired French beauty.
And if he suspected there was much more to her than met
the eye, well, he'd also long figured Sam was more than
just an international lawyer.

"I see where you're going with this." He reached over,
snagged the pop from her hand and took a drink. She
narrowed her eyes at him. "But it isn't that I don't approve of Ana's husband. He's just not the kind of guy I
expected her to end up with."

"Let's see. Someone nice and boring like an insurance
salesman? Someone who'd build her a house down the
street from the family home with a white picket fence and
a dog?"

The observation was close enough to the mark to sit
uncomfortably. "Maybe." Instead, she ended up with an
ex-CIA agent who'd seen and experienced too much.
"What the hell, if I have to entrust my sister's safety to
anyone, I'd just as soon it be Jones." There was no question the man was capable of protecting her. And no denying he'd give his life to do it. That kind of devotion
went a long way toward overcoming Cade's reservations.

"So your early solicitous tendencies drove you to seek a career with the NOPD, to continue your need to serve and protect." He reached for the pop can again, but she moved it out of his range and toasted him with it before she drank.

He folded his arms over his chest. "Nope. I wanted to be a cop so I could drive fast and carry a gun."

"True hero quality," she affirmed. "I hope you wrote that down on your application. It's very impressive."

He grinned foolishly, enjoying the look of her. Draped against the couch, she was as relaxed as he'd ever seen her. The creamy skin bared by her top glistened, inviting a caress. And because he was tired of fighting the urge to do just that, he said, "Last time I was here you asked me to stay. If you were to ask tonight, my answer would be different."

She studied him, her gray eyes wide and serious. And God help him, he didn't breathe until he heard her say "Stay for a while."

The breath seeped out of him a bit at a time and, he dropped his feet to the floor. Obeying the urge that had ridden him all night, he reached out and lifted the strand of hair that had worked loose from the knot and wound it slowly around his index finger, his knuckle brushing her jaw. Her skin would feel just that soft all over, he thought, like the rose petals in his grandmother's gardens. He had to fight a sudden urge to discover every silky spot on her body. Now. To explore the places that made her sigh and ravage the spots that made her moan. He released her hair to trace his finger over her lips, battling the desire to take her hard and fast and furious. There was satisfaction to be had in taking it slow.

And he was going to do all he could to satisfy them both.

With a quick movement he had her scooped up and on his lap, settling them both comfortably in the corner of the couch. She looked a little startled at his action, and her gaze grew wary as she looped an arm around his neck to steady herself. Distracted by the pulse pounding in her throat, he pressed his mouth to it.

"We'll be more comfortable upstairs." Her words were breathy.

He found the cord in her neck and scored it gently with his teeth. "I'm pretty comfortable right here." He inhaled her perfume, something subtle and inviting, and felt his senses shred. No, he wasn't going to hurry this. Wasn't going to race toward the inevitable conclusion. Hooking his finger in the thin strap of her top, he dragged it over her shoulder, tasting the skin he'd bared with his mouth. He'd thought about this moment much too often to want to rush through it.

"Cade." Both hands were pressing on his shoulders, and when he lifted his head, he'd have sworn he read embarrassment on her face. "It's not that I don't appreciate your seductive techniques, but they're unnecessary. You've got a sure thing here."

A smile played around his mouth. "Still trying to set the rules?" he murmured, dropping a kiss at the corner of her mouth. "Ever wonder what would happen if you just forgot about controlling the situation and let go?" He didn't wait for her answer, didn't need one. He suspected that loss of control was the one thing in the world Shae O'Riley feared.

His hand stroked her back, feeling the tense set of muscles, the rigidity of her spine. His fingers worked at the tightness there, slow and soothing, as he trailed a lazy path of kisses along her jaw. After a few moments he was rewarded when he heard her issue a faint sound and sag a little against him. Despite her protests, he'd give her romance, because he'd never known a woman more in need of it. And in the seduction, allow himself to be seduced.

She slid her hand into his hair and brought his mouth to hers. Her kiss was direct, much like her personality. He found he liked that about her. Too much. Their breath mingled as he sank into the flavor of her. Mouths mated, tongues tangled, first quick and darting, then slowing to a languid glide. He gathered her closer to him and changed the angle of the kiss, demand edging in, fierce and sharp as a blade.

As if she recognized the change in him, she pulled away, her gaze never leaving his. She grasped the bottom of her tank top with both hands, sliding it up over her head before tossing it aside. He reached up and tugged at the pins holding her hair. One by one, he released thick strands to tumble below her shoulders. Only then did he reach for the front clip of her bra to release it.

Her breasts were soft perfect cones and fit his hands as if made for them. And with the bra tossed aside, her hair draped over her bare shoulders, she looked like a marble goddess come to life. Except she wasn't a cold statue, nor was she the frosty doctor he'd first met. She was a fallen angel, tempting him to join her descent into wicked pleasure. It was a journey he was anxious to share.

He shifted position to press her shoulders against the arm of the couch and drew one of her tightly beaded nipples between his lips. He laved it with his tongue, quick teasing strokes, before sucking more fiercely on it. She gave a little gasp and pressed closer to him, forcing a deeper contact. He complied, covering her other breast with his hand, kneading lightly, and felt all his other senses dim.

There was the taste of her, exquisitely feminine, and the feel, curves layered with heat. Everything inside him was focused on her. On diving into those flames and allowing desire to scorch them both.

He lifted his mouth, rubbed his unshaven jaw against the wet swollen nipple he'd released, then swallowed her cry of pleasure. Her hands tugged at his shirt, but he wasn't in the mood at the moment to help her. There was something too gut-wrenchingly sexy about holding her half-naked body on his lap. About savoring first one breast, then the other, and feel her twisting against him.

It was both heaven and hell, he discovered, to take things slow, especially with a woman who'd been a fever in his system for too long. He hadn't had sex since before the shooting, but he didn't fool himself into thinking abstinence was the reason for his rapidly eroding control. The reason was the woman herself. She cleared his mind of all that had come before her and filled it with thoughts only of her. Of this moment.

She struggled to an upright position and then straddled him, dragging his shirt from the waistband of his pants. Her hands slid beneath, trailing fire in their wake. Her fingers stroked his sides, slid to his back, flexed against the muscles. Her touch torched his blood. He could feel it surging through his veins like a Thoroughbred straining toward the finish line. And thought began to recede.

He undid the buttons of the shirt with quick savage movements, and when it was open, he splayed his hand against her back and brought her against him. Flesh to flesh. Curves to angles. Heat to heat. Her breasts flattened against his chest, he went in search of her mouth, kissing her with a measure of the hunger that was welling up inside him.

Her hands pressed between them and reluctantly he released her mouth. Her palms skated over his torso, slowing when she found the injury that had nearly ended his life. He didn't want to think about that now. Not when he felt more alive than he had in years. Not when every breath he took had to be battled out of clogged lungs. When every one of his senses was awash in her.

She leaned forward, dragging the tips of her breasts across his chest, and with every sensual stroke a corresponding bolt of lust tightened low in his belly. She nipped at his shoulder, the tiny sting of pain honing his desire to a sharper edge.

His hands settled on her hips, pressed her more closely against his aching length. He wanted to be buried inside her to the hilt. Wanted to plunge into her velvety softness until the need exploded for them both, leaving only pleasure in its wake. And he wanted, quite desperately, for that to be enough.

An alarm sounded at the back of his mind warning him that one taste of her wasn't going to be enough to quench the fever in his blood. That one night, however pleasurable, was never going to sate a desire that simmered whenever he was near her.

He rose, hands gripping her bottom, urging her legs around him to clasp his hips, and made his way to the staircase. When he got to the bottom of it, she twisted against him until he released her, and with one arm wrapped around his waist, she ascended the stairs with him. Each step notched the anticipation up even higher. The longing even stronger. And when they got to the top, she stepped into his arms once more.

The bed lay behind her, the rumpled covers dappled in the moon glow slanting in through the skylight. He remembered the first time he'd been up here, that time without her permission. His focus hadn't been on the bed, but he'd carried the picture of it in his mind long after, none-theless. Had had a mental image of her spread out in the middle of it, nude and painted with starlight. With his body stretched out atop her, buried in her.

Her fingers danced along the top of his jeans, teasing, knuckles brushing his belly. Hooking his thumbs in the sides of her pants, he dragged them down over her hips, baring the tiny scrap of panties she wore beneath. She wiggled her hips to aid him, distracting him for a moment, before the pants slid down her long slender thighs.

Kicking them aside, she swayed toward him, her gaze direct, her eyes smoky, as her hands worked to release the button on his jeans. He splayed one hand over her bottom and brought her closer, dragging his lips over the side of her throat before taking the lobe of her ear in his teeth to worry it gently.

"Do you have protection?" He'd never put her at risk, and if she didn't have something, he did.

But she nodded as she worked his zipper over the bulge in his fly. "In the nightstand."

He released a shaky breath and filled his hands with her bottom, squeezing gently. He traced the edge of the elastic where it met the tops of her thighs, the back of his knuckles grazing her silk-clad mound. Finding her mouth with his, he kissed her deeply, his tongue stroking hers in rhythm with the brushing movements of his fingers. He could feel the damp heat of her behind the thin barrier of silk. Could imagine that slick wet softness opening for him, surrounding him.

Then her hands were freeing him, cupping him, her firm strokes sending restraint careening away. He withstood her teasing as long as he could, until the breath was strangling his lungs and his vision began to turn hazy. Then he stepped back, kicked out of his remaining clothes and reached for her again.

He tumbled her down onto the bed, pausing to appreciate the way the moonlight gave her skin an alabaster sheen. Her hands were greedy, her mouth demanding, as she drew him down to her. But he wasn't ready for this to be over. Not yet. Not until he'd tasted every inch of her. Explored all the curves and hollows where her scent lingered, her pulse throbbed.

The skin on her stomach was like satin. He moved his mouth over it, pausing to dip his tongue in the delicate swirls of her navel. He felt her muscles quiver as she guessed his intent. Felt the bite of her nails on his shoulders a moment before he pushed her panties over her hips and down her legs. He slid his hand up her satiny thighs and parted them.

"No, Cade." Her whisper was slightly panicked as he traced the seam where her leg met her hip with his tongue. "I don't want..." The rest of her words were lost as his mouth found her sensitive flesh and feasted.

He relished the low moan she released, the feel of her fingers sliding into his hair, tightening. The taste of her was liquid fire, and it called to something primal within him. He couldn't get enough of her. Couldn't taste enough. Touch enough. His tongue found the cluster of sensitive nerves hidden in her folds and her hips arched off the bed.

Yes, he thought savagely, as he heard the cries she made. This was what he'd wanted. The feel of her pressing closer to his mouth. The scent of her in his blood. Her flavor intoxicating his senses. He'd wanted to strip away every vestige of control she might cling to. To shred every defense until she was a mass of sensation, a creature driven by need.

He entered her with one finger, exploring her inner softness, as she twisted against him. His name on her lips fulfilled one need, summoned a hundred more. His hunger for her was ravenous, spiked with each tortured cry she gave, by the involuntary clenching and unclenching of her fingers. Her body bucked more and more rapidly beneath him, tightening, signaling her imminent release. And when it came, ripping a shattered cry from her throat, need slashed through him like a blade.

Lifting his head from her sated body, he reached blindly for the drawer on the table beside him. His movements were clumsy with pent-up hunger. It took longer than it should have to rip open the package.

Then Shae's hands were pushing his aside to roll the latex over his shaft. Cade closed his eyes as just that touch alone was nearly enough to send him hurtling over the edge.

It was too late to think of finesse. He pressed her back on the bed, made a place for himself between her thighs. When he paused there for a moment, desperately reaching for a control that seemed suddenly elusive, her hips arched, urging him on. He focused on her face as he entered her in tortuously slow increments. Her eyes went wide, then slid to half-mast, and she reached up, curled her hand around his nape, as her legs climbed his hips.

The position opened her to him in an invitation he was helpless to resist. He sank into her, burying himself as deeply as he was able, and fought to get air into his lungs.

She was tight, exquisitely so. He withdrew partway before giving a firm surge against her, burying himself deeply again. He wanted to watch her. Wanted to commit every change of expression to memory as he began to thrust into her with a slow heavy rhythm. But his own climax was rushing in on him, making restraint impossible. His pace quickened until he was pounding into her, her heels digging into his hips, her nails biting into his shoulders. And when his release came, in a sudden powerful explosion, he thought of nothing but her.

He lay there afterward, listening to her slow breathing, feeling his own return to a normal pace. His arm was draped over her waist, keeping her curled against him, his hand brushing lightly over the curve of her waist and hips. The night sky was studded with a million stars. He could see why she'd been reluctant to ruin this view with bars. It gave an illusion of freedom and of solitude. He knew Shae well enough to know that both were important to her.

Neither of them spoke, and he was content with the silence. His palm skated over the silky line of her back, feeling each vertebra, surprisingly delicate for a will so strong. And felt a sliver of peace, one that had been conspicuously absent for far too long.

He'd imagined all too often how it would be between them, all reckless need and explosive passion. But he would never have guessed at how easy it would be to hold her afterward. How right it would feel. And how quickly he could become accustomed to it.

He wasn't sure how long they stayed like that. Long enough to begin the gradual drift into slumber. He'd have sworn she already slept. Her voice, when it came, sounded like it. "I have an early day tomorrow. How about you?"

Fogged by sleep, his answer was slow in coming. "Not bad. The usual." She said nothing else, but something in her silence brought him alert.

Shae rolled away from him, sat up in bed. The lace-edged covers bunched around her waist, highlighting her femininity. She pushed her hair back over one shoulder and smiled at him. And he wondered exactly what it was in that smile that felt false. "I'll never make it through my shift if I don't get some sleep."

He leaned over to brush her mouth with his, lingered a moment. "You're kicking me out?"

Her hands slid to his chest, kneaded gently. "I have to."

Maybe it was only ego that had him imagining the tinge of regret in her voice. Maybe he needed to hear it there. Although it was the last thing he wanted, he threw back the covers, went in search of his clothes.

She accompanied him downstairs, wrapped in a filmy invitation of a robe, and while he finished dressing, she loaded the videos back into the box. She stuck a piece of tape on the one that had yielded the images of LeFrenz.

Sliding his arms into his jacket, he picked up his cell phone and put it in his pocket. Then he crossed to her, drew her into his arms and lowered his head to rub his mouth against hers. "Last chance," he murmured against her lips. "I'm not bad to wake up to and I make a mean omelette."

"I'll have to take your word for it." She gave his bottom lip a quick nip, then reached up to smooth the hair from his forehead. He could have told her the action was in vain. He'd never found a way yet to keep it tamed.

"Okay, then." Lingering wasn't going to strengthen his resolve, so he turned away and picked up the box. "Don't forget to call my cell if you need to." She nodded. "And set the alarm when I leave." Again she nodded, then reached for the door.

Something about her too-bright smile, her easy agreement, had his instincts heightening. Slowly he moved out into the hallway. "I'll call you to—" The door was already swinging closed after him.

And as he stood studying its raised panels, listening to the quiet snick of the lock engaging, he had the distinct impression that he had been neatly, efficiently dismissed.

# Chapter 11

Shae finished suturing the eleven-year-old boy she was treating and said, "There you go. You're going to have a real cool scar to show your friends."

"Awesome!" the boy said, bending his arm around, trying to see the stitches she'd put in it.

"Next time try wearing elbow pads and a helmet when you're skateboarding," she advised, picking up the clipboard with her patient's history on it.

"There won't be a next time if he doesn't," the boy's mother said.

"Oh, Mom."

Shae finished scribbling notes for his follow-up care and handed the sheets to the woman. "Bring him back in seven to ten days to have the stitches removed. Until then keep them dry and covered with a Band-Aid. Let us know if the wound gets puffy or red. That might indicate infection."

The woman rolled her eyes and nodded. "Believe me, with Evel Knievel here, I know the drill."

Shae smiled, checked the boy's history again. "Since he hasn't had a tetanus shot for a few years, we should probably give him one now."

"A shot?" The boy's earlier excitement melted into fear. "I hate shots."

Patting his shoulder, Shae walked by him and checked the drawers in the supply cabinet for some vaccine. "Not as much fun as stitches, I know, but that rusty wire you got caught on could do even more damage if we don't give you a shot to guard against it."

Finding no serum in the drawers, she excused herself and went to the door, leaving the woman to deal with her son's protests. "Jan." The head nurse was striding down the hallway. "I can't find any..." Her voice tapered off when she got a good look at the woman's harried expression. "What's wrong?"

"Wrong? Well, let's see. I've got three nurses out with the flu, another four I called can't cover because they have symptoms, and I'm starting to feel a bit nauseated myself." The woman bared her teeth. "Did you need something?"

The way she uttered the words sounded like a dare. Shae smiled in commiseration and held up her hands. "Nope. I can do it myself." Jan hurried on her way, muttering something about wishing the other doctors felt the same way, and Shae strode down the hallway to the drug closet.

She was waylaid by Tim Pearson, who fell into step with her. "We're going to be shorthanded today."

"I just got done speaking to Jan."

"Fowler and Kendall called in sick, too." He named

two of the E.R. doctors. "I can't promise we'll be able to let you go when your shift is over."

Shae nodded. "I can help out."

"Good. That's good. You don't have any plans that'll be screwed up, huh?" He continued walking alongside her.

Her brows arched. "Obviously not."

When it was evident she wasn't going to be more forthcoming, he said, "I just thought…you and that detective seemed to be getting kind of chummy. Tremaine."

"I'm not sure where you got that impression," she said coolly, neither confirming nor denying his statement. The truth was, it was none of his damn business, and both of them knew it.

He shrugged. "Hospital talk, you know. Didn't believe it, anyway. He's not your type. I can't see you dating a cop."

She stopped and stared at him, before saying, "Really? But then, you never did have a clue about what my 'type' was, did you, Tim?" The man flushed and turned, walking stiffly away. For once she hadn't used diplomacy when dealing with him and she didn't much care about the fallout. If the situation hadn't been so annoying, she would have been amused. What Tim had really meant was that he couldn't imagine her dating a cop after turning him down.

She squirmed inside at the thought of being the subject of any hospital gossip. Her private life was just that. And the thought that anyone had linked her to Cade made her uncomfortable on several levels.

*Chummy.* The word didn't begin to describe her relationship with Cade. It couldn't come close to applying to their interlude last night, when they'd nearly burned up in a scalding inferno of desire.

A shiver skated down her spine at the memory. She hadn't expected the experience to be so shattering. Hadn't expected it to affect her emotions as it had her senses.

And she'd certainly never believed it would be so difficult to send him away afterward.

Shae dismissed the errant thought. She'd done the right thing. The only thing. Her defenses had been constructed by design. And if they kept Cade Tremaine at a distance, as well—she shrugged off the pang that pierced her chest—then that was for the best in the long run. She wasn't a woman who believed in long-term relationships.

But a sly inner voice reminded her that it had been a long time since she'd needed to remind herself of that.

Stopping before the closet, she took a set of keys from her pocket and selected one. She fitted it into the lock and shoved the door open, then walked inside, stumbling to a halt as she realized two things. The light was already on and she wasn't alone in the space.

Recognition didn't come quickly enough to prevent reaction. One hand flew to her throat, and she couldn't prevent a startled gasp from escaping.

"Didn't mean to scare you, Doctor." Matt Brewer, one of the orderlies, gave her a reassuring smile. "Guess you weren't expecting anyone else to be here, huh?"

"No." It was maddening to discover that her heart hadn't settled back to a normal beat yet. And infuriating to realize that LeFrenz was the cause for her jumpiness. Brewer brushed by her, readying to leave, before comprehension kicked in.

"Matt?" He turned to look quizzically at her. "What were you doing in here?" Only medical personnel had keys to the drug cupboards, theft being a primary concern, and both the closet door and the cupboard door storing the drugs were kept locked.

He lookcd uncomfortable. "I don't want to get anyone in trouble."

"If you don't want to be the one in trouble, you'd better tell me."

He sent a quick glance at the door, as if contemplating escape. "The head nurse sent me in here to do the inventory. You know they're shorthanded and all." He shrugged, clearly ill at ease. "I was just helping her out."

Shae felt a quick surge of irritation. However pure the intention, the scenario was a minefield of legal and ethical implications. Jan had taken a huge risk sending an orderly on such an errand. And it was going to fall to Shae to tell her so.

Scowling, she unlocked the cupboard and withdrew the tetanus serum, wishing futilely that she'd sent the nurse after it so she could have avoided what promised to be an unpleasant encounter.

It was another hour before she sent her eleven-year-old patient on his way and then helped take care of the new patients that had come in. Seeing Jan stride by the exam room lit her memory, and Shae excused herself from her patient to step outside the room. "Jan? Can I have a word with you?"

The woman stopped, clearly impatient. "Yes?"

"In private?" Shae led her to the nearest lounge area and, finding it empty, picked out a corner where they wouldn't be overheard. "I know you're busier than usual today, but I think you'd be wise to consider the consequences before you cut corners," she began.

Jan shook her head. "What are you talking about?"

"Matt." When the nurse still looked uncomprehending, Shae went on, "I caught him in the drug closet taking inventory for you. You know better than to give your keys to an orderly."

"Matt Brewer?" Jan's dark eyes snapped with anger. "Why the heck would I let Matt Brewer take inventory for me? I'm shorthanded, not short brain cells."

Her vehement denial took Shae aback. For some reason it hadn't occurred to her to doubt the orderly's story. "He wasn't helping you out?"

Jan shook her head. "Are you crazy? I could lose my job for pulling a stunt like that. Did he really say I'd sent him there?"

Shae's tone was grim. "Yes, and the door was locked when I walked in on him, which means he has a key. You'd better check the inventory, see if anything is missing. Then let me know."

The woman heaved a sigh. "This is all I needed to make the day complete. I'll be right back." She hurried away.

Two patients and fifteen minutes later, Jan motioned Shae into the hallway. "I've got two bottles of Darvocet unaccounted for. Should I alert security?"

It was on the tip of Shae's tongue to say yes. Then a thought made her hesitate. "Not yet. Let me check into something first. Then I'll take care of it." She went in search of Tim. When she found him at the admissions desk, he didn't appear all that happy to see her. But when she told him what had occurred that morning, his expression turned serious. "I'll report it."

His hand went to the phone, but she stopped him. "Before you do, could you find out if Matt was working the night the prisoner escaped from I.C.U.?"

Tim stared at her, comprehension dawning in his expression. "That's quite a conclusion to jump to. From stealing drugs to killing a cop."

"The epinephrine was stolen from the E.R. drug closet. Matt has keys to it he shouldn't have. Not to mention the fact that the inventory is off since he was caught in there today.'' She worked her shoulders, not totally comfortable herself with what she was accusing the man of. "Maybe it's farfetched, but we owe it to that dead cop to check it out, don't we?"

Without another word, Tim dialed a number, spoke a few terse sentences, then waited. Moments later he hung up and punched in a new set of numbers, then said to Shae, "He wasn't scheduled to work that day, but he came in to cover for one of the other orderlies. I'm alerting security first, then administration."

Shae nodded shakily and moved away, drawing her cell phone from the pocket of her white coat. Tim could call security. She was calling Cade.

Josh Birtch walked to the window of the empty hospital office they were using and lifted the shade to look out. "I don't know, Matt, to me your story just doesn't seem to hold up. Does it to you, Tremaine?"

Cade shook his head, watched as the man they were questioning took out a cigarette with shaking hands and attempted to light it. Reaching forward, he flicked it away. "Trying to light up in a hospital? What are you thinking, Brewer?"

"C'mon, guys, cut me some slack." The orderly's face wore a light sheen of perspiration. "I lifted a couple bottles of pain medication, okay? Didn't think it was serious enough to bring in the cops."

"You have a cell phone, Matt?" Cade leaned back in his chair, watched Birtch roam the room. They'd agreed how to play this on the way over to the hospital. Light. Friendly. Guy-to-guy. The last thing they wanted to do was give the guy a reason to lawyer up before finding out what, if anything, he knew.

The question took the man by surprise. "Yeah. So?"

"Did you happen to leave it anywhere recently?" Birtch asked from the window. "Lose it, maybe?"

Brewer looked from one of them to the other. "No, it's in my locker here at the hospital. In my coat pocket. Is that why you guys are here? Someone lost a cell phone?"

"What's your cell number?" Cade asked. "Maybe we can get this whole thing cleared up right away." He slid a tablet of paper and a pen across the table to the man. "Write it down for me."

Brewer appeared eager to do just that, quickly jotting the digits down.

Cade reached for the tablet, glanced at it and then handed it to Birtch. The other detective pulled a sheet of paper from his pocket, unfolded it and began scanning the list. In a moment he looked up, caught Cade's gaze and nodded.

Tone hardening, Cade leaned toward the orderly. "I think we have a problem here, Matt. You were working the night Jonny LeFrenz was broken out of I.C.U., weren't you?"

Brewer stared at him. "Hey, what's a couple boosted bottles of pills got to do with that, huh? I already talked to some detectives about that. Everyone on shift that night did. They cleared me."

"No one was cleared," Cade corrected. "We just didn't have reason to talk to anyone again. Now we have reason to talk to you."

"What?" Brewer's gaze darted from side to side. "Why?"

"'Cause we're thinking you had reason to help your friend Jonny get out of here, Matt." Birtch strolled over, braced his palms on the table and shook his head pityingly. "Just your bad luck that a policeman was killed while you were doing it."

The man nearly came over the table. "No way! You can't prove that!"

"I'll tell you what we've got, Matt." Cade kept his voice matter-of-fact, hinting at none of the adrenaline spiking inside him. "We've got you at the hospital that night. Weren't even supposed to be working, were you, but you were here, anyway."

"I...a friend of mine was sick. I was just filling in for him. Nothing wrong with doing a favor for a friend."

"Is that what you did for LeFrenz that night? A favor?"

Sweat rolled down Brewer's face. "Not LeFrenz. Mason, another orderly. I filled in for him 'cause he wanted to go to a Saints game."

"But you didn't do a favor for LeFrenz?" Birtch questioned, his face close to Brewer's.

"No! I didn't even know the dude!"

Birtch slammed the table, making the man jump. "Then how come your cell phone number is listed in his book of contacts?"

The man looked dazed. "I don't know. I'm not...hey, do I need a lawyer here?"

The two detectives looked at each other. "Does he need a lawyer?" Josh asked.

Cade shrugged. "Beats me. We haven't taken him downtown." His gaze went back to Brewer. "You agreed to talk to us, right?"

"Is there something you're afraid to tell us?" Birtch asked. "'Cause maybe then you do need a lawyer."

"No, there's nothing like that," the man muttered.

"Look, I'll tell you what we're going to do," Cade told him, leaning back in his chair. "You play straight with us, tell us what we want to hear, and we'll write down that you were cooperative. That goes a long way when sentencing rolls around.''

''Sentencing?'' The man tried for a laugh and failed. ''Sentencing for what?''

Birtch looked at Cade. ''Accessory to murder?''

''Definitely. Aiding and abetting. Plus, my guess is he supplied the murder weapon. Could go down as the killer. I'm betting that's the way LeFrenz will tell it when we catch up with him.''

Brewer crossed his arms and tried for bravado. ''If you were going to catch LeFrenz, you'd have done it already.''

''Want to play those odds?'' Cade gave him a chilly smile. ''Maybe you think he'll leave your name out of it when he's cutting a deal with the D.A. He'll be facing the death sentence. You can't believe he won't use everything he's got to save himself.''

''You be the first to flip, Matt, and you get the best deal you can for yourself.'' Birtch sat on a corner of the table and lowered his voice persuasively. ''Spin the story your way and you might not do much time at all. You owed LeFrenz some favors, right? He was your dealer and he kept you supplied with anything you wanted. Maybe even handed out a freebie now and then, a goodwill gesture or something.''

Cade took over. ''Must have been a shock for you to find out he'd been put out of commission. Guy has a habit like yours, he can't afford to go without for long. Maybe you checked on him a couple times, just to get an idea of whether you needed to find yourself a new source.''

The orderly swallowed hard and said nothing, just looked down at the table. ''Maybe you didn't even know what he was planning,'' Birtch said. ''He asked you for a syringe full of stuff—hey, it's no big deal, right? You had no idea what he was planning.''

"That's right." The man pointed his finger at Birtch. "I had no idea. He never told me nothin' about why he needed it."

Cade sat back in his chair. "Just that he needed your help, right? So you should get yourself to the hospital that night and be available. You come up with the football tickets for your friend? Offer to work for him so he could go?"

Brewer swallowed. "I had no idea what Jonny was going to pull. And I sure wasn't the one to stab that needle into the guard's heart."

"Sure, we know how it went down. You got caught up in something bigger than you planned on." Birtch gave him a commiserating look. "You can write it up that way, too. Give your side of things. But first tell us how you got the guard in there. Who else helped? It wasn't just you and LeFrenz, was it?"

The man shook his head miserably. The shaking in his hands had increased dramatically. "Some other dude was in there when I came in. It was 1 a.m., just like Jonny said. I thought the guy was a doctor. He had I.D. clipped to his pocket."

The two detectives exchanged a glance. More than likely the I.D. had been fake. "Did you see his face?" Cade asked.

"He had operating scrubs on." The man gestured. "Had his hair covered up and a mask on his face. Covers over his shoes. All I could see was that he was a couple inches taller than me, had blue eyes and wore glasses."

Working in tandem, the two detectives drew out the rest of the details of that night. How Brewer had told the guard he was needed in the room. How the officer had pushed the door open to watch the two men pretend to work on LeFrenz. And when LeFrenz had acted as though he was going after the phony doctor, the guard rushed to the bed to help subdue him. Brewer had gone to close the door and the fake doctor had jabbed the syringe into the police officer's heart, killing him almost immediately.

"Did you hear the other man speak?"

Brewer nodded. "He's the one who told me to take Jonny out the way I'd told him…I mean, to take him down to the morgue entrance," he corrected himself. "He met me there with an ambulance, we loaded Jonny into it and he drove off."

"Would you recognize his voice if you heard it again?" Birtch asked.

The orderly shook his head. "His voice was muffled from the mask, and he was talking in whispers mostly."

"How about LeFrenz? Did he ever call the man by name?"

Brewer's limbs were trembling now. Cade wondered how long it'd been since the man had had a fix. He'd had to have been desperate to take a chance breaking into the drug closet today. "If he did, I didn't hear it."

After another half hour it became apparent that the man had nothing else to tell them, so they prepared to take him downtown. Pushing open the door, Cade saw Shae standing in the hall. He sent a quick glance to Birtch. "Put him in the car." The younger detective moved to do so, but not before taking a look at Shae, one long and thorough enough to have Cade narrowing his gaze at him.

She waited until they'd walked away to say, "Did Matt know anything about LeFrenz?"

"Your instincts were right on the money," he told her. "He helped with the escape that night."

She went pale. "Matt…helped kill that officer?"

"He supplied the drug. Helped smuggle LeFrenz out of the hospital." Cade went over and propped one shoulder against the wall, facing her. "He couldn't give us much help about the other guy helping LeFrenz."

Because it seemed too long since he'd last had the opportunity, he took his time studying her. She looked good. Her hair was pulled back with some sort of clip, and there were small gold rings in her earlobes. Until he noticed them, he hadn't considered the fact that he'd rarely seen her wear jewelry.

"You did the right thing to call me," he said, and gave her a friendly nudge. "You're getting pretty good at this detective stuff."

"Yes. Well." She looked discomfited by the compliment. "Was that your new partner who took Matt out?"

The term still didn't sit well with Cade. He wondered if it ever would again. "That's Detective Birch. He just graduated kindergarten."

That elicited a smile, a real one this time, not the strained, too-bright sample she'd given him last night as she'd ushered him out of her apartment. "He doesn't look much younger than you."

He shrugged uncomfortably. "He's a good cop." The words were true enough. They shouldn't have felt like a betrayal to Brian. "We're paired for the duration of this case."

She shoved her hands deep into the pockets of her lab coat, as if uncertain what to do with them. "We're short-handed here. I don't know when I'll get off."

"I'll tell the guys on detail to check in with you. I want you to ride home with them."

Shae nodded, but made no move to leave. "Will I see you tonight?"

He hadn't expected the question, but then, he never really knew what to expect from the woman. She was a mass of contradictions and it would take a lifetime to unsnarl them all. He'd always been a sucker for a puzzle. He was beginning to think that when it came to her, he was just a sucker, period. "I'm not sure. I've got another engagement and I don't know how long it'll take."

Something flickered in her eyes, as fleeting as it was intriguing. Her voice was stilted when she said, "Of course. I'll talk to you later, then."

She turned to walk toward the elevator, and he stopped her with one hand on her elbow. "If it's not too late, I'll call you tonight."

Her gaze dropped to his hand, then raised to his face. And her voice had warmed several degrees when she said, "Call me either way."

The sign outside advertised restaurant/bar, but it looked like a typical yuppie place to Cade. He shoved open the door of the establishment and felt instantly ill at ease. It was the kind of place you'd maybe bring a date, or the wife and kids. It wasn't the sort of place you met a guy for drinks, even when you were only pretending the meeting was cordial. He suspected Morrison had chosen the place on purpose.

He saw the man sitting at a small table in a corner of the bar area and brushed by the hostess when she would have led him to a seat. Cade was hoping he wouldn't be here long enough to have to pretend to choke food down. There was a limit to his acting ability.

"Tremaine." Morrison waved him to the seat opposite his and slid a complimentary basket of popcorn at him. A perky waitress met him at the table. "What are you drinking?"

"Miller Lite, bottle." He waited for the woman to move away before looking around. "Nice place. I've never been here before." And would never have chosen to come here, had it been up to him. The place featured polished oak, brass and hanging baskets of ferns. Cade had never trusted a bar that had live plants in it. How the hell did they keep them alive in the dark interior? And if they were fake, what was the point?

"I come here a lot," Morrison said. "At least I used to when my wife was alive."

The statement elicited an unwanted thread of sympathy. "I'm sorry."

The other man lifted a beefy shoulder, his gaze on his bottle. "Cancer. What are you gonna do, right?"

Since there seemed no real answer to the question, Cade directed his attention to the waitress headed toward them balancing his lone beer on a large tray. He imagined it would have been simpler just to deliver it by hand, but he suspected he just had a bad attitude tonight, anticipating the distasteful scene ahead of him.

He tilted his bottle toward the man across from him in a silent salute, before tipping it to his lips.

"So." The Internal Affairs detective studied him. "I thought we'd have to force things with your lieutenant to finish the meeting that was interrupted last time."

"The lieutenant has been on my case about getting it done," Cade lied. He'd told Howard exactly what he was planning and gotten the man's blessing. "But it probably won't shock you that I wasn't in a hurry to meet with your sidekick again."

Morrison gave a shrug. "Torley's not so bad."

"He's an ass." The statement might be the only one he uttered here tonight that was perfectly honest. "So I figured, if I could meet with just you—away from headquarters—we could get this thing over."

"I've said all along that we don't have to be adversaries." The I.A. detective paused to sip his draft. "I'm aware of my partner's faults. I like the guy well enough, but I know what he is. I wonder if you can say the same about your ex-partner.''

Cade's beer was suddenly difficult to swallow. "I knew Brian as well as anyone.''

"But you didn't know what he was up to.''

Setting the bottle down on the table, Cade looked the other man square in the eye. "See the thing is, you haven't convinced me that he was up to anything. You've thrown out lots of innuendoes and allegations, but I haven't seen anything that comes close to evidence.''

The man's eyes went shrewd. "You're not the person we need to show evidence to.''

Cade shrugged, took another swallow.

When he stayed silent, Morrison said, "We had a warrant for his car, his house and his bank records. You think they just give those things out with nothing to go on?''

Running his thumbnail under the label on his beer, Cade countered, "There's a lot of back-scratching that goes on in this town. No telling who owed you a favor.''

The other man shook his head as if in disgust. "You don't want to see what's right in front of you.''

Leaning forward, Cade said, "No, you're the one who doesn't see. Brian was like a brother to me. You got a brother, right?''

Morrison nodded, belched. "I hate his guts. But I see where you're going with this. That's nice for you, that you and your partner were so close and all. But you and your brothers, I mean your real brothers, well, you're all on a whole different financial plane from ol' Brian, aren't you?''

The personal shift in the conversation blindsided Cade. "What are you getting at?''

"I mean, you boys were born rich. Your sister, too, I

guess. Silver spoon in your mouths and all that. It could begin to gnaw on a man who wasn't born that fortunate.'' Morrison smiled, revealed a chipped incisor. ''Brotherly feelings or not.''

For a moment it was difficult to remember just why he'd thought Morrison was the least offensive of the two IA agents. Cade wanted nothing more than to plow his fist into the man's square face. Instead, he clenched his jaw and muttered, ''I guess.''

''No guessing about it. You can't imagine what it's like to want more, since you've always had plenty. Hell, your family probably spends more on hiring people to manage their money than most of us make in a year.''

''Yeah, well, none of this has anything to do with Brian.'' Cade didn't have to manufacture the note of stubbornness in his voice.

''No?'' Morrison withdrew a slim folder from his breast pocket and slid it across the table. A bank book. ''You might be interested to know that we found this in our search of your buddy's place. It was buried at the bottom of his toolbox in the garage. Either he's been having a lot of bake sales or he was into something dirty—up to his neck. He was putting away some nice-size payments pretty regularly.''

Cade stared at the book, strangely reluctant to pick it up. It didn't matter what was in there, he thought. Wouldn't matter. He knew Brian. Knew what he was capable of. And what he wasn't.

He saw his hand reach out as if disconnected from his body pick up the book, flip it open. Saw Brian's name, what looked like his signature.

And saw the weekly payment entries. Nine of them.

As if it singed his fingers, he dropped the bank book

on the table. "Anyone could have planted that book there. Anyone could have made the deposits."

Morrison pursed his lips, nodded as if in agreement, and reached for some popcorn. "But anyone didn't. Hollister did. Bank camera caught him on film in the bank lobby on at least two occasions. And guess what? Both times he was with his pal, Freddie." He tossed the kernels in his mouth, munched loudly. "Guess he was more than a snitch, after all, huh?"

It was like taking a fist in the solar plexus. There was a roaring in Cade's ears. A vise tightening in his chest. There had to be another explanation. Everything Morrison had shared was circumstantial. Damning, but not absolute proof.

But it was more proof than Cade had expected to face.

Aware that the other man was looking for a reaction, he gave him one. "This isn't…I don't know." Jamming his hand in his hair, he gave a credible impression of someone who'd just had the rug pulled out from beneath him. "I wasn't expecting this. I didn't…" He drew in a deep breath. "I can't believe it."

The I.A. agent picked up the bank book and tucked it back into his pocket. "Hey, I'm not a total jerk. I feel for you. Has to be a shock to discover the guy you thought you knew was running dirt right beneath your nose."

Below the table, Cade's hand fisted. "Yeah. A shock."

"I could get my ass in a sling for telling you this much, you know," Morrison paused, as if waiting for Cade to thank him. Fat chance. "But I figured you for a stand-up guy. Just sticking up for a friend he believes in. Now that you know—" he shrugged, washed some popcorn down with a swallow of beer "—things might look different."

Cade shook his head as if dazed. "You put a whole new light on things and everything changes, you know?

You start to rethink things you saw, what you heard…''
He let his words taper off.

"Exactly." Morrison leaned forward, genial exterior
gone for the moment. In its place was a hard-nosed cop
moving in for the kill. "All I'm asking is for you to rethink things Hollister might have said or done. Given this
new light on things, your interpretation of events could be
totally different."

Cade pushed his half-full bottle away. He didn't have
to feign a sudden distaste for it. "I'll need some time."

"You do that. Then call me." Morrison slid a card
across the table, and Cade made himself pick it up. Look
at it. It had the I.A. detective's numbers listed on it. "Why
don't you give me a call in a few days?"

Nodding, Cade rose and strode away, the image of a
man anxious to escape the truth. Or run from it.

The air outside seemed fresher somehow, and Cade
hauled as much as he could into his lungs. He needed to
clear his head. To shake the doubts that had crept in like
sly thieves in the night. When emotion had receded, he'd
be able to think more clearly. Be able to figure out an
explanation for everything Morrison had told him. Everything he'd seen for himself.

Head down, he went toward the parking lot where he'd
left his car and heard his name called behind him.

"Hey! Tremaine, right?"

Cade looked up, recognized the task force detective that
had taken over his and Brian's case. Quentin. "Yeah. Hi."
Although he wasn't in the mood for conversation, he
waited for the man to reach him.

"I thought that was you in the restaurant. I was getting
ready to leave about the same time you walked out." He
made a face. "Lady stood me up. Again. Don't know why
I put up with her."

"Any news on the case?"

Quentin fell into step beside him. "Well, you were right about Reggau. He's moved up on the food chain, but he isn't big enough to be the guy you were after. I still like Davies, though. My men are starting to get some real interesting stuff on him. Think he could be our guy."

Cade unlocked his car with the remote. "Hope you catch up with him soon, then."

"Hey." There was an oddly tentative note in the man's voice, stopping Cade as he was about to open the door and climb in the car. "Inside...I couldn't help but see you were with Morrison."

Instantly wary, Cade responded, "Yeah. So?"

There was a flicker of sympathy in the man's dark eyes. "So I figure he ran his half-assed theory by you."

Leaning against the car, Cade folded his arms across his chest. "Which one would that be?"

"That Hollister had set up the meeting at City Park that night with the intention of having you killed." He shook his head in disgust, missing the frozen expression on Cade's face. "Those I.A. pricks have some imagination, huh?"

"Yeah." Cade's head was reeling. "Some imagination."

"Listen." The man looked around, lowered his voice. "I don't have any more love for I.A. than the next guy, so I thought I'd give you a head's up. From my conversation with them, I think Torley's the one whose holding on to that scenario. But Morrison in there, he's a real piece of work. He doesn't think Hollister was alone in this. So watch your back, man. Word is, the job is looking at you, too."

# Chapter 12

Shae opened her door to find Cade leaning against the jamb. His smile was lopsided. "I decided not to call."

"I noticed." She let him in, noting the weariness in the set of his shoulders. It had been a surprise to hear his voice on the intercom. And even more of a surprise to feel the quick flutter of pleasure at his unexpected visit.

Under normal circumstances her reaction would worry her, but right now she was more concerned about him. She'd grown used to seeing exhaustion in his expression. But this time there was more than lack of sleep responsible. He looked discouraged, and more than a little disillusioned.

He'd walked halfway into her apartment, then stood in place, as if wondering what he was doing there. She was beginning to wonder the same thing. "Any news on the case?" For a moment she thought he had bad news to share and was grappling with a way to word it. But he looked startled at her question, and she relaxed muscles she hadn't realized had gone tense waiting for him to answer.

"No. We've got a list we're following up on with the partial plate number. Something should kick on that soon."

Because he looked a little too lost standing there, a little too vulnerable, she went to him and subtly guided him to the couch. Whatever it was that was bothering him, he'd tell her when he was ready. He shrugged out of his jacket and tossed it over the back of the couch before sinking down in its cushions. But when she was about to sit beside him, he tugged her down onto his lap, burying his face into her hair.

Shock held her immobile. There was nothing sexual in his touch; that she would have been able to handle. It was comfort he was seeking, and she wasn't used to dispensing comfort, at least not in her personal life. Tentatively one arm went up to rest lightly on his shoulders. His heart thudded in her ear, solid and dependable.

She'd never been a lap sitter. But she could get used to the feel of Cade's arms around her holding her tightly, as if he drew solace from having her close. And though the simple pleasure she derived from the contact was just short of terrifying, she could give him this. He appeared to need it.

It was a long time before he spoke, and when he did his voice was quiet. Contemplative. "Did you ever think you knew someone so well that nothing he did could surprise you? Then find out he had this whole different life, a side to him you never would have believed possible?"

Immediately her thoughts went to Liam. The baby brother she'd watched out for. Believed in absolutely. She'd seen in him exactly what she wanted to see. And she was still devastated by the fact that she hadn't known him at all. "Yes." Her voice was as quiet as his.

Her agreement didn't seem to surprise him. His arms just tightened around her. "Internal Affairs has been investigating my late partner. They've been talking a lot of dirt about him, all of it, I figured, without solid proof. That he was taking money from the very scum we work to put away. That maybe he wanted me dead so I wouldn't find out." She jerked at that, she couldn't help it. She knew how he felt about the man he'd partnered with. If it turned out that he was responsible for Cade's near death, she wondered how he would bear it.

"In my family home there's a crest that hangs over the front door as you enter. As long as I can remember, the Tremaines have lived by the words on it. Honor. Duty. Devotion. Old-fashioned, I guess, but there you go."

It was, Shae thought, more than old-fashioned. It was completely outside her realm of experience. Her father had lacked all three traits. Would never consider the lack a failure.

"There comes a time when you have to wonder where loyalty leaves off and naïveté begins." He stroked a hand over her back, to the base and back up again. "I don't know if I hate myself more for having doubts or for not being able to refute them."

It was hard not to ache at the baffled sadness in his voice. Hard not to want to soothe the regret from his face. And because she wanted, badly, to do both, she found herself sharing far more than she ever had before. "Liam, my brother, is in prison." The words were difficult to voice. More difficult to hear. "When I heard he'd been arrested, I was indignant. Terrified for him, but full of righteous rage that such an obvious mistake had been made. I bailed him out, hired him an expensive attorney and threw myself into proving his innocence. Because I was convinced of it, you see. And he never said anything to disabuse me."

She could see quite clearly now that he'd been afraid to. Ashamed. "So we spent months putting together a defense, and I wouldn't allow the lawyer to even talk about a plea bargain. Then we went to court." She remembered the feeling exactly. Having illusions stripped away, one at a time, each with a quick vicious yank that left its own wound. "The evidence was so damning. The detective on the stand kept talking, and every word he said built this wall of evidence that just kept going higher and higher. But still I didn't quite believe it. Not until I looked across the room and saw that Liam couldn't meet my eyes. Then I knew."

It had been too late by that time, of course. Too late for a deal or to mount an argument based on his lack of priors. His plea of innocence in the face of such overwhelming proof smacked of a complete lack of remorse. The ambitious prosecutor had asked for, and received, the stiffest sentence possible.

"Then I expect you know how I feel about the evidence I saw against Brian." His voice was grim, regretful. "I still can't believe it. I can't ignore it. And I'm having a hell of a time explaining it. But I want to. God, do I want to."

She tipped her head to look directly at him. "If the proof exists, you'll find it." She was certain of that. She'd never met a man more tenacious. And if proof didn't exist...well, he'd learn to live with that, just as she had. To readjust what he thought he knew about his partner and continue to love the best part of him.

The softness in his eyes as he studied her had her pulse thrumming. Her inner alarm shrilling. Now was the time to discreetly disentangle and send him on his way. Before more vulnerabilities could be exposed. Before weaknesses could be exploited.

But it didn't feel like weakness when her lips parted under his. Didn't feel like a mistake to exchange a kiss as soft as gossamer, so achingly tender that her limbs threatened to melt in a gooey puddle right there in his arms. Somewhere in the distance was a ringing sound. She traced the seam of his lips with the tip of her tongue and let herself drift in the languid lazy pleasure of it.

A moment later Cade was pulling away to cock his head. "Is that your phone?"

Their gazes met. Comprehension returned sluggishly. Shae struggled to her feet, would have stumbled if Cade hadn't steadied her. On legs that were a little too wobbly for her liking, she crossed to the phone on the kitchen counter. Pride demanded that her spine be a little straighter, that her mind be a little less fuzzy. But she hadn't accomplished either by the time she picked up the receiver.

"Angel Eyes."

Blood that had slowed and thickened only moments before abruptly chilled. Shae tried to swallow, found she couldn't. Her gaze went to the man who'd risen from the couch. "Jonny."

Cade's expression transformed with stunning suddenness. Gone was the disillusioned friend, the tender lover. The grim-faced cop was back.

"I been thinkin' about you, Doc." Cade had already taken the cell phone from his jacket. He was talking quietly into it as he took the stairs two at a time to her bedroom and the second phone. His action brought her a measure of calm.

"I've been thinking about you, too. Wondering where

you were." That, at least, was the truth. "When are we going to meet?" Cade was coming back down the stairs with the other phone, and he glared at her from across the room, violently shaking his head.

"Soon." LeFrenz crooned the word. "Won't be much longer now. I got things to take care of first. Business before pleasure, ya know what I mean?"

"Sure, I know. How's the injury coming?"

"Healin' real good. Ain't gonna slow me down when you and me get together. Don't worry about that."

She took a deep breath. "You wait much longer and we're not going to get together at all." Cade's eyes narrowed dangerously as he strode toward her, still holding both phones.

Deliberately she said, "I've got a vacation planned in a few days. I won't be around for a while."

It was all too easy to read the words Cade mouthed at her. *What the hell do you think you're doing?* But she knew exactly what she was doing. She was bringing things to a head. She was taking control of her life again, whether he approved of the way she did it or not.

It was apparent from the fury on his face that he didn't approve at all.

"In that case I'll have to work something out, Angel Eyes. I'll be seeing you real soon. Until then you give Tremaine a message for me."

Her heart stopped. She stared up at Cade, eyes wide. "Tremaine?"

"I know he's been around. Seen him go into your place a time or two. Didn't much like to think about you two together." LeFrenz's voice was ugly. "You tell him next time he comes round that I'll be seein' him, too. And he's going to pay. For everything."

The line disconnected. Cade turned away to speak into

the cell phone. "What's the address?" He listened for a moment, then ran for the door.

"Wait." She followed him, saw him race down the hallway.

"Lock your door!" he ordered over his shoulder. "And stay put!"

Cade's car screeched to a halt outside a crowded blues bar on Bourbon Street, the auxiliary light flashing on his dash. The street was crowded with black-and-whites and rubber-neckers. He elbowed his way through the people, flashed his shield at the uniform attempting to do crowd control.

"They chased your man down the street there, Detective."

Cade jogged in the direction the man had pointed until he saw a cluster of officers from his district. He began cursing, savagely. If there was good news to report, they wouldn't all be standing around. "How'd he get away?" he asked flatly, walking up to the group.

Josh Birtch spoke. "Couple of patrolmen were in the vicinity and were first on the scene. I was next, along with Pascan and Pearce. When LeFrenz saw the patrolmen he ran into a tour group." He made an expression of disgust. "They lost him in the crowd."

Cade looked around. It didn't matter the time, the day or the season. Bourbon Street, a tourist mecca, was in a constant state of revelry. Ghost tours, graveyard tours, voodoo tours…LeFrenz couldn't have chosen a better place to disappear.

He heaved a sigh. "Canvass started?" Birtch nodded. "Okay. Let's split up."

With the disappointment of the previous night still burning a hole in his gut, Cade pulled up outside Security

First Federal and parked in the bank's lot. The tap and trace had worked beautifully. The phone company had gotten them the number in record time. And still somehow LeFrenz had managed to slip away. They'd canvassed the area until near dawn and came up with people who'd seen LeFrenz, but not where he'd gone. Cade was beginning to believe the guy lived a charmed life. But not for long.

Because he was going after Shae. Cade shook out a couple of photos from the envelope on the seat next to him and got out of the car. He'd known what she was doing last night, and if he'd had the time, he would have given her the hell she deserved. She'd been inciting the man to act. Sooner, rather than later. When he'd heard her words, his blood had turned to ice. This case was going to be solved without using Shae as bait. He didn't even want to think about LeFrenz getting that close to her and was going to do his damnedest to prevent it.

Pushing open the bank doors, he surveyed the area carefully. A half-dozen tellers were open. He glanced up at the ceiling, found the cameras spotting the area. The same cameras that Morrison claimed had caught Brian on tape.

He headed to the teller closest to him, intending to work himself down the counter. His meeting with Morrison had had an unintended advantage. He could openly do some checking on the evidence the man had shown him. And he couldn't prevent the stubborn ray of hope that he was going to discover something that would clear his partner, a hope that survived despite the cloud of doubts.

"Can I help you, sir?" The teller was young and had a polite smile. Cade flashed his shield and pulled a picture of Brian from his pocket. He slid it across the counter toward her. Before he could say anything, she looked at it and nodded. "Oh, yes. I remember him."

A swipe to the jaw would have been easier to bear. "You do?"

She nodded. "The other detectives that were here? They showed pictures of this man, too."

Cade took a deep breath, released it. "Do you remember ever waiting on him?"

She shook her head firmly. "No, and I told them that."

He thanked her and went to the next line, waiting his turn to play the same scene with that teller. And then the next. And the next. By the time he'd talked to all the tellers, instinct was stirring. How was it possible that no one remembered waiting on Brian?

It was such a small thing, he reflected, heading back to the car, to raise his spirits once more. Apparently it didn't take much for hope to elbow aside those pesky doubts.

At Lieutenant Howard's invitation, Cade pushed open the man's office door with barely concealed impatience. His superior looked up from the paperwork spread on his desk and scowled. "You better have a damn good excuse for missing the meeting this morning."

The session with LeFrenz's investigative team. By going to the bank first thing, Cade had known he'd miss it, but had figured it would be easier to ask forgiveness than permission. "You can catch me up." The scowl turned thunderous. Cade pushed a chair up closer to the man's desk and dropped into it. "I had a little talk with Morrison last night. Before the LeFrenz thing broke."

Howard's expression lightened. Cade wasn't off the hook yet, but it was a start. "And?"

"So I played it like we talked about. Got him to meet me without Torley, and he laid out some of what they've got on Brian. He showed me a bank book with cash deposits."

"See a signature?"

"It looked like Brian's," Cade admitted. "Morrison claimed they found it in his garage. Said they caught him on camera in the bank lobby."

Rubbing a hand over his forehead, the lieutenant said morosely, "Well, I knew they had to have something to go on. Damn."

"Listen, though. I went to the bank this morning and showed pictures of him around, and get this. No one remembers him. Oh, sure, they remember I.A. flashing pictures, but not one teller could say she'd ever waited on him."

The lieutenant dropped his pen and clasped his hands on his desk. "Cade," he said gently, "there comes a time when even we have to look at the evidence."

Stunned, Cade stared at the man. "Haven't you heard a thing I've been saying? No one saw him there. There's not one eye-witness account. Morrison even said the camera caught him in the lobby. Not in a teller line, in the lobby. They have one of those desks set up in the center of the place that they staff with one of those perky older ladies with fancy hair and perfect teeth?" The woman had reminded him of his great-aunt Edith without the facelift. "It's their job to direct customers, offer coffee—she never saw him, either. Never talked to him." Cade could see he wasn't convincing the lieutenant. The man couldn't seem to look at him.

Leaning forward, Cade braced his hands on his superior's desk. "I stood there and watched the woman for fifteen minutes. If they get within twenty feet of her desk, she's talking to them. But if someone just walks in through the doors, stays by the windows, they'd be caught on one of the cameras." Lieutenant Howard looked up finally, contemplated him.

"I talked to the gal in charge of opening new accounts, too. According to the dates in the bank book Morrison showed me, there were nine transactions dating a couple months before Brian's death. But she didn't remember waiting on him, either. Neither did any of the tellers in the drive-up line."

"Exactly what are you suggesting?"

"That the book was planted. That the deposits were set up to make Brian look dirty. Hell, anyone with a copy of his signature could do a decent job duplicating it."

"And this same person went to the trouble of having identification made with Brian's name on it so that they could open an account there?"

Recognizing the disbelief in the man's voice, Cade crossed his arms. "It could happen."

"Then tell me why. Why would someone go to that trouble? Better yet, tell me who. You don't think I.A. planted that evidence, do you? What reason would they have?"

"I don't have it all figured out yet," Cade admitted.

Howard folded his arms on his desk and leaned forward. "I know what Hollister meant to you. What he meant to this squad. But none of this helps clear him. You see that, don't you? It doesn't look good for him at all."

Cade knew how it looked. Last night he'd battled those same doubts. The kind that swirled up from the bottom of the mind like a nasty little fog, obscuring everything he'd once been certain of. But today was different. Something about this whole thing didn't add up. Cade didn't know how to make the lieutenant see that.

"Brian was a smart guy, wouldn't you agree?"

Howard shoved away from the desk in apparent disgust.

"With all the cases he worked," Cade went on, "drugs especially, he knew a hell of a lot about laundering dirty money. Doesn't it strike you the slightest bit odd that he'd waltz right into a busy bank complete with security cameras and plop the extra dough there?''

''I know what you're saying.'' The patience in Howard's voice was difficult to take, but not as difficult as the note of sympathy. ''Keep looking into it, if you want. Just don't…don't bring any I.A. attention on yourself in the process.''

Cade's gaze met his superior's. The man's words reminded him for a moment of Quentin's warning last night. *The job is looking at you, too.* If the narcotics task-force officer was right, the lieutenant's warning came much too late.

He felt a slice of disappointment at the knowledge that he'd failed to convince his lieutenant of all the holes in I.A.'s case. But he hadn't been told to stop nosing around in it. He'd take what he could get for now. ''Any sighting of LeFrenz since last night?'' he asked.

Howard shook his head in disgust. ''Guy's like a ghost. But we're working down the lists for the plates, his cell phone and the contacts in his notebook. Here's yours.'' Cade took the paper the man held out, looked at it. ''Birtch has been waiting for you. Take him along.''

Recognizing his dismissal, Cade turned to go. He got to the door before Howard's voice stopped him. ''Tremaine?''

Cade looked at him.

''I hope you're right about Hollister. I really do.''

Nodding, Cade left. It was going to take a helluva lot more than luck to get the proof he'd need to offset the evidence I.A. had against Brian. And more than a little luck to find it.

Shae answered the intercom, a smile playing around her mouth when she recognized Cade's voice. ''Forgotten how to use a telephone, Detective?''

''You should be more polite to a guy intent on feeding you.'' His voice was amused, a teasing note alive in it.

''If you're holding a pizza, I'll buzz you up.''

''I'm not, so you better come down. We'll go out and find one.''

''Hmm. I'm not in the habit of going out with every strange guy who rings my buzzer.''

''I'm not all that strange, am I, kid?''

Shae could hear TeKayla's giggle in the background. She must be playing on the stoop again. Shae grabbed her jacket and purse and let herself out of her apartment. What she'd told Cade wasn't the complete truth. She didn't make it a habit of going out with many men, whether they promised to feed her or not. She didn't want to consider what made her change her routine now. Didn't want to admit that the reason was Cade himself.

When she got outside, she found man and child sitting on the steps, telling knock-knock jokes. ''Careful,'' she told Cade, closing the door behind her. ''She can keep that up for hours.''

''Yeah?'' Cade cocked an eyebrow at the girl, who nodded vigorously. ''Well, I'm all out, so I'll have to get some new ones before I come back next time.''

Lingering on the steps, Shae asked, ''Is your mom home?''

TeKayla shook her head. ''She's workin'.''

Shae stifled a sigh. The girl was too young to be left unsupervised, especially outside. ''Then I think you should go back into your apartment and wait for her, okay?'' A thought occurred then, and she sent a quick glance at Cade. ''I know we were supposed to go to the gator farm this weekend, but—''

"I can't wait!" The girl bounced on the step, her pig-tails jiggling. "I been drawing alligators and crocodiles at school and I told all my friends I was going, too."

Shae's stomach rolled. Squatting down, she looked into the girl's face. "You know I want to take you, but something's come up and I can't do it this weekend. But we will go another time."

The little girl's lip jutted out. "But you promised."

"I didn't…" Shae stopped. The girl wasn't going to understand her verbal gymnastics. To a child, any intention stated by an adult was a promise. And if the child was very lucky, she or he never learned the disappointment that came from believing too deeply in someone else. "I will still take you. Just not this weekend."

"When?"

Shae looked helplessly at Cade. "As soon as I can." It was the best she could do, but it wasn't enough to wipe the crestfallen expression from the girl's face or erase the disappointment from her eyes. Without another word, TeKayla stood, walked dejectedly up the steps and went into the building. Leaving Shae fighting memories of her own childhood that still had teeth.

Her father had been full of promises. Shae rounded the car and got in silently. Each time he'd come home bearing presents and glittering stories of the places he'd been, the things he'd done. But Shae had hung back. The house would be full of excitement as her mother and brother would clamor for his attention. She'd always wondered why they opened themselves up for that time after time. Allowing the man close enough to raise hopes, to spin dreams. Hadn't they known how painful the reality would be when he disappeared again?

Cade pulled away from the curb. "She'll be okay. Kids are resilient."

"No," she murmured. "That's what people think. But sometimes they're not." Given enough disappointment over a long enough time, and some stopped believing. Stopped expecting. And started to erect defenses that would prevent hope from ever taking root again.

Cade glanced at her oddly. "I'm sure by tomorrow she'll be—" His cell phone rang, and he used his free hand to withdraw it from his coat pocket.

"Carla." It was the warmth in his voice that caught Shae's attention, not the name of another woman. Curiously she listened to his side of the conversation, which ended with Cade promising to call her later that week.

"Brian's widow," he said by way of explanation. He wore a slight frown. "She's been staying with her folks for a while, but her boys are getting to be too much of a handful there. She's thinking about bringing them home."

"Sounded like you were trying to convince her otherwise."

"I'd rather she stay put for a while. This whole I.A. thing hasn't run its course yet. And once she's back in town I'm afraid they'll be badgering her again."

Shae felt a flash of sympathy for the unknown woman. "Maybe there's somewhere else she could go."

He thought for a moment before shaking his head. "Brian's folks retired to Arizona, and I don't think she wants to go that far. Her dad has a cabin on one of the bayous, but it's not exactly Carla's favorite place." Brian had liked to go there. The memory was unaccompanied by a pang. He'd always said a weekend spent there fishing and catching crawdads with the boys was better than taking a week's vacation.

The memory clicked like a shifting gear. *Brian had liked to go to the cabin.* Had even taken Cade once. And it was fairly close to the city. Questions flooded his mind, and he knew he wouldn't rest until he got some answers. He skated a glance to the woman at his side. "How do you feel about taking a road trip?"

"Well, that was an adventure." Shae gamely shook off the effects of the airboat ride and accepted his help onto the dock. "Something tells me there isn't a pizza place around here, either."

The driver of the boat cackled. "I could find ya a place that serves a mean gator stew, if that's to your liking."

Despite the darkness, Cade was certain he saw Shae pale. "Don't tell me. It tastes just like chicken."

The man laughed again and Cade leaned down with a folded bill in his hand. The driver backed away. "Forget it, man. I brought the guy and his family out here more times than I can count."

Cade nodded. "I appreciate it. This might take a half hour or so."

The driver shrugged and slouched down in one of the seats. "I'll be waiting."

Taking Shae by the elbow, Cade guided her down the dock to the small cabin ahead. Using touch alone, he felt above the doorjamb for the key Carla had assured him was still kept there.

He'd had to call her back to get information about how to get here and who to contact to boat them over here. It had been difficult to field her questions when he had more questions than answers himself. He just hoped he wasn't raising the widow's expectations, only to have to dash them later.

He hoped he wasn't raising his own.

Pushing open the door, he found the battery-operated lantern on a small table right over the threshold, exactly where Carla had told him he would. Flipping it on, he and

Shae went around turning on all the other lanterns until the small area was filled with light.

"Cozy," Shae said, looking around.

*Rustic* was the word Cade would have used. There was a wooden stove with a portable kerosene one sitting atop it. A round woven rug sat in front of an overstuffed sofa, flanked by a couple of rockers. All were situated before the native-stone fireplace. A small table and chairs were tucked into one corner of the room. If memory served, a postage-stamp-size bedroom completed the building, with an outhouse in back.

"Tell me again, what are we looking for?"

"Anything that looks like it shouldn't be here." It was the best he could do. She immediately went to the cupboards above the stove while he checked in the bedroom. When he came out minutes later, she had the cushions off the couch, the covers unzipped and her hands inside.

Dropping to his hands and knees, he went over the floorboards, looking for a loose one. He almost hoped he wouldn't find one. God knew what lived under the floors as close to the swamp as this place was.

Fifteen minutes later he was willing to admit the floor was solid. His gaze landed on the fireplace. "Come and help me with this, will you?"

Shae joined him. "What are we doing?"

"Checking to see if any of the stones are loose." While she complied, he got down on his back and squinted up into the chimney.

"Find Santa up there?" she inquired.

Because he could reach her, he nudged her with his foot. "Can't see a damn thing. Bring me one of those smaller lanterns, will you?" While he waited, he reached for one of the pokers sitting beside the fireplace. She placed the lantern in his other hand.

Setting the lantern inside the fireplace, he ran the poker along the inside. The facing was rough, with a small ledge around the inside about two feet up as the chimney narrowed. It was this ledge he directed his attention to now.

And was rewarded when a manila envelope, soiled with dirt, dropped to land beside the lantern.

Shae kneeled beside him. "What is it?"

Edging out of the fireplace, Cade sat up, the envelope clutched in his hand. A locomotive was racing through his chest, making it difficult to breathe. If he could have spoken, he'd have told her that it was probably an answer to all his questions about Brian's death.

And holding it in his hand, not being able to guess at the contents, he was more terrified than he'd ever been in his life.

# Chapter 13

Shae had known something was very wrong when Cade had insisted she get in the driver's seat once they'd returned to the car. She looked from the keys he'd pressed into her hand to him. "Are you sure?" she asked dubiously.

"Yeah. If you drive, I'll be able to take a look at what's inside this." He'd indicated the envelope he still clutched in his hand.

But it had taken him a full half hour to reach up to turn on the interior light. They'd hit the city limits before he undid the clasp on the envelope. She didn't think it was her imagination that his hand trembled slightly.

Shae's mind flashed back to something he'd said the previous night. *I don't know if I hate myself more for having doubts or for not being able to refute them.* She hoped, for his sake, that the papers in his hands would put his doubts to rest once and for all.

Because she didn't want to disturb him, she drove the

powerful sports car around the city aimlessly, waiting on tenterhooks for Cade to speak. Caring, more than she should have, what he would say.

When he finally lifted his head, she could restrain herself no longer. "What'd you find?"

"Secrets," he muttered, his voice sounding rusty. He cleared his throat. "Stuff Brian was looking into on his own. Stuff that probably got him killed."

A chill ran down her spine. "What do you mean?"

He took a deep breath, released it slowly. "These are notes from some conversations he had with one of his informants. The same guy who set us up in City Park. His name's Freddie. He was just a junkie snitch. Never had much more than street gossip."

Cade stopped then, looked around. "Where are we going?"

"I have no idea."

He gave her some directions and then continued. "This guy called Brian a few weeks before and claimed he had something big and wanted real money for it. I.A. claims there was nothing on the logs, so I'm guessing Brian never paid him. Probably wanted proof of what the guy was telling him. It sounded pretty farfetched."

"How farfetched?"

"That the entire illegal drug market in the area was being reorganized into one cohesive unit."

Something in his voice alerted her, and she turned to meet his gaze.

"And that the people at its helm are cops."

When she stopped before the building he'd directed her to, her brows rose. "This doesn't look like a pizzeria." Located on Decatur in the French Quarter, they were within walking distance of Café du Monde. Rows of renovated historic buildings lined the street, complete with lacy wrought-iron balconies and hidden gated courtyards.

"I know for a fact that we can get pizza inside." He reached over, took the car keys from her and got out of the car. It wasn't until she'd joined him on the sidewalk that she first noticed the yellow curb.

"This also doesn't look like a parking place."

"It's okay. I know someone who can fix my tickets."

"Really?" Her brows skimmed upward. "Doesn't exactly fill the average citizen with faith in the local law enforcement."

He used his keys to unlock the wrought-iron gate. "Lucky for me you're not the average citizen."

She took the banter as a sign that his earlier grimness had eased, at least enough for her to ask, "What are you going to do?"

He didn't pretend to misunderstand her. "About Brian's papers?" He unlocked the side door to the building and showed her into a foyer filled with antiques. "I'll take it to my lieutenant. See where he wants to go with it. If Brian was on the right track, though, it's going to be damn difficult to know just who to trust."

Rather than using the artfully concealed elevator, he guided her up the stairs. "I live on the fourth and fifth floors. The rest are rented out."

The statement had her brows arching again, and sidetracked her from her earlier question. "Tremaine, do you *own* this building?"

His smile was satisfied. "My accountant told me ten years ago it'd be a good investment. But I'd already gotten addicted to beignets. It seemed more convenient to stick close to Café du Monde."

Comprehension flooded in then, and she couldn't believe she'd never put it together before. First the luxury car, and now the exclusive property. "Tremaine Technologies? That's you?" The security software company was the largest employer in nearby Tangiphoha Parish.

"Mostly it's my brother James. He's run it practically since birth. He likes running things, and it keeps him out of our hair, at least most of the time." He took out a key and pushed open a door, ushered her in.

The interior was vast, decorated with comfort in mind and with an eye to the history of the area. The result was at once arresting and intimate. Shae dropped her coat and purse on a chair and wandered around. There were two sets of French doors, one overlooking the street and the other, she discovered upon exploration, the courtyard.

"What kind of pizza do you want?"

"I'll eat anything." She followed his voice into a kitchen that would do a chef proud, and a smile twitched at her lips. "Frozen pizza? You really know how to treat a lady."

He looked up from preheating the oven and shot her a devastating grin. "There goes my plan to pass it off as homemade. Pour some wine, will you?"

There was a bottle whose label she couldn't pronounce on the counter with two wineglasses. Amusement filled her. Frozen pizza and fine wine. The dinner of champions. She handed him his glass and lifted her own to her lips to sip. "I was chauffeured to and from work today."

"Sullivan and Hanson?" She nodded. The two men assigned to her detail had been polite but insistent. She'd figured Cade had seen to that. "They said LeFrenz slipped away again last night."

"I don't want you to worry about that," he began.

"I'm not worried. Not anymore." And it was true. She'd decided last night that she was through letting her life be curtailed by fear. She was taking back control. And if that meant encouraging LeFrenz to act... She gave a mental shrug. At least the waiting would be over.

As if he read her thoughts, Cade said, "You were taking an unnecessary chance, baiting him like that."

"I wasn't baiting him."

"It was like waving a red flag to a bull," he disputed. "You all but dared him to make his move."

"I want this over," she said flatly. "I want my life back."

"And I want him caught before he comes after you."

"Have you ever wondered what's stopping him?" Because she'd spent too much time wondering that very thing. "He said something last night about business before pleasure." With effort she restrained the shudder the memory brought and tried to remember his exact words.

"He said he had something to see to first. I've figured for a long time that there had to be a reason he was staying in the area. Something other than you."

"Like what?"

He shoved the pizza into the oven. "I'm figuring it has to be drug-related. He's got a big shipment coming in, got a deal going he can't walk away from..." He shook his head. "I don't have the details figured. The point is, thanks to your statements last night, he might decide not to wait until his business is taken care of."

"Isn't that what you want? To make him reckless enough to make mistakes?"

He took her elbow in his free hand and drew her close. "Not if his mistakes involve you."

A warm frisson of pleasure jittered down her spine. There was no mistaking the concern in his eyes, and something else. Something that turned the blood in her veins molten, scorching her from the inside out. "I really don't want to think about him anymore."

For a moment he looked as if he'd say something more. Then he nodded, slipped an arm around her waist. "Okay." He walked her into the area adjoining the kitchen, the one overlooking the courtyard. This looked like the room he spent the most time in. Bookcases lined one wall. Every shelf not holding TV or stereo equipment was crammed with books and framed pictures. He stopped in front of the stereo and fiddled with some knobs. To the accompaniment of a wailing sax, a legendary blues singer sang plaintively of lost love.

Shae reached out and picked up a picture that showed Cade, two other men and a diminutive blond woman. "Your family?" He nodded. "Sam, James and Ana." He pointed each of them out in turn. "That was taken last year." She studied the photo intently. There was an easy camaraderie among them that the photographer had managed to capture, an intimacy that came from family.

At least, it came from some families, she thought, setting the frame down. "None of you look much alike."

"Well, Sam's got green eyes, too, but you're right, I did get the looks in the family."

Shae smiled, as she was meant to. "All the modesty, too."

He dipped his head, nuzzled her neck, making her shiver. "I also got all the dancing ability. Wanna see?" He set his wine on one of the shelves. Took her glass and set it next to his. Then, drawing her into his arms, he moved her to the music.

He was making it all too easy to forget everything but this moment. This man. She'd never been much of a dancer, but he wasn't doing anything fancy. Just holding her close and swaying to the sound of the sax.

His mouth went to her neck, and she arched it to give him better access. The room was shadowed; the only light was that spilling from the kitchen. He did a quick twirl, weakening her knees and elevating her pulse. And the rest of the world was forgotten for the moment.

Because she'd spent most of her life being strong, she'd never realized how wondrous it could be to feel protected. And since she hadn't ever let herself need anyone, she'd failed to discover the sensual pleasure of leaning on a man. Even if it was just for a moment.

When she would have put a sliver of distance between them, he pressed her closer, his hand firm against the small of her back. With his other hand he reached out and opened the French doors, then moved them both onto the balcony without missing a beat.

She smiled at the practiced move, but her voice was more breathless than she would have liked when she said, "You've done this before."

"Not with you," he murmured, and the intensity of his gaze had the smile fading from her lips. The night sky was clear, but the fall air was chilly. He pulled her closer, sharing his heat.

Of their own volition, her fingers went to his shirt, tugging it from his waistband and unbuttoning it. Once it was open, she slid her hands inside. The flesh on his sides was smooth, the muscle beneath firm. Shae brushed her lips against his chest, skating her hands over his back. Being this close to him was its own seduction. She remembered too well the pleasure of exploring his body. Sleek taut skin stretched over plane and sinew. He was still too lean, but there was no missing the muscles roping his arms, padding his chest. And there was no denying that she wanted to discover them all over again.

She pressed her lips to his chest, strewing a trail of kisses from one masculine nipple to the other. His hands slipped down to cup her bottom, bringing her hips into contact with his every time they moved. He was already aroused, and the rhythmic brushing of their bodies had a hot ball of desire lodging in the pit of her belly.

He took her earlobe in his teeth and worried it gently while she traced his collarbone with the tip of her tongue. And then because she needed the taste of him, craved it, she went on tiptoe to open her mouth on his.

His flavor was distinctive, staggering, each time a shock to the senses. She met his tongue with her own and engaged in a short sensual battle before giving a little sigh and leaning into the kiss. Trailing her fingers down his chest, she found the silky ribbon of hair that descended into his jeans and lower. When she stroked it lightly she could feel the muscles in his belly jump. The evidence of his excitement brought a heady kind of thrill.

A dizzying spiral of heat swirled through her, turning her boneless. She couldn't have stood without support. His mouth was hungry against hers, a hint of desperation in his hands as they unfastened the buttons on her shirt, then splayed against her skin.

The pleasure of that first touch, fingers skating over flesh, sent her senses reeling. He unfastened her bra, covering her breasts with his palms, and the contact had her back arching. Her nipples were tight, achy. He cupped them in his palms, flicking his thumbs over the sensitized tips, before bending to take one in his mouth.

He wasn't gentle. She didn't want him to be. She held his head closer, wanting to deepen the pressure. The hot wet suction contrasted sharply with the chilly air. His tongue was working dark magic on her system, pressing her nipple against the roof of his mouth and lashing it with quick liquid strokes. Desire fired a path from her breasts to her womb.

She wasn't aware of moving until she felt the door at

her back. Her eyes fluttered open and she tried to focus, disoriented. Cade lifted his head only long enough to guide her through the French doors and kick them shut with his foot. Then urgency took over.

They sank to the floor, hands battling with clothing, limbs tangling in it as their mouths melded. Somehow clothes were discarded, along with their rapidly dwindling control. Shae stretched out on top of him, breasts crushed against his chest, hip to hip, thigh to thigh. With a sudden dizzying movement he rolled them so they lay on their sides facing each other, his knee between both of hers.

Reaching down, she cupped his heavy masculinity, stroked his heated velvet length. The need to have him buried within her was a constant throbbing ache, one impossible to deny.

The position of his leg held her open, and he worked a finger inside her as his mouth went to her ear. Her throat. Her breast. Sensations careered through her system, one slapping against the other until they couldn't be individually identified.

"Now." The word was delivered on a moan that sounded too much like a plea. "Now, Cade."

He fumbled for his jeans, withdrew a condom, while she kneaded his thighs, his hard masculine buns. The curse he muttered when the package proved difficult to open sounded desperate. The tremors in his hands as he sheathed himself spoke of dark and reckless needs.

She gave neither of them time to consider. When his arms went around her, she pressed him back and sat astride him. His eyes glittered as he watched her, allowing her to take control of their lovemaking. She positioned his shaft at the opening of her femininity and took him in, one fraction at a time.

That first bolt of pleasure had her head lolling, lungs

growing strangled. One hard thrust would end things for both of them. She didn't want to end it. Not yet. She kept her movements shallow, sliding teasingly before lifting away, denying them both the ultimate contact.

Cade's face was sheened with sweat. His fingers clutched her hips as he endured the torment for long moments. She thought she heard him say something. It was difficult to know. There was a rushing in her ears, her eyes couldn't focus as need battered at her, demanding release.

She sank down on him, sheathing him deeply with a suddenness that had them both gasping. And then it was a battle to move the fastest, to rock the hardest, each reckless lunge spinning her closer and closer to release.

His hands came up to cover her breasts, and the dual pleasure catapulted her from driving urgency to a shuddering crest. His hips kept hammering upward, pounding him into her with uncontrolled passion. And when he climaxed beneath her, his big body jerking in helpless pleasure, they drifted back to earth in each other's arms.

It was difficult to move through an unfamiliar apartment in the dark. Especially when Shae was so desperate for quiet. The clock on the bedside table had highlighted the early hour. The panic in her heart had warned it was much too late.

Cade slept, his arm flung out in the huge four-poster bed for a woman who wouldn't be there. Nasty little needles of guilt stabbed her, and despite long practice she wasn't quite able to assuage them. She'd told him last night, she rationalized, finding her shoes only by tripping over them, her socks by happenstance. Sometime between the smoke alarm and gorging themselves on wine and blackened pizza, she'd told him she'd have to go. Offered to get a cab.

Bra and shirt had landed together, making that search a bit easier. Haste made her movements clumsy. Her fingers couldn't seem to work the buttons. She'd allowed herself to be convinced to stay longer. And staying had meant making love again. A second and third time. By the final act they'd made it to the bed, and afterward she'd even dozed a bit.

And awoke, frantic that he was gone. Even more panicked that he was there.

She couldn't let him matter this much. *Wouldn't* let him. The trick to shielding a heart, she'd found, was distance. The cab she'd called would provide that, physically at least. Emotionally was another matter.

The kitchen light snapped on, and she froze. Cade stood surveying her, hair rumpled from sleep and from her hands. His jeans were unfastened, showing a wedge of hair-roughened skin, as if he'd donned them hastily. And his face… Her stomach plummeted. There was hurt lurking beneath the anger. But neither emotion sounded in his voice.

"I take it you're leaving."

Shae moistened her lips. "I…I called a cab. I didn't want to disturb your sleep."

"You sure do have a time waking me." It wasn't an agreement. Not delivered in that sardonic tone. And he was making this harder than it needed to be.

"I just don't sleep well with someone else in the room." She shrugged, as if it was perfectly natural.

"Is that what you tell yourself? That it's about sleep? In that case, let's go back to bed. We won't sleep at all. Stay the night."

"I can't."

His eyes were dark with emotions she was afraid to consider. "You choose not to. I recognize the difference even if you don't."

Because her lips threatened to tremble, she firmed them. "It's only sleeping arrangements, for heaven's sake."

"No, it's about intimacy." He rounded the couch and propped his hips against the edge, folded his arms across his chest. "It's about you running from it, refusing to accept it. Refusing to give it."

His statement arrowed a little too close to the truth. "This doesn't have to matter." She was shocked at how desperate she was for that to be true. "Don't let it matter."

"I can't do casual, not with you, Shae. I'm an all-or-nothing kind of guy. You can't pick and choose what you'll accept, what you'll give and what you won't."

His words brought a quick surge of stunned pleasure. Had she ever mattered so much...to anyone? But then panic crowded in, the strength of it nearly choking her. She had avoided emotional entanglements for just this reason. Inevitably someone expected too much. Wanted too much. Something she doubted was inside her to offer.

A horn sounded outside the apartment. Her cab. She grabbed her coat, her purse, holding them tightly to her chest. "It doesn't have to be so scary, taking that first step." His words were dark magic, and they were weaving a spell on her. She urgently wanted to believe them. Was terrified that she would.

He unfolded his arms to hold his hand out. The horn sounded again. "If you don't stop running now, when will you? Make the decision, Shae. Choose now."

She stared at him, eyes burning with unshed tears. He didn't know how tempting it was to take what he was offering. Or how disappointed he would be when he found how little he received in return.

She made the only choice she could. The only one there was for her. Turning, she walked across the apartment and out the door.

"This changes everything," Cade insisted, arms braced on the lieutenant's desk. The man had been in meetings until afternoon, and it was the first chance he'd had to speak to him privately. "What are we going to do about it?"

Brian's notes were spread across the desktop. Frowning, Howard studied first one page, then another. "If this is true, the department's in for a firestorm. The politics will take years to die down."

"The problem is who to trust. Do we take it to I.A., the task force, federal?"

Howard rubbed his face, looking suddenly old. "Luckily that's not my decision. I take it to the superintendent and he'll decide from there." He shook his head, an expression of intense sadness in his expression. "I gotta tell you, I'm hoping it's not true. That Brian was murdered by cops and you nearly were." He dropped his hand from his jaw, looked at Cade. "Why didn't he share any of this with you?"

That question, and others, had been haunting Cade since he'd found the papers. Would it have changed anything if he had? Would Brian still be alive? Would they both be dead? He shook his head. "I don't know. I'm guessing that that was what the meeting was supposed to be about in City Park. Maybe he wanted me to hear the information from Freddie and get my take on it. But either Freddie was playing him all along or someone else got to him and flipped him, set up the double cross."

Howard picked up the sheets of paper one by one, his movements methodical as he folded them and put them back in the envelope. "I'll take care of these. Do you need to take some time?" His gaze was piercing. "You've been through a lot lately."

For a moment the scene with Shae came hurtling back with startling clarity. The gut-wrenching agony of seeing her turn away from him. Walk out that door. "I'm okay." The words were as much to convince himself as his superior. "And I've got a case to work."

The man gave him a nod. "Okay, then. A match came in today on that partial plate and one of the contacts in LeFrenz's book. He's been questioned once, but now that we've got a maybe on his car, why don't you and Birtch go grab him up again?"

Cade nodded, a flicker of relief filling him that the lieutenant hadn't pushed harder for him to take some time off. Because right now he needed the job to buffer thoughts of Shae, to keep the mingled fury and pain at bay. Work had been enough for him once, it would be again.

It had to be.

"I'm telling you, guys, that car was stolen." Hank Logan's rodentlike features were twisted into an expression that was supposed to pass for innocence.

Cade shook his head in disgust, looked at Birtch. "I'm not in the mood for this. Are you?"

"I'm never in the mood to get jerked around," Josh said. "Especially by a lowlife punk who's already lied to detectives in this squad about knowing LeFrenz."

"Hey, some cops come to the door and want to know do I know a drug dealer they're looking for—what am I gonna say?" He spread his hands. "So, okay, I used to like to snort a little, which I don't anymore and haven't for a long time. And maybe I did business with LeFrenz a time or two. But I've been clean for a year and I got drug tests at work to prove it.''

"Well, I'm glad to find out you finally found a test you could pass," Cade told him. "Probably made your mother real proud. But we're not gonna believe you didn't report the car stolen." When the man opened his mouth, Cade slapped his palm against the table. "Don't bother lying anymore. You're just going to piss me off, and my fuse is already short. We pulled your sheet. You did time in lockup just eight months ago and nearly got yourself killed there. You wanna go back?" The guards had barely gotten the cell unlocked in time to pull Hank's huge cell mate off him. Cade shot a look at Josh. "We could probably go grab up Marcus, couldn't we?" Just the mention of the man who'd had the choke hold on him had Hank blanching.

Josh nodded, going along with the ploy, and checked his watch. "He's just getting home this time of night. Got a job bouncing at a strip joint. I hear he gets real surly when he's short on sleep."

"Knowing Marcus, he'll have drugs on him, too, which would be a violation of his parole." Cade heaved a sigh, pretending not to notice that Hank had sunk lower in his chair. "Now if I have to go clear over there, grab him up, do the paperwork on it, I'm gonna be feeling a little mean myself."

"Mean enough to make sure you guys are bunk buddies in lockup again," Josh said, his face close to Hank's. "Hope the guards on duty are as quick as they were last time."

"That guy's crazy," Hank whined. "Said he'd kill me if he saw me again."

Cade shrugged. "So what's it gonna be, Hank? It's your call."

The man clutched the table with his fingers until his knuckles went white. "Listen, I hadn't seen LeFrenz for a while, you know? So when he shows up at my house in the middle of the night, it's like, what the hell?"

"We don't need your every thought, Hank, just the facts," Josh said. "He asked to use your car."

"I told him no way, I need it to get to work. And if I miss work once more, my boss is gonna fire me, and then my parole officer will be all over me." Cade rolled his eyes. Clearly there was no hurrying this guy. "But finally I say yeah, okay, here's the keys. 'Cause he promised he'd bring it right back, but he didn't. So now I want to report it stolen." He looked at Josh. "Is it too late to do that?"

"Those aren't the details we're looking for, Hank." Cade folded his arms. "That's just the sort of runaround crap that's going to make me think throwing you in a cell with Marcus is exactly what you deserve."

The man licked his lips. "He was talking big, you know? Like he'd landed on the gravy train. And then he said that when he brought the car back, he'd take me over to his new place. Got a place in one of them developments, over by the lake? It's got a pool and everything, heated, inside the house. Real fancy. But he said he was laying low for a while, so don't worry if I don't hear from him right away.

"He was lying, right?" Hank looked first at Josh, then at Cade. "I figured a little rat like him couldn't have gotten that high in the network so fast like he said. But he claims that sh—stuff is going down and he's gonna be one of the top dogs when it's all over."

"Did he mention any names?" The punk's brow furrowed and Cade elucidated. "Did he say who he was working with? How he was connected?"

Hank shook his head. "No. Just said he was in a sweet

deal with guys at the top that no one could ever take down. I shoulda known he was just blowin' smoke. I mean, who could he work with that the cops couldn't touch?"

"You've got a visitor, Shae."

Shae looked up at Boyd DuBois's announcement, a tiny bubble of hope bouncing through her veins. "Who is it?"

"Guy says he's your dad. Looks enough like you I guess it's true."

Hope died, reminding her, once again, just how dangerous it was to harbor it. She hadn't expected Cade to show up here, anyway. After last night, it had been only too apparent that any further dealings she'd have with the man would be professional.

It was for the best. She thought it and tried to believe it. He pushed too hard, asked too much. She'd always known that it was dangerous to let someone else close enough to tempt her to want more. And Cade Tremaine was all about temptation.

"The guy's a real card."

Boyd's laughing remark jerked her attention back to him.

"Your dad. He's in the staff lounge waiting for you. Cracking jokes, doing card tricks I never could figure out."

She gave a sigh. "How much did he take you for?"

The intern looked startled, then sheepish. "Twenty. Would have been more, but I left my wallet at home."

A wise decision when Ryan McCabe O'Riley was around. Straightening her shoulders, Shae strode resolutely down the hall to extricate her father from her place of work. And hopefully from her life once and for all.

She shoved open the door of the staff lounge, and was met with the sight of her father sitting at the table, surrounded by four hospital employees. Ryan had some plastic-foam coffee cups lined up before him as a slick patter spilled from his lips. "You can do it. Just watch closely. Where'd your money go? Which one is it under?" She watched his sleight of hand with a world-weary cynicism. He hadn't been able to pull that one on her since she was six.

"This one?" He lifted a cup someone had pointed to and groaned aloud. "Oh, no, thought you had it that time, I surely did. Have to tell you I don't even know where it's at myself."

"Look in your pocket," Shae suggested. All eyes in the room turned toward her. Pushing away from the door, she approached the table. "Give them their money back, Da. Every cent of it."

He looked up and beamed. "Shae, angel of my heart, look at you, beautiful as an Irish morn."

Since the closest her father had been to Ireland was a pub in Queens, the compliment lacked sincerity. "The money?" Her voice was edged in steel. "Now." Their gazes did battle for a moment, before he moved the cups around with lightninglike speed and then lifted one with a flourish, producing delighted murmurs from the group.

"There you go now," he told them magnanimously. "Never had any intention of keeping a dime of it." The fact that he could utter such a bald-faced lie without batting an eyelash was a testament to both long practice and absent conscience.

Shae waited until the money had been collected before saying, "If everyone wouldn't mind, I need a little privacy with my father." She watched grim-faced as his newfound friends gave him friendly goodbyes before filing out of the room.

Ryan beamed at her. "Look at you in those scrubs and coat. You look just like a doctor."

"I *am* a doctor. And this is a hospital. You aren't welcome here, Da, and if I ever find out you've been running your sidewalk scams here again, I'll call security."

He stacked the cups neatly on top of each other. "You left me no choice, Shae girl. Wouldn't answer my calls. Wouldn't call me back. Couldn't even get in to your apartment to see you." He gave her a wink. "That's a dandy little security system you got for yourself, by the way. Topnotch."

"Some people might take all those things as hints."

"You don't want to give me names for potential clients." He shrugged hugely. "I can accept that. All I want is a wee spot of cash to get my latest business venture started and I'll leave you alone."

"No names. No cash."

It was as if he hadn't heard her. He probably hadn't. Ryan O'Riley only heard what he wanted to. And *no* wasn't a word he was fond of. "I'll pay you back, of course. In lieu of interest, I can let you in on this deal, too. Make your investment back and then some."

She gave an incredulous laugh, shaking her head. He'd even fleece his own daughter without a second thought. "You'll never change. I don't know why that always surprises me. Maybe I'm more like you than I thought, because I won't change, either. I didn't fall for your lies when I was a kid and I won't now. You're wasting your breath."

Amazingly her words seemed to convince him. The ever present smile was wiped from his face. A surge of bitterness filled her, resentment for what this man had taught her about distrust. A lesson she'd learned all too well.

"I know you've always held your childhood against me." The sigh he gave could have been real. Probably wasn't.

"Thanks to you, I didn't have a childhood. I had an absent father, broken promises and more tutoring than necessary in the dangers of letting people too close."

He looked away. Swallowed hard. "Well, if that's true, then I am sorry for that. Because it's a cold world out there with no one close to you, Shae girl. Maybe I didn't make the best choices all the time when you were a kid. Maybe it hurt you in ways I never considered. But you've been grown up for a long time now. You can't blame your choices on your da anymore."

He got up, for once seeming every one of his years. He moved to the door slowly, then paused to look back at her. "You were always the toughest sell I ever tried to make. I could come home after being away months and dangle the silliest, sparkliest little bauble in front of you and you'd never once reach out for it. I could see in your eyes how much you wanted it sometimes. But you wouldn't make a grab. What I'm hoping is that if something comes around now, you'll take that step. Life is pretty dull without taking chances."

Blinking furiously, she said, "Ryan O'Riley's life motto."

He said nothing else. Opened the door and prepared to walk through it. She'd watched him walk away a hundred times before. She would never know why she stopped him this time. "Da." She moistened her lips when he looked back at her. "I... One of my patients is wanted by the police. He's called me, so there's a device on my line. It lets them trace the calls." Ryan's eyes widened. "There are a couple detectives outside when I'm here or at home.

I just wanted you to know, so you don't get caught up in that.''

He stared at her for a moment before smiling boyishly. ''Well, I appreciate that, Shae, I surely do.'' One eye slid shut in a sly wink. ''Don't you worry about me, though. I've always been careful.''

She watched his retreating back, reflecting on his last words. Yes, she'd always been careful, too. For the first time in her life, though, she was wondering if it was possible to be *too* careful.

# Chapter 14

"**I** don't know what we can do about it." Cade and Josh were walking back to the squad room after releasing Logan. "It's not like we can start searching every house on the lake that has a pool on the off chance we find LeFrenz in one of them."

"Maybe we should start patrolling that area, looking for the car."

The suggestion would take manpower they couldn't afford. "Maybe the lieutenant can get that turned over to the patrol units." Cade's voice stopped once he got back to the squad room and saw the man standing beside his desk. Walking away from Josh, he drawled, "Aren't you afraid the company's going to go belly-up with you running to the city every chance you get?"

James Tremaine, turned, grinned. "The mark of a well-managed company is that it doesn't need the CEO there every minute in order to operate smoothly."

The two men clapped each other on the back. "So what

brings you to the city?'' Dropping into his desk chair, he motioned for James to pull up a vacant seat. ''Run out of that fancy wine you're so fond of?''

''Since you pilfer my wine cellar every chance you get, if I found myself short, I'd know where to look for it.'' James sat, with an eye to maintaining the crease in his trousers. ''I need some information.'' With effort Cade hid his surprise. It wasn't often that James admitted to needing anything even from his family. ''I'm looking for a private investigator who was in business years ago. This was the name of the company.'' He handed a slip of paper to Cade. ''I can't find any record of it now, and I don't know the name of the employees who worked there.''

''How long ago was it?''

''Twenty years.''

''Okay.'' Cade put the paper in his notebook, where he'd remember it. ''What's going on?''

James was already rising. ''Just an old case the company hired out. I ran across some records and started wondering about it.''

The explanation didn't quite satisfy Cade. ''Twenty years ago you weren't even at the company. Why's it matter now?''

His brother gave a shrug. ''Maybe I have too much time on my hands. It's a puzzle I want solved. I have to get back. I promised Sam and Juliette I'd pick up the wedding invitations.''

Cade let that go, although the thought of James playing errand boy was laughable. There was no point in questioning his brother further, because it was obvious he wasn't in the mood to share more, at least not at the moment. But as he watched James's retreating back, his gaze fell to the slip of paper, and his naturally inquisitive nature took over. Two decades ago would have been the time of the accident that had taken their parents' lives.

He looked at the doorway James had disappeared through. What sort of twenty-year-old case would be puzzling his brother enough to request help for it? And what did it have to do with Tremaine Technologies?

His thoughts were interrupted when Lieutenant Howard came out of his office, looking grim. "An officer in Eighth just found a body in burnt-out car. Color and plates could match the one of the security tape at the Quik-Mart."

Cade was already shrugging into his jacket. "Do they know who it is?"

"The upper body is burned beyond recognition. Someone torched the car and guy. But they found I.D. on him belonging to Jonny LeFrenz."

The Orleans Parish coroner's office was never Cade's favorite destination. He and Birtch had waited in a couple folding chairs at the end of the hallway for their guy to get his turn with the coroner. Given the workload of the place, he knew how fortunate he was to get the case prioritized.

But now, standing next to the stainless steel table that held the stiff, it was hard to feel lucky. The stench of burned flesh and singed hair filled the room. He sent a glance to Birtch, who was making a valiant attempt to keep from retching. "Here." He passed him the bottle of wintergreen oil to rub on the inside of his mask. "Use this. It helps."

"If you're going to toss your cookies, do it in the sink over there. I'm expecting company." This attempt at a joke was accompanied by a cackle of merriment. The coroner, Herb Clements, was the best Cade had ever worked with, but his sense of humor left something to be desired.

Cade had often thought the man resembled a cadaver himself. Tall and thin, with a low brow and deep-set eyes, the man was rumored to curl up and nap on one of the autopsy tables when things were slow. It suited Cade not to believe that.

"So who's your friend, Tremaine?"

He knew Herb well enough to know that he was talking about the corpse, not Birtch. "I.D. says it's Jonny Le-Frenz. We want to be sure."

Herb looked up at him. "The guy who downed one of your men at Charity?"

Cade nodded. "He was seen the night before last on Bourbon Street. We don't know anything after that until he was found in the car. Looked like the vehicle had been set on fire."

"So the guy was probably dead when it was torched." Birtch was keeping his gaze fastened on his shoes.

"We'll see," Clements said reprovingly. He didn't like anyone drawing conclusions before he'd had a chance to do his examination. He took out his pocket-size tape recorder and turned it on to record the date, time, and identity of people in the room. Cade watched as he walked around the table, dictating the condition of the body and the clothes it was clad in.

Then he took photographs of the body from every angle before enlisting the detectives' help disrobing it. Each article of clothing was carefully placed in a separate bag and labeled. The shirt had to be cut away, and the remaining pieces dropped into another bag.

"So what's your priority, today, Tremaine? Time of death, cause of death or I.D.?"

Cade knew the examination today would answer all three questions, but there was really only one he was interested in. "Identification first." He had to be certain that the bastard was dead. That was the only way Shae would be safe again.

"Any identifying marks you know of?"

"He had a tattoo on his back. Right shoulder blade. A skull and crossbones."

Clements rolled the corpse over, pursed his lips. "Probably won't be able to be sure, at least not right away. Looks like the back of him took the brunt of it. Seat probably caught fire behind him."

"Any chance of getting a fingerprint?"

"Depends on the extent of the burns. Let's see." Clements picked up one of the hands. The burns had made the fingers curl into the palm. Setting it down, he walked around the table to examine the other. "You might get a decent print from the middle finger over here. It's not as bad as the rest on this hand."

Cade could hear Birtch take a deep breath, as if the sight of those blackened gnarled hands had made him queasy again. "Ink and cards in the same place?" He was already moving over to the set of cupboards in one corner.

"Don't get in a hurry," the coroner admonished. Cade waited impatiently while the man carefully searched beneath the fingernails of the corpse for trace evidence, before cutting the nails and sealing them in yet another bag. Then Cade pulled on a pair of gloves and, with no little difficulty, inked the fingertip Clements had suggested. The finger was stiff, making it difficult to roll across the card for a full print. When he was satisfied with the result, he looked over at Birtch. His face around his mask had a faintly green tinge, but he was still on his feet and looked steady enough.

"You going to be okay here?" When the other man nodded, he looked at Clements, who had picked up what looked like a pair of pruning shears. "I'm going back to headquarters to see if I can make a match. If this doesn't do it, we'll have to try DNA. We should be able to get samples to match from LeFrenz's apartment.'' He took off the mask and used it to wipe the wintergreen oil from his nose. Then he peeled off the gloves and tossed them away. The stench was going to be more difficult to get rid of. He knew from past experience that it would be in his hair, in his clothes.

''Call me when you find out,'' Birtch said. Nodding, Cade headed out the door.

Once back in his car, he reached for his phone and called the hospital while he drove to the Records Division. A nurse at the desk informed him that Dr. O'Riley had already left for the day. He was about to try her at home, then hesitated. On second thought, there was no reason to talk to her until he had a positive I.D. to report. And that was the reason he put his phone away again, he told himself firmly. Not because of a streak of cowardice he hadn't known he possessed.

Cade's eyes were trained on the city traffic, but his thoughts were on the scene in his apartment last night. It was difficult to imagine, given his expertise dealing with skittish witnesses, how he could have handled the situation any more poorly. But the situation had been too important, too personal, for finesse. Finesse would have only delayed the inevitable, at any rate.

He pulled into the building's parking lot, cruised for a spot. Every time he thought he'd reached Shae on any level, she fought to regain distance. Physically. Emotionally. And each time was like a keen-edged blade slicing into his chest. He didn't know when he'd let it matter this much. And he sure as hell didn't know what he was going to do about it.

Cade took the card with the corpse's fingerprint and

handed it to the records division officer at the desk. The man would scan the print and feed it into the Automated Fingerprint Identification System. His cell phone rang, distracting him from the nerves knotted in his stomach as he waited for a match.

Lieutenant Howard's voice greeted him. "I got some news while you were out. Quentin's task-force team scored a big bust last night when they arrested that Trax gang member, Justus Davies. Davies was shot, but before he died, he admitted to being behind the shooting in City Park."

Cade felt a vise squeeze his chest. "Did he…" He took a deep breath, scrubbed his free hand over his jaw. "Do we know why yet?"

"Not yet." Sympathy tinged Howard's tone. "Maybe as they round up the rest of the gang, some might spill more details. But this is partial closure, at least, for Carla. Do you want to tell her?"

"Yeah." The lieutenant ended the conversation a few moments later, leaving Cade to his ghosts. Brian's killer had been caught. He tried to feel something. Anything. But there was no sense of justice. No feeling of retribution. Only emptiness. Because a good man was still dead, and they still didn't know why. Life wasn't always neat. And some questions never found answers.

He released a breath. He'd call Carla later, once he'd gotten home. He hoped she'd get more satisfaction from the news than he did.

Several minutes later, the machine signaled a match. A measure of tension seeped out of him. This at least, would close the door on the danger facing Shae. He knew how important it was to her to get her life back under control. Without complications. Without him in it.

He leaned forward to examine the information on the computer screen. Then he froze. Blinked. Stared again.

The computer had come up with a match all right. Trouble was, the print didn't belong to Jonny LeFrenz, but one Frederick "Freddie" Latham.

Brian's missing snitch.

Someone had gone to a great deal of trouble to make sure everyone thought Jonny LeFrenz was dead.

Cade bolted away from the computer and headed for the door. A feeling of foreboding descended, dark and heavy. And it wouldn't be lifted until he'd seen Shae again and made sure she was all right.

When her doorbell rang, it took conscious effort to quiet her rocketing pulse. Logically she knew it wasn't Cade, even if he'd found someone to let him in. But logic didn't always dictate emotion.

Looking through the door's peephole, she saw TeKayla's gap-toothed grin. The little girl was giggling. Something inside Shae lightened. Hopefully the child had gotten over her disappointment and forgiven her. Smiling, she flipped off the alarm system, unlocked the door and pulled it open. "You don't know how happy I am to see you."

"Angel Eyes." Jonny LeFrenz stepped away from the wall he'd been leaning against. Beside the door. Out of sight. With lightning speed he had his hands on the little girl's shoulders, holding her in front of him. His smile was ugly. "I'm glad to see you, too. Let us in."

Her gaze riveted on the grip he had on the girl, Shae had no choice but to swing the door open, allow them both entry. Blind panic had wiped her mind clean. All she could think was that the worst had happened. Someone else had been caught up in the situation because of her.

"Surprise, Dr. Shae!" The little girl's squeal was delighted. "You din't know your cousin was coming to see you, did you? Did I do good, Dr. Shae? He made me promise not to ruin the secret."

She couldn't even manufacture a plastic smile. "You did real good, honey. Now maybe you should go back outside. Let me talk to...my cousin."

"Cute kid." LeFrenz's hands flexed on the girl's shoulders. "Maybe she should stay."

Icebergs bumped in Shae's veins. "We have a lot of catching up to do. It'll be easier to do alone."

"Maybe you're right. I know where to find her if I need to." His warning couldn't have been clearer.

"Go to your apartment, honey." A thin thread of desperation sounded in Shae's voice.

But TeKayla was already skipping out the door. "I can play outside. My mom's home and she said so."

Her phone began ringing. Once. Twice. Again. She made no move toward it. Instead, she watched helplessly as LeFrenz swung the door shut and stalked toward her. "You look surprised. Don't know why. I promised you I'd be around to see you, didn't I?"

"You did. I've been looking forward to it."

Her calm manner seemed to take him aback. He grabbed her roughly, pulled her against him. She could feel the gun in his coat pocket. "You don't wanna be playin' no games with me, Angel Eyes. 'Cept the ones I tell you to."

"No games," she gritted, trying for a smile. "I bought a special wine after your last call. I was hoping you'd make it before I left on my vacation."

"What I got planned for you, baby, is gonna be better than a vacation." Revulsion shook her as he grabbed her breast, kneaded it roughly.

She managed a laugh, then pressed lightly on his shoulders. "What's your hurry? Can't we have some wine first?"

He stared at her suspiciously. She must have been a better actress than she'd thought because he relaxed a little. "Okay. Yeah, sure. Why not?"

Inwardly quaking, she went to the refrigerator and took out a bottle of white Zinfandel. As she turned and opened a drawer under the counter, LeFrenz reached forward, gripped her hand tightly. "What are you looking for in there, Angel?"

"Corkscrew."

He pulled the drawer out further and looked down at the instrument in her hands. "Okay, then." Stepping back, he motioned for her to continue. "Let's get that bottle opened."

Her hands were trembling so badly it took twice as long as it should have to remove the cork. "Glasses are in the third cupboard to your right," she said. And when he had his back turned for that split second, she shoved the corkscrew under her shirt into the waistband of her pants.

He watched her narrowly as she poured them both some wine. "I thought you were putting me on when you told me you were looking forward to me coming here. I thought you was scared of me."

"Did you?" Her throat was dry, but when she tried to take a sip of the wine, she nearly choked. "Maybe I was at first. A little. Then it started to get…exciting." She could barely force the word out. "There's not much excitement in my life, Jonny."

"That's about to change." LeFrenz's gaze traveled up and down her figure. "Lose the shirt."

Shae froze. "What?"

"The shirt. Let's get started on that excitement right now." He grabbed her by the arm and pulled her roughly to him. It would be only an instant before he'd discover the corkscrew. Shae tensed, got ready to use it.

The doorbell rang. The familiar noise was so jarringly out of place, so unexpected, they both stared at the door. In the next moment Shae's fingers went in search of the corkscrew, determined to use the distraction to her advantage.

Then a voice sounded, calm yet commanding. "I know you're in there, Jonny. Open the door."

LeFrenz's face went completely white. He swung his head from side to side, as if looking frantically for a way out.

"Now, Jonny. Before the situation gets too far out of control."

To Shae's stunned amazement LeFrenz finally obeyed, going to the door and pulling it open to admit a man she'd never seen before. One wearing a gold shield around his neck and holding a gun steadily on LeFrenz.

"You know the drill," he told him.

"I din't mean to—"

"Save it," the man barked. "Against the wall, hands behind your back." He frisked the man, finding the gun and sticking it in his waistband. Pulling out a pair of handcuffs, he said, "Are you all right, ma'am?" he asked, never taking his eyes of the sullen LeFrenz.

"I…" She was beginning to shake with shock and adrenaline. "Yes."

Expertly the man secured the handcuffs around first one of LeFrenz's wrists, then the other. "Damn lucky for you that I got a tip from one of LeFrenz's buddies that he was on his way over here.'' He cuffed LeFrenz on the side of the head. "How'd you happen to make it by the two cops out front, huh, Jonny?''

"Came in the back with the kid,'' he muttered.

"Bad idea, Jonny. But I think you're beginning to realize that you misjudged the situation, aren't you?''

A pounding started on her door. "Shae, are you all right?''

Her body heaved with relief. "Cade!'' She skirted around the police officer, making sure to give LeFrenz a wide berth, opened the door and walked into his arms. Her system was on overload, her mind grappling with the rapid-fire events of the past quarter hour.

Cade squeezed her once, hard, then set her away. "Detective Quentin. I don't know what you're doing here, but I'm damn glad you are.'' In an aside to Shae he said, "The detective here leads the city's narcotics task force. Last night he took down the guy who killed Brian.''

"Tremaine.'' The other detective nodded. "Sorry as hell about your partner, but at least the scum responsible for it is dead.''

"Seems you were right about one of the guys you were watching,'' Cade remarked conversationally. Hands shoved in his coat pockets, he seemed incongruously relaxed. "Did you find out anything that points to why he did it?''

"Not yet, but we'll be shaking down the rest of the gang for information.''

Cade's gaze skated to LeFrenz. "Jonny. The deal I offered in the hospital still stands. You give up the head of your organization and maybe the D.A. can work something out.''

Shae frowned. Why in heaven's name was he offering the man a deal? Especially now.

LeFrenz's jaw worked, but he said nothing. ''I'm sure he'll flip once I get him downtown,'' Quentin said. He holstered his gun and shoved LeFrenz toward the door. ''Let's go.''

''I'm afraid I can't let you leave with him.''

Shae never saw Cade reach for his gun, but it was in his hand now, pointed at the other detective, who looked as incredulous as she felt.

''Tremaine, what the hell are you doing?''

Cade smiled, a grim stretch of the lips. ''Making sure he makes it downtown and doesn't pull a miraculous escape. Or even wind up with a bullet in his head. Drop your gun. Both of them.''

''Have you lost your mind? Is that it? Post-traumatic stress from your shooting?''

''Drop the guns.''

Quentin must have read the purpose in his voice, because with quick vicious movements he did just that. ''You're going to feel pretty stupid about this when you explain it to our superiors.''

''I'm willing to take that risk. If I'm wrong, I'll even apologize. Shae, pick up his weapons.''

''Tremaine, there's stuff you need to know,'' LeFrenz said, his gaze sly. ''Stuff I can help you with.''

''Shut up, Jonny!''

At Quentin's thunderous order, puzzle pieces clicked into place for Shae. Memories came flooding back of the papers Cade had found belonging to his partner. The man's theory that the drug market was being reorganized. *And that the people at its helm are cops.*

Her comprehension came moments too late. LeFrenz threw himself at Cade, knocking him off balance. Quentin bent down as Shae went to Cade's aid. And then her blood congealed when she saw the task-force detective straighten, a small gun in his hand. Operating on sheer instinct, she reached for the corkscrew and flew at him, jamming it as hard as she could into his gun hand. She was shoved violently away, tripped and slammed her head against the table. The last thing she heard before unconsciousness claimed her was the sound of a lone shot.

The hospital door was pushed open and Cade peeked his head inside. "Is it safe to come in yet?"

Although her heart leaped at the sight of him, she wasn't done being angry. "Where have you been? And the only answer I want to hear is that you've been downstairs signing me out."

"You're a strict conversationalist." He strolled through the door. "I also hear you're the worst patient this floor has seen in a decade."

Because the statement was most likely true, she chose to ignore it. "I don't have a concussion and I want to go home."

"You could have a concussion, and you've been admitted for observation," he countered.

Shae glared at him, suspecting that he had had something to do with convincing the attending physician to admit her.

"I just got some good news." Pulling a chair close to the bed, he turned it around and straddled it. "Quentin's hanging tight, but LeFrenz is spilling his guts. And he's named Quentin and three others on the task force as being behind the drug reorganization.''

She sobered immediately. ''So Quentin was responsible for you being shot and Brian killed?''

''Sounds like it.'' The look on his face was savage enough to have her shivering. ''There's a special kind of hell reserved for cops who turn on their own kind. You can be damn sure that Quentin and the others will pay. It was his idea to turn I.A. on to Brian in the first place. Freddie, one of Brian's snitches, got wind of some of what was going down and tried to sell the information to Brian. Brian couldn't prove it, but the deeper he dug, he must have started to get the impression there was some truth to it.''

Shae frowned, already growing confused. ''But I thought the snitch set you both up.''

''He did.'' Memory clouded Cade's face. ''LeFrenz found out what Freddie was up to and tipped off Quentin. They paid him to set up the ambush, then LeFrenz stashed Freddie away and kept him high until he could be useful again.''

''Why would Quentin set I.A. on Brian? What was the point once he was dead?''

''To make him less credible.''

''You mean, no one was going to put much stock in information gathered by a dirty cop.''

''Exactly.'' Cade nodded. ''He was starting to feed I.A. material that would point to me, too. I guess he figured if I was busy defending myself from an I.A. investigation, I wouldn't have time to look at him. They have a huge shipment planned for the day after tomorrow. He was desperate that nothing mess that up.''

''The business that LeFrenz spoke of,'' she murmured. She thought for a moment. ''So how did he know LeFrenz had come to my place? Did he follow him?''

''He knew about Jonny's obsession with you.'' He made a disgusted sound. ''Hell, he probably picked that up by accessing our reports. He couldn't afford to get rid of LeFrenz, not before the shipment. So he was keeping close tabs on him. Most likely he monitored the radios, found out that a body had been found with LeFrenz's I.D. and figured Jonny was going to make his move.''

She shook her head in disbelief. ''My life used to be pretty uneventful.'' The last several days had set that particular description on its ear.

''It's back under your control now,'' he told her, his face sober. ''I know how important that is to you.''

Her gaze met his, then skated away. ''It is, yes.'' At least it always had been in the past. ''When I was a kid there was so little I could depend on that I got used to counting on nothing at all. And on no one.'' For a long time she'd thought that was the wisest way. Certainly it had been the easiest. Right now her heart was hammering so hard she was certain he could hear it. Her palms went damp as she searched for the words that would make him understand.

''My father came to see me yesterday.'' Her smile felt more like a grimace. ''Had to throw him out before he fleeced the entire hospital staff, but he said something that made me think.'' She moistened her lips and discreetly wiped her palms on the hospital sheet. ''He reminded me that I've never taken a chance on anything in my life.''

''Easy enough to figure why.'' As if he couldn't stay still any longer, he pushed up from the chair to roam the room. ''We're all a product of our environments in one way or another. Only way to face that is head-on.''

Shae waited, but he said nothing more. She wasn't surprised by his silence. She'd recognized from the start that the man had complication written all over him.

''You see things in black and white,'' she murmured, feeling a thread of panic. ''It's all or nothing with you.'' It was like standing on the edge of a precipice, survival instinct battling with an overwhelming urge to fly.

''That's right.'' His eyes glittered when he strode back to lean over the rail of her bed. ''All or nothing. So choose now, Shae. Which will it be?''

She reached up, linked her fingers with his and leaped. ''All.''

His eyes slid closed for a moment, his grip tightening around hers as if in relief. ''Thank God. I have a habit of pushing too hard when things are important.'' He opened his eyes and looked at her, and the light of emotion in them made her heart expand. ''And nothing is more important than you, Shae. I guess I realized that about the first time you kicked me out of your apartment. I love you.'' When she would have spoken, he rushed on, ''I know that under normal circumstances, that's likely to send you running, but there's nowhere to run right now. I'm willing to give you space, time, whatever you need, but I'm not willing to let you push me away when I get too close.''

''You were quicker than me. I didn't know I loved you, or at least,'' she corrected herself, ''I didn't admit it to myself until I heard gunfire right before I blacked out. I lost consciousness afraid that you'd been shot again.'' The memory made her voice shaky. ''I love you.'' It wasn't as difficult as she'd imagined to say the words, even with her throat, her heart, full. ''I'm not promising it's going to be easy or quick. But for the first time I'm going to take a chance on something in my life, reach out for it, and that's going to be you.''

''I'll be there,'' he said softly, bending down to brush his lips over her cheek. ''And I'll be here. All night.''

The words lacked the power they'd once had to alarm her. ''I won't sleep,'' she warned him, her arms going around his neck.

His lips moved to her mouth, lingered there. ''I'm counting on that.''

\* \* \* \* \*

*Now that the third Tremaine has found a match, there's just one to go. What was in those papers? Find out in early 2004 with Kylie Brant's exciting conclusion to*

THE TREMAINE TRADITION!

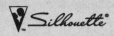
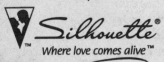

# eHARLEQUIN.com

The eHarlequin.com online community is *the* place to share opinions, thoughts and feelings!

- Joining the community is easy, fun and **FREE!**

- Connect with **other romance fans** on our message boards.

- Meet your **favorite authors** without leaving home!

- **Share opinions** on books, movies, celebrities…and *more!*

**Here's what our members say:**

"I love the friendly and helpful atmosphere filled with support and humor."
—Texanna (eHarlequin.com member)

"Is this the place for me, or what? There is nothing I love more than 'talking' books, especially with fellow readers who are reading the same ones I am."
—Jo Ann (eHarlequin.com member)

**Join today by visiting
www.eHarlequin.com!**

If you enjoyed what you just read,
then we've got an offer you can't resist!

# Take 2 bestselling love stories FREE!
# Plus get a FREE surprise gift!

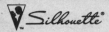

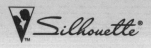

Silhouette®

# COMING NEXT MONTH

**INTIMATE MOMENTS®**

### #1243 NIGHT WATCH—Suzanne Brockmann
*Tall, Dark & Dangerous*

U.S. Navy SEAL chief Wes Skelly had come to Los Angeles on an unofficial assignment, and he was most certainly *not* looking for love. But a blind date with Brittany Evans brought him friendship—and finally passion—where he least expected to find it....

### #1244 FATHERS AND OTHER STRANGERS— Karen Templeton
*The Men of Mayes County*

When Jenna Stanton discovered the identity of her thirteen-year-old niece's father, she made the agonizing choice to introduce them, even though she knew she risked losing the girl she'd raised as her own. But was the girl's father, embittered loner Hank Logan, ready to accept an instant family...and the possibility of love?

### #1245 DEAD CALM—Lindsay Longford

Cynical police detective Judah Finnegan was used to facing the evil that men do, but finding an abandoned baby in a storm pushed him to the edge. Dr. Sophie Brennan had once tried to heal Judah's wounded soul and failed. Could this tiny lost child bring these two opposites together—forever?

### #1246 SOME KIND OF HERO—Brenda Harlen

When private investigator Joel Logan was hired to find a friend's long-lost relative, he didn't count on falling madly in love with beautiful Riane Rutherford-Quinlan, the woman he sought. Nor had he expected to unearth a secret that could rock her politically prominent family to the core and might destroy any hope he had of winning her heart.

### #1247 NIGHT TALK—Rebecca Daniels

Radio personality Kristin Carey, aka Jane Streeter, had a stalker, so ex-cop Jake Hayes was recruited to keep her safe. He'd been a secret fan of her show ever since he first heard it, but he didn't want to tell *her* that. Now it was up to Jake to protect her—and not let his growing feelings disrupt his duty.

### #1248 TRUST NO ONE—Barbara Phinney

After she witnessed her boyfriend murder an innocent man, receptionist Helen Eastman decided that faking her own death was the only way she would be safe. But she didn't know that undercover detective Nick Thorndike had witnessed her "suicide" and vowed to protect her—and win her heart!